THE WORDSMITH

EMERSON PASS HISTORICALS, BOOK SEVEN

TESS THOMPSON

PRAISE FOR TESS THOMPSON

"I frequently found myself getting lost in the characters and forgetting that I was reading a book." - ***Camille Di Maio, Bestselling author of The Memory of Us.***

"Highly recommended." - ***Christine Nolfi, Award winning author of The Sweet Lake Series.***

"I loved this book!" - ***Karen McQuestion, Bestselling author of Hello Love and Good Man, Dalton.***

Traded: Brody and Kara:

"I loved the sweetness of Tess Thompson's writing - the camaraderie and long-lasting friendships make you want to move to Cliffside and become one of the gang! Rated Hallmark for romance!" - ***Stephanie Little BookPage***

"This story was well written. You felt what the characters were going through. It's one of those "I got to know what happens next" books. So intriguing you won't want to put it down." - ***Lena Loves Books***

"This story has so much going on, but it intertwines within itself. You get second chance, lost loves, and new love. I could not put this book down! I am excited to start this series and have love for this little Bayside town that I am now fond off!" - ***Crystal's Book World***

"This is a small town romance story at its best and I look forward to the next book in the series." - ***Gillek2, Vine Voice***

"This is one of those books that make you love to be a reader and fan of the author." -***Pamela Lunder, Vine Voice***

Blue Midnight:

"This is a beautiful book with an unexpected twist that takes the story from romance to mystery and back again. I've already started the 2nd book in the series!" **- *Mama O***

"This beautiful book captured my attention and never let it go. I did not want it to end and so very much look forward to reading the next book." **- *Pris Shartle***

"I enjoyed this new book cover to cover. I read it on my long flight home from Ireland and it helped the time fly by, I wish it had been longer so my whole flight could have been lost to this lovely novel about second chances and finding the truth. Written with wisdom and humor this novel shares the raw emotions a new divorce can leave behind." **- *J. Sorenson***

"Tess Thompson is definitely one of my auto-buy authors! I love her writing style. Her characters are so real to life that you just can't put the book down once you start! Blue Midnight makes you believe in second chances. It makes you believe that everyone deserves an HEA. I loved the twists and turns in this book, the mystery and suspense, the family dynamics and the restoration of trust and security." **- *Angela MacIntyre***

"Tess writes books with real characters in them, characters with flaws and baggage and gives them a second chance. (Real people, some remind me of myself and my girlfriends.) Then she cleverly and thoroughly develops those characters and makes you feel deeply for them. Characters are complex and multi-faceted, and the plot seems to unfold naturally, and never feels contrived." **- *K. Lescinsky***

Caramel and Magnolias:

"Nobody writes characters like Tess Thompson. It's like she looks into our lives and creates her characters based on our best friends, our lovers, and our neighbors. Caramel and Magnolias, and the authors debut novel Riversong, have some of the best characters I've ever had a chance to fall in love with. I don't like leaving spoilers in reviews so just trust me, Nicholas Sparks has nothing on Tess Thompson, her writing flows so smoothly you can't help but to want to read on!" ***- T. M. Frazier***

"I love Tess Thompson's books because I love good writing. Her prose is clean and tight, which are increasingly rare qualities, and manages to evoke a full range of emotions with both subtlety and power. Her fiction goes well beyond art imitating life. Thompson's characters are alive and fully-realized, the action is believable, and the story unfolds with the right balance of tension and exuberance. CARAMEL AND MAGNOLIAS is a pleasure to read." ***- Tsuruoka***

"The author has an incredible way of painting an image with her words. Her storytelling is beautiful, and leaves you wanting more! I love that the story is about friendship (2 best friends) and love. The characters are richly drawn and I found myself rooting for them from the very beginning. I think you will, too!" ***- Fogvision***

"I got swept off my feet, my heartstrings were pulled, I held my breath, and tightened my muscles in suspense. Tess paints stunning scenery with her words and draws you in to the lives of her characters."- ***T. Bean***

Duet For Three Hands:

"Tears trickled down the side of my face when I reached the end of this road. Not because the story left me feeling sad or disappointed, no. Rather, because I already missed them. My friends. Though it isn't goodbye, but see you later. And so I will sit impatiently waiting, with desperate eagerness to hear where life has taken you, what burdens have you downtrodden, and what triumphs warm your heart. And in the meantime, I will go out and live, keeping your lessons and friendship and love close, the light to guide me through any darkness. And to the author I say thank you. My heart, my soul -all of me - needed these words, these friends, this love. I am forever changed by the beauty of your talent." - ***Lisa M.Gott***

"I am a great fan of Tess Thompson's books and this new one definitely shows her branching out with an engaging enjoyable historical drama/love story. She is a true pro in the way she weaves her storyline, develops true to life characters that you love! The background and setting is so picturesque and visible just from her words. Each book shows her expanding, growing and excelling in her art. Yet another one not to miss. Buy it you won't be disappointed. The ONLY disappointment is when it ends!!!" - ***Sparky's Last***

"There are some definite villains in this book. Ohhhh, how I loved to hate them. But I have to give Thompson credit because they never came off as caricatures or one dimensional. They all felt authentic to me and (sadly) I could easily picture them. I loved to love some and loved to hate others." - ***The Baking Bookworm***

"I stayed up the entire night reading Duet For Three Hands and unbeknownst to myself, I fell asleep in the middle of reading the book. I literally woke up the next morning with Tyler the Kindle beside me (thankfully, still safe and intact) with no ounce of battery left. I shouldn't have worried about deadlines because, guess what? Duet For Three Hands was the epitome of unputdownable." - ***The Bookish Owl***

Miller's Secret

"From the very first page, I was captivated by this wonderful tale. The cast of characters amazing - very fleshed out and multi-dimensional. The descriptions were perfect - just enough to make you feel like you were transported back to the 20's and 40's.... This book was the perfect escape, filled with so many twists and turns I was on the edge of my seat for the entire read." - ***Hilary Grossman***

"The sad story of a freezing-cold orphan looking out the window at his rich benefactors on Christmas Eve started me off with Horatio-Alger expectations for this book. But I quickly got pulled into a completely different world--the complex five-character braid that the plot weaves. The three men and two women characters are so alive I felt I could walk up and start talking to any one of them, and I'd love to have lunch with Henry. Then the plot quickly turned sinister enough to keep me turning the pages.

Class is set against class, poor and rich struggle for happiness and security, yet it is love all but one of them are hungry for. ......Where does love come from? What do you do about it? The story kept me going, and gave me hope. For a little bonus, there are Thompson's delightful observations, like: "You'd never know we could make something this good out of the milk from an animal who eats hats." A really good read!" - ***Kay in Seattle***

"She paints vivid word pictures such that I could smell the ocean and hear the doves. Then there are the stories within a story that twist and turn until they all come together in the end. I really had a hard time putting it down. Five stars aren't enough!"

- ***M.R. Williams***

ALSO BY TESS THOMPSON

CLIFFSIDE BAY

Traded: Brody and Kara

Deleted: Jackson and Maggie

Jaded: Zane and Honor

Marred: Kyle and Violet

Tainted: Lance and Mary

Cliffside Bay Christmas, The Season of Cats and Babies (Cliffside Bay Novella to be read after Tainted)

Missed: Rafael and Lisa

Cliffside Bay Christmas Wedding (Cliffside Bay Novella to be read after Missed)

Healed: Stone and Pepper

Chateau Wedding (Cliffside Bay Novella to be read after Healed)

Scarred: Trey and Autumn

Jilted: Nico and Sophie

Kissed (Cliffside Bay Novella to be read after Jilted)

Departed: David and Sara

Cliffside Bay Bundle , Books 1,2,3

BLUE MOUNTAIN SERIES

Blue Mountain Bundle, Books 1,2,3

Blue Midnight

Blue Moon

Blue Ink

Blue String

EMERSON PASS

The School Mistress of Emerson Pass

The Sugar Queen of Emerson Pass

RIVER VALLEY

Riversong

Riverbend

Riverstar

Riversnow

Riverstorm

Tommy's Wish

River Valley Bundle, Books 1-4

LEGLEY BAY

Caramel and Magnolias

Tea and Primroses

STANDALONES

The Santa Trial

Duet for Three Hands

Miller's Secret

❀ Created with Vellum

THE WORDSMITH

For my editor and friend, Erin Crum, who fixes all my commas and other errors I won't mention, as well as provides encouragement, patience and flexibility to this absentminded and harried author. May we one day meet in a cafe in Paris to celebrate our long partnership!

1

ADDIE

THE AIR SMELLED OF LOVE THAT AFTERNOON IN THE JUNE OF 1934, A combination of wild roses and pine needles. I was a fanciful young woman, prone to daydreaming, but today it was as if all my senses were on high alert. Under the shade of the awning, my sister Fiona and I waited for James West's train to arrive from New York City for his annual summer visit to our little mountain town in Colorado. James. James West. He was my secret and most likely unrequited love. I'd been only a child when he'd first come to Emerson Pass. Now I was grown and ever hopeful that this would be the summer he noticed me.

Noticed me. What did that mean, really? Would he suddenly see me as a woman instead of his best friend's younger sister? My stomach fluttered as if the bees that currently jumped from flower to flower were alive within me.

Around me, people waited on the train platform, most of whom I recognized, chatting or merely standing in silence. Were any of them as anxious as I to see the train pull into the station? Did anyone else have a secret, as I did? If so, were they secrets of the heart, as mine was?

Emerson Pass was still a small town, although it had grown by thousands before the depression hit the country. We'd stagnated since then but still considered ourselves lucky. Other parts of America were suffering much more than the people in our small community. We looked after one another here. No one went hungry in Emerson Pass, my father often said. "Even if I have to feed them myself."

"It's terribly hot, isn't it?" Fiona asked, breaking into my thoughts. "I'm rather done with the heat, and the summer's barely begun."

I glanced at her, surprised. She was not one to complain. Her cheeks were pink from the summer heat, and tendrils of her hair escaped their careful arrangement and curled at the nape of her damp neck. Dark smudges under her eyes told me she hadn't been getting enough sleep. None of this took from her beauty. In fact, she appeared as she always had, despite her challenging work demands. She remained petite and slight, with dark hair and fair skin. Her tiny waist gave no hint that she'd carried twins just four years previous. It was only the fine lines around her mouth that had deepened. Only slightly, mind you, considering she was raising four boys while keeping up with her musical career. Two sets of twins, no less.

She'd surprised us all when she gave birth to twin boys four years ago. She somehow juggled her two sets of twins with grace and what seemed like ease. I knew it wasn't always as idyllic as she made it seem. She'd been my age—only twenty—when six years ago, she and Li had adopted eight-year-old boys they'd found living on the streets of Paris. My parents had worried she was too young to have a sudden family, but they needn't have fretted. Fiona was born wise beyond her years and with the heart of a saint. At least that's how she seemed to me.

"Are you feeling all right?" I asked her now, suddenly worried.

"I'm fine. Tired." She covered a yawn with her fist. "We've been up late composing, and the little boys wake with the rooster and never seem to run out of energy." She and her husband, Li, had fallen in with the motion picture people out west and now composed musical scores. It was too exciting.

"It's been a long week and I've been looking forward to seeing James, but all I want is a nap." Fiona tilted her head to rest against my shoulder for a moment. I was four inches taller and had white-blond hair and light blue eyes. Anywhere but here in town, no one would have known we were sisters. In Emerson Pass, however, the Barnes family was somewhat infamous. Our father had built the town from his own will and desire to create a thriving community for his children. He'd succeeded. Now that he was older, he'd slowed down quite a bit, handing over a lot of his business to my brothers and brother-in-law.

"I can look after James for you," I said. "Entertain him today, I mean."

"He'll like that very much. He's very fond of you. Also, I may have mentioned to him about your manuscript. He offered to take a look at it for you."

I gulped, nervous just thinking about someone as esteemed as James looking at my work. "We'll see."

"I think I may be having another baby," Fiona said casually, as if it were an afterthought. "Hopefully only one this time."

"Really? Fiona, are you sure?" Another baby? Before she knew it, she'd have seven kids like our parents.

"I'm not entirely sure, so I'm keeping it to myself for now."

"Except for me?" I smiled, pleased. She and my sister Cymbeline were close confidants. I was flattered to have been told such news first.

"I do hope dear James is doing well," Fiona said. "His last letter hinted at trouble. Perhaps with his work?"

"I hope not."

"It may be only a matter of exhaustion," Fiona said. "We'll put him back together before sending him back to the chaos of the city."

He'd been away an entire year this time. Between editing

projects, he came "home" to Emerson Pass to rest and recuperate. He had several famous authors he worked with and he'd confessed to me the summer before that they'd temporarily robbed him of his health and spirit. I had asked why and he'd said they were difficult in various ways. One was a drunk, and James had to cajole him to finish projects. I couldn't even imagine it, but I knew James would not exaggerate.

We were here for him, regardless. Whenever he needed to be buoyed or pampered, we were here like the cushions in our sofas, soft, reliable, and comforting.

The first time I ever laid eyes on him I thought I might faint dead away. I'm not exaggerating, either. My legs had actually wobbled. I made a mental note at the time to use it in one of my future novels, this feeling of being utterly smitten with a man. I'd never have thought it possible. I had always been more of the studious, quiet type, happy with my books and my paper and pen.

My breath caught as the train came around the bend and chugged into the station, bringing the scent of oil and smoke. Steam rose in clouds around the engine as it squeaked to a stop. I searched the windows of the first-class car for James. "There he is," I said, breathless. At last he'd returned to us.

Fiona, perhaps sensing my excitement, glanced my way. Her brow worried into a crease and those eyes of hers, those all-seeing eyes, could perhaps see straight through me. Did she suspect my secret feelings for James? I'd told no one, not even Delphia. Not Cym or Jo or even my mother. It was too embarrassing as well as possibly mortifying if my affection was seen as a foolish little girl's crush.

He appeared in the doorway of the passenger car and then, seeing Fiona and me standing together, waved. Grinning, he bounded from the train and headed our way. His smile, etched into my memory and my dreams at night, had the same effect it had the first time I ever met him. I'd been only fourteen that summer my sister and Li brought him home with them from

Paris. A penniless nobleman, Fiona had said. James had dreamt of being a book editor back then. He'd made his dreams come true, working at one of the New York publishing houses. Despite the depression that had swept the nation, he had managed to keep his job. He worked with several successful novelists, and it was said that without him the books would not have seen the light of day. Fiona believed the reason for their success was James's excellent taste and nurturing guidance. I had no doubt that she was correct.

I thought of my finished manuscript. Would James think it had promise, or would he pat me on the head and send me off to my dreamland? Never mind that. James was here. That's all I cared about for now.

The sunlight glinted off his thick copper-tinted dark blond hair. A lock had broken free of the pomade and hung attractively over his forehead.

"Only two of the infamous Barnes sisters here to greet me?" James asked, teasing us in his delightful English accent. "Have I fallen out of favor with the others?" He kissed Fiona's hand and then turned to do the same to mine.

I breathed him in. He smelled of soap and another scent that I could think of only as James. Different than anyone else. A scent I wished I could keep on my pillow and have with me every night as I fell asleep. Although perhaps that would have kept me from sleep. His scent wakened desires a proper young lady should not have. Nonetheless, they were there, calling to me, begging James to touch me with his long, graceful fingers.

Deep blue eyes studied each of us in turn. He had a way about him that reminded me of a clergyman, curious yet compassionate. I'd noticed that I wasn't the only one who wanted to tell James every detail of my life, both for redemption and counsel. All of my sisters reacted to him in a similar fashion. Mama, who shared many qualities with James, had once said she thought he'd missed his calling as either a teacher or a pastor. Perhaps this was the secret to his editing genius? It took a combination of the two when partnering with a writer. Were these the qualities from which a writer's finest work evolved?

"You know the answer to that, dearest James." Fiona held her cheek up for him to kiss. "You could never fall out with our family. You belong to us, you know."

"How I love to hear it." James looked from one of us to the other. "I can't say either of you look anything short of exquisite. In fact, you've both grown lovelier since my last visit."

"That's what we do." Fiona tossed her dark curls and gave him one of her heart-melting smiles. There wasn't a time or circumstance that my sister's glow and compassionate heart couldn't make everything better. Or almost everything. She could not distract me from my undying devotion to James West or the fact that he looked at me with the eyes of an older brother. How would I live without his love? At some point, I would have to let go of my fantasy world. There would be a time when he disembarked from a train with a wife on his arm. That would be the day that part of me died.

"Come, the car's parked in the shade." Fiona hooked her arm through his. "Wait until you see the new road. Roosevelt's sent his WPA workers here, you know. And they're making the road to Louisville as smooth as a baby's cheek."

James grimaced. "It wouldn't take much to improve that road. The last time we were on it, I thought the contents of my brain would be scrambled like one of Lizzie's egg dishes by the time we were through."

"That was Cym's driving more than the road," Fiona said. "A preamble to the rest of that decadent, eventful evening, if I recall correctly."

They laughed. A private joke between them. One that excluded me because I was too young. Perhaps, even, too fragile. In their eyes, anyway. I'd been sickly as a child and had almost died. Until clever Theo figured out that it was anything with wheat that was making me so ill. After I quit eating the delicious-smelling stuff, my health restored. I was as robust as Delphia these days. Not robust, really. That would imply a curve or two. Instead, like my mother, I was straight as a board. Delphia was a few inches shorter than I and shaped like an hourglass. Her skin was pink and pretty, like a peach, whereas I was more like a pristine white rose.

My hair was almost white and indistinguishable from my milky skin. Sometimes I thought I looked like a ghost. Often I felt like one, roaming around the world unseen. I tried to convince myself that being uninteresting and quiet made me a better writer. While the rest of the Barnes family were making others laugh or capturing their attention with stories of their antics, I was in the corner observing. The wallflower.

Still, I had hope that perhaps this summer James would notice me. He might see the spark that lived inside me, ready to be pulled out by the right man.

We arrived at the car, parked under an aspen tree. The dust of the parking lot covered my shoes. I'd have to shine them tonight before bed, I thought, absently. James tossed his suitcase into the back.

"Is that really all you've brought with you?" Fiona asked.

"Your mother told me to pack lightly," James said. "She's arranged for Mr. Olofsson to make me two new suits this summer. I'll have to send them home through the postal service."

"Don't even think about that," Fiona said. "You have two full months here with nothing to do but relax."

A shadow passed over James's face. His cheekbones seemed more prominent than last summer. His face had thinned. Was he worried about something?

"What is it?' Fiona asked, stopping and looking over the top of the car at him. "What was that look?"

He sighed and held open the passenger-side door for me. "My path's a little uncertain at the moment."

"What? What happened?" Fiona asked.

"My publisher sold out to a bigger publisher. It's rather complicated. We can speak of it later."

"Should we be concerned?" Fiona asked, her sweet face scrunched slightly with worry.

He flapped his hand in a dismissive gesture. "Not at all. Nothing to worry over. I'm here now, and that's all I care about."

"You can stay with Mama and Papa as long as you'd like," Fiona said. "If you decided not to go back."

He gave her a strange look, as if she'd come from behind and scared him, but didn't say anything further.

"Tell me, Miss Addie, what have you been doing to keep yourself occupied and out of trouble?" James held out his hand to help me into the back seat of my sister's car. His accent, crisp consonants and vowels, were like fully open daisies, bright and wide and a salve to my soul.

I allowed myself a quick peek into his eyes. They were the prettiest of blues, almost turquoise in the light of the afternoon. "I've been reading and writing. Spending time down at the creek, swimming and picnicking and helping Mama with volunteer duties at the church." I cringed at the singsong tone of my voice. I sounded rehearsed. It was true to some extent. I'd thought over the details of this summer many times—what I would say, how I would hold myself so that he might have an inkling of what we could become together.

"The creek. How I've missed it," James said. "On hot days in the city, I think of the cool, clear water and almost salivate, as if it were a great meal and I a starving man."

"It's not changed," I said, leaning forward from the back seat as they settled in the front. "Nor has anything else."

"Thankfully." James adjusted his tie. "You ladies have no idea how much I've looked forward to these two months here."

I had an idea. It couldn't be as much as I'd looked forward to seeing him.

As we bumped along the dirt road, a cloud of dust behind us, Fiona caught James up on the happenings of the Barnes family.

The older twins, Bleu and Beaumont, were fifteen and had grown into tall, muscular young men. Neither of them had any interest in music but loved academics. In addition, they were athletic like my sister Cymbeline and her husband, Viktor. Winters were spent skiing and summers swimming or hiking through the woods. They were fluent in English now with only a trace of their French accents. Traces the girls in town swooned over.

The little boys were musical like their parents, always singing, and had already begun lessons on the piano. Although many people couldn't tell them apart, I had no trouble at all. Alexander was like his namesake, my papa, adventurous and mischievous with eyes that twinkled. James, named after James West, of course, was quieter and more cerebral.

"They're getting into all kinds of mischief," Fiona said to James now. "Mostly Alexander. He reminds me, God forbid, of Flynn."

"How are Bleu and Beaumont?" James asked.

"They're rascals," Fiona said. "Sometimes I wonder if I was too young when I became their mother. They're as wild as these mountains. The lost little boys we knew are no longer."

"Praise God," James said. He'd been there when Fiona and Li had found the twins living homeless on the streets of Paris.

"Cym and Viktor are doing well," Fiona said. "Their little girls are darling." She sighed. "And smell so nice all the time."

Cymbeline, the tomboy of our family, had surprised us all by having two girls one after the other. The first, Annie, had come soon after Fiona and Li had returned from Paris. She favored her father, with reddish-blond hair and his light Nordic eyes. She was soon to have her sixth birthday. Holly had come right before Christmas the next year. Our miracle, as there was a snowstorm that night and Theo and Louisa hadn't been able to make it to help with the birth. Viktor had delivered her himself. Holly looked like Cym and Fiona, fair but with dark curls and blue eyes. Oddly enough, Cymbeline seemed to have adjusted fine to having girls. Because the children were all so close in age, Fiona and Cym were second mothers to the other's children. On any given day, the kids were in and out of the two houses, built only a half acre apart. They loved it that way. So did I, as I adored them all.

We were pulling up to my parents' home by then. The late June flowers and shrubs were in full bloom, including the rhododendrons in their pink glory. Bees traveled from one honeysuckle flower to another. Fiona claimed she could hear the insects buzzing this time of year.

She parked in the front and turned off the car. She looked over at James with a sweet smile. "Mr. West, we're glad you're back where you belong."

He gazed back at her with a serious expression on his handsome face. "Do you really think I belong here?"

"You belong wherever you want to be," Fiona said. "And if it's here with us, then I'm delighted."

Before anything else could be said, Delphia came running out the front door to greet us. She may have looked like a pink-cheeked porcelain doll, but she was tough and fast, like Cym. Like our older sister, she ran on high speed all of the time, until she crashed into bed at night and slept so hard I had to shake her awake in the morning.

"Goodness gracious, is it my best girl?" James called out as he exited the car.

Delphia threw herself into his arms. "Oh, James, we thought you'd never get here. We're all terribly excited, and the time was going slow, slow, slow. Like we were stuck in molasses."

He held her by the shoulders for a moment. "I didn't think it was possible, but you're all grown up. It's broken my heart, if you must know."

She grinned, her pink cheeks rounding like crab tree apples. "I'm a young lady now, James. I have heaps of beaux. Or, they want to be, at any rate. I'm unable to like any of them."

"But why?" He put his hand on his heart. "They must be heartbroken."

"I don't like any of them much. I'm waiting for *my* Viktor—a man just like him is what I want."

"That's going to be hard, isn't it?" James asked, eyes dancing.

"I refuse to compromise," Delphia said. "I'm holding out for true love."

"A worthy goal." James laughed as he gazed down at Delphia with obvious fondness. "But you're only sixteen. You've plenty of time."

By now, Mama and Papa had come out to greet their guest. Mama, in a white linen dress, looked as fresh as a daisy. Her brown eyes shone as she reached out to James. "James, it's wonderful to see you. We've missed you so."

He kissed her hand. "I've missed you all as well. There's much to discuss." He turned to Papa. "Thank you for having me, Lord Barnes."

"Dear boy, you must stop calling me that," Papa said. "It's Alexander or Papa to family." He and James had the same accent, having come from the same part of England. Very posh and noble, I always thought.

"Come in for tea, darlings," Mama said. "We can catch up properly before dinner."

I hung back, enjoying the sight of James walking into the house with my family. If only he would stay forever.

2

JAMES

The sight of Fiona and Addie on the platform had given me a lump in my throat. They were both lovely in their summer dresses, so pure and fresh after the long train trip from New York. Fiona was my dearest friend and had been since we met in Paris. Her husband, Li, was a close second. They'd quite literally given me a new sense of purpose when they'd invited me to return with them to America. During that first visit in the summer of 1928, I fell in love with the entire Barnes clan. They were my truest and closest friends, a second family when I desperately needed one. It may be that I needed them more this summer than I had the very first one. How would I tell them all that this might be the last? Even if I were to come in future summers, it would be with Lena by my side. I couldn't imagine her here. Not as my wife, anyway. This would be the last of my idyllic summers with the Barnes family.

I'd answered Fiona honestly about my work, but I'd not told her about my personal life. The company I worked for had been bought by Maxwell Masters, one of the richest men in America. Many of my colleagues had been let go. I had kept my job. At first, I had not known why. Now I knew the terms. I knew what he wanted from me.

Last week, I'd been summoned to Maxwell Masters's offices and escorted into a room with a large desk. Behind it sat Mr. Masters. Plump and red-faced and dressed impeccably, he'd offered me a drink at eleven in the morning. I'd declined, thinking of my father and what drink had done to him.

The office smelled of cigars, good whiskey, and new money. I could practically taste the newly printed bills. The depression had hit even the richest of New York City. There had been suicides and disgraces splattered all over the streets of the city in the early days after the crash. Masters had taken advantage of this, buying up property and businesses for pennies. All good businessmen seemed to have a sixth sense for this kind of thing. If only my father had, I would not be in my current predicament. Currently, Masters was set to rule the world.

"I suppose you wonder why I've sent for you?" He pressed his fingers into his white mustache and looked across the desk at me. Green eyes, I noted. Like Lena's. Instead of placed in her pretty face, on Masters they seemed to peer at me from doughy pink folds between his forehead and cheeks.

"Yes, sir." I swallowed. Had I been brought here because I'd taken his daughter, Lena, out several times? Once for dinner and a play, another time for a stroll in Central Park. We'd met at a party in the early spring and had immediately liked each other. Like the soiree, she'd been light and funny, a welcome distraction from the seriousness of the times. "Is it because of Lena? Because I can assure you I've been nothing but a gentleman." Was I going to get sacked for dating the new boss's daughter?

"I'm aware of your courtship. Lena tells me everything, you see. She's quite taken with you."

"And I with her, sir." I'd not thought much about her, if truth were told. She was out of my reach. I was a penniless editor living in a one-room apartment eating beans and stale bread for dinner.

"James, did you know I know your father? We met years ago, right after the war."

I sat there, shocked, waiting for what was coming next. Was this why I'd kept my job? "How do you know him?"

"It's a long story that I won't go into today," Mr. Masters said. "Suffice it to say, we had business dealings that were more advantageous to me than him."

Most were, I thought. Especially those done over the poker table.

"He's informed me of his troubles," Masters said. "Of the situation with your family."

Situation. The *situation* was that my father had gambled and drunk away the family fortune, or what was left of it anyway, and now they were unable to keep up the estate or staff. The gardens had gone to ruin, the damp and dark house infested with vermin. Father had written to me earlier this year that all of the money was gone. There was no place for them to go. He'd asked for too many favors from my mother's only relative, a rich aunt. He didn't know what he was going to do, and could I send a little something to help them? *Think of your sister,* he'd written. What money, I'd thought? I'd written back to him. *I have none to give you. Not the vast amounts you need.* Not any amount, for that matter. I barely made enough to afford my apartment and meager meals.

"It's quite sad, isn't it?" Mr. Masters asked. "A man like your father. Such potential. I was always envious of his station in life. Nobility and all."

"Yes, sir." I didn't know where this was headed, but I bristled. Why would he care about stations? Masters was an American. None of that mattered here.

"I've been in contact with your father," Mr. Masters had said. He leaned back in his chair, placing his hands over his stomach. "We've come up with a plan that I think will be agreeable to all of us."

"A plan, sir?"

"You are to marry my daughter Lena at the end of August. In exchange, I'll take care of your father's financial difficulties."

My mouth went dry. "What?" Surely I'd heard him wrong? Marry Lena? I hardly knew her.

Masters shifted in his chair, causing it to squeak in protest. He was not a small man. "You two are the perfect match. She has a bit of a wild streak, you know. You're respectable and handsome, plus your noble birth. This is of great use to us."

I didn't know, but nodded anyway. Lena had seemed perfectly tame to me. Charming, well-educated, and absolutely stunning to look at, with big green eyes and a pointy little chin and thick auburn hair. The few times we'd spent together, I'd quite enjoyed her company. There had been a definite hint of attraction. Still, marriage hadn't occurred to me for obvious reasons. "Why would you want her to marry me? I'm nearly penniless, and you obviously know about my father."

He set his elbows on his desk and leaned forward. "I'll be honest here. Lena has been shut out from society because of me. I have a reputation, as I'm sure you've heard."

I nodded, not knowing what to say. There were rumors about shady business deals and possible illegal activities during Prohibition. Regardless, I didn't pay much attention to any of that, too busy with my books. In hindsight, maybe I should have.

"We're not respected by the society women in this town, and they run the world here. You may not be aware of what that means to us. Lena wants to be accepted and invited to their ridiculous parties. So do I, for that matter. It's good for business. You bring titles and all that."

I couldn't believe my ears. "Sir, I'm not sure about this. What does Lena think of me? Of this idea?"

"She sees the logic in my thinking. With you, doors open for her that have been slammed right in her face."

"Aren't there other men that could solve that problem?"

"She wants you. She says you're kind and witty and God knows you have the looks. In fact, she thinks she's in love with you. Her mother died when she was a baby. It's just been the two of us. I've never seen her this way before."

"Really?" I hadn't thought we'd spent enough time together to fall in love. Maybe I was missing something?

I closed my eyes for a moment. My father's last letter had sounded even more desperate, hinting at my mother's depression and poor health, implying that it was my fault because of my lack of business skills. All my life I'd wanted to please him, get his approval. Instead, he'd been disappointed with everything about me.

"Listen, young man, let me lay this out for you. If you don't do this, you'll no longer have a job in publishing. I own this world now, and a few calls will ensure you won't ever work again. And your father and mother will be ruined."

My life would be over. The one I'd built over the last six years. Unless I married Lena. She would be the answer to all of my problems. I thought of my little sister. She'd not been able to find a match because of my father. This would change things for her, too.

"I need time to think," I said at last.

"No time for that. The offer expires at midnight."

I sighed and looked down at my hands. Left-handed, I had a permanent stain on my index and middle fingers from my ink pen. "I have a trip planned for Colorado. My friends live there. I go every summer. Can I have one last visit with them first? When I get back, we can marry." Saying it out loud felt a little like jumping off a bridge.

"I'll make the arrangements." His lips smacked, as if he'd eaten something sweet. He'd gotten what he wanted. I had a feeling he almost always did.

Now, I put all that aside as I was ushered out to the backyard for tea. The day was cloudless and warm, without the humidity I'd left. A man could breathe here. I looked out over the rolling lawn, littered with the remnants of a croquet game. Surrounded by the lovely Barnes sisters and their mama and papa, I was a rich man.

"Here, darling, have another of Lizzie's cookies," Quinn said, thrusting the plate toward me. "Have you eaten since you saw us last? You're much too thin."

I smiled, pressing my hand against my chest before reaching for another of the sugar cookies. Having Quinn mother me while I was here made me feel like truly part of the clan. "I've missed Lizzie's cooking, I'll say that."

"We've finally convinced her to put more sugar in the cookies," Alexander said.

"And to call them cookies," Fiona said. "When we were kids she called them biscuits, which confused us."

"The problems of a mixed household," Quinn said, eyes twinkling at her British-born husband.

"Toss our French twins in there and we're even more complicated." Fiona smiled as she lifted a teacup to her mouth. The cup and teapot were painted with pretty pink roses. They reminded me of the Barnes sisters.

"A big, wonderful mess of a family," I said. "I'm glad to be here with all of you."

"I have another Englishman to keep me company for a few months a year. I'd rather have you here all the time, but we'll take what we can get." Alexander clapped a hand on my shoulder. "It's good to have you back."

If only I could stay forever, I thought. Give up all my ambition and move here to Emerson Pass. Of everywhere I'd lived in my life, this was the place that felt like home. For a second, I let myself imagine what it would be like to move here. Alexander would find work for me—something to earn my keep. Maybe they'd help build a cottage as they had the others. And then what? I'd live alone forever? Would I become a bitter old man, alone and nearly penniless? *You'd have a family,* I reminded myself.

No, my fate was decided. I would marry Lena and save my family. I would still have the job I loved. I would immerse myself in the work, as I'd done for the last six years. Lately, it had seemed less and less gratifying.

Was my admiration for Lena enough? It was not the kind of love Fiona and Li shared. Or any of the other Barnes couples who seemed to have chosen solely on love without factoring in anything else. Love matches, my mother called them. My parents had been a love match, and what good had that done? Eventually, because of my father's choices, they grew to despise each other. Couldn't the opposite happen? Could I fall in love with Lena if I gave it enough time?

Fiona's twins, James and Alexander, had now arrived with their nanny. Fiona stood from the table laid out for tea and held out her arms. They almost knocked her over with the enthusiasm of their hugs. "Darlings, look who's here. Mr. West has come all the way from New York City."

They turned to me with solemn eyes, sizing me up from the looks of it. More beautiful children I'm not sure I'd ever seen. A combination of Li's Chinese ancestry and Fiona's English one had created the most exquisite children, with large brown eyes and dark hair that shone under the afternoon sun.

"I don't know who he is, Mama," James said. "Am I supposed to?" His brow furrowed, as if trying to remember me but coming up empty.

"He's the man you're named after," Fiona said.

"He is?" James seemed dubious but stuck out his hand anyway. "Pleased to meet you, sir."

"Pleased to meet you." I shook his small hand and gave him my best smile. He simply stared at me with suspicion. Clearly, he had no recollection of the fun we'd had the previous summer. I'd swum with them at the creek many days. They'd liked me to pretend I was a sea monster and chase them around the shallow parts of the creek.

"Come here, love." Quinn gestured for James to come to her. "Have some tea."

"May I have a cookie?" James asked his mother.

"Yes, but just one," Fiona said.

"I'm named after my grandpoppy," Alexander said to me, rather proudly. "See there." He pointed to Alexander, who was now bringing James onto his lap for snuggles. As soon as he was settled, James bit into his cookie. Crumbs cascaded from the corners of his mouth onto Alexander's linen suit. Grandpoppy seemed unconcerned. What a contrast Alexander was to my father. Neither he nor my mother would have ever taken a child onto their lap. Especially one who had a cookie dangling from their mouth.

"I know you were," I said, returning my gaze to Alexander.

"But everyone calls me Alex. Otherwise people get confused."

"Well, Alex, I'm pleased to see you again. Do you remember last summer? I was the sea monster."

"No, sir." His eyes flickered to his mother, as if he might be in trouble for not remembering.

"You were a lot smaller back then," I said quickly. "It's a whole year since we saw each other last."

"I shall remember you this year." Alex spoke stoutly. He would will it into reality, I thought. Like his grandfather, he would be a force in the world.

"Is it James West in the flesh?" I looked up to see Cymbeline striding across the lawn toward us. Her two little girls each held on to a hand until they saw their cousins and left their mother to come tearing across the grass.

I stood to greet Cym, kissing both her cheeks, feeling the strength of this fine woman in the grasp of her hands in mine. "It is I once again, Mrs. Olofsson."

"Has the city starved you?" Cym sized me up and found me lacking. "We'll have to fatten you up before we send you back to that awful place."

I knelt to say hello to the girls. "You've both grown since I saw you last."

"We know," Annie said. As the older one, I'd noticed she

often answered for her and her sister. She looked so much like her father, I thought, as I looked more closely at her light blue eyes. "I'm almost six and Mother just measured me for the wall."

"The wall?" I asked.

"Where Mother writes down the date and then makes a line over my head. I've grown two inches since last year."

"Two inches. My God, what is your mother feeding you?" This prompted a fit of giggles from both girls. "Holly, how many inches did you grow?" I asked her.

"I don't know." She buried her face in her mother's skirt, dark curls covering her cheeks.

"She's going through a shy phase," Cym said, without sympathy. "I don't know why."

"I understand." My knees popped as I straightened.

"Can we have cookies?" Annie asked.

"Yes, but only one each," Cym said. "And then play with your cousins. Wear yourselves out." She said the last part under her breath, before turning back to me. "James, you look well, other than your thinness and this suit." She ran her fingers down the threadbare arm of my jacket. "Viktor's father will have you looking dapper by the time you leave."

"I'm a poor city mouse," I said. "And all my money goes to books, not suits."

"You poor darling," Cym said. "Don't worry. We'll take good care of you until it's time for you to go back to that dreadful city. We're delighted you could come. Do you have a young lady yet? Every summer, I fear it will be the last when some feline gets her claws into you."

"There is a girl, in fact," I said. "I'll tell you all about her later."

"A girl?" Fiona asked, sitting up straighter. "Why haven't you mentioned her before?"

I shrugged, as if it were nothing. "It's rather new. Quite serious," I added, knowing I would have to tell them the entire sordid story. Not today, though. Today I wanted to enjoy their company and pretend that the life waiting for me at home was meant for some other man.

Behind me came the sound of porcelain crashing into the floor of the porch. I turned to see that it was Addie's teacup, which was now in a half dozen pieces. She was already stooping to pick it up but I brushed her aside, swooping in to gather the broken pieces myself. "We don't want your writing fingers cut, now do we?" I asked gently, taking in her flushed cheeks and neck. Something had upset her. "Are you all right, Addie? You didn't cut yourself, did you?"

"No, I'm fine." Addie met my eyes briefly. Long enough for me to see that hers were glassy with tears.

A bell of alarm went off in my head. What was wrong? Was it the heat? I looked over at Fiona, but she and Cym were huddled together talking. Had anyone else noticed the broken cup? Alexander and Quinn were busy with all four of the children, doling out cookies and asking for promises that later they must eat their dinner, including all their vegetables.

"Addie, come with me," I said, offering her my hand. "I'd like to see the flowers, and you can tell me all about your life."

She nodded and allowed me to help her to her feet. "Excuse us," I said. "We're going to stroll around the garden for a moment."

"Yes, enjoy the garden, but be sure not to get overheated," Quinn said, more to Addie than me. She'd been ill as a child, and Quinn had never quite been able to discard her fears.

"Take him out to see our newest addition in the barn," Cym said. "You'll be tickled, James."

I would be tickled to see all the animals, as I was the house and gardens and my dear friends. What was it about this place that gave me so much comfort and felt so much like home? *This is not my home,* I reminded myself. These were merely my friends kind enough to share their home and lives for two months every summer. I didn't belong here. Other than as a charity case, I had nothing to offer them or the community. I was unskilled, other than editing books or playing the part of an impoverished nobleman. I had to go back to New York and the Masterses. The sooner I accepted my fate, the better.

3

JAMES

I TUCKED ADDIE'S HAND INTO THE CROOK OF MY ARM. WE strolled, silent, each of us…each of us what? Was Addie as tortured as I was about the future? Had she worries I wasn't cognizant of? An ill-advised love affair perhaps? God forbid. She was too sweet to be under the spell of a cad. Any man who would make lovable Adelaide cry would have me to answer to, that was for certain.

"Is something troubling you, Addie?" I squeezed her forearm. "You can talk to me about anything, if you ever need an ear."

"I cannot speak to you about this thing." Her mouth tightened as she looked away from me.

I left it at that. If she were having romantic problems, her sisters probably knew about them. They were much better suited than I to give her counsel. "What have you been working on?" I knew she would understand the question. The very first time I ever came here, Addie and I had formed a connection, bonding over books. She'd shyly confessed to me, at the tender age of fourteen, that she wanted to be a writer someday. I'd encouraged her, of course, hoping she had talent and telling her to send me anything she wanted a second set of eyes upon.

"I have a secret," she said. "A secret project."

We stopped at the rose garden. She let go of my arm and dipped her head to smell a white rose, so like her skin that it took me aback. *If only I were a writer,* I thought. *Then I would know how to describe their similarities.* "Would you like to tell me about it?"

"I suppose it couldn't hurt if you knew." She brushed a wisp of her hair from her cheek. Her loveliness was almost startling. Like a blue sky here on a clear day, so pretty it doesn't seem real. She'd always been a pretty child, but the last few summers she'd blossomed into a true beauty. Did she know? I guessed not, sheltered as she was by her large family. My earlier worries about her falling for a cad were no doubt unfounded. No one in this family would let a man hurt their innocent Adelaide.

"I've written a book about my siblings, taken from the stories they told me when I was small." Addie wrinkled her nose. "They used to distract me from my illness by telling me stories, especially Cymbeline and Josephine. The stories were so real to me that sometimes it felt as if I'd been there, too. I wasn't even born when they were small children. You know that, of course."

"I do." I smiled as I brushed aside a bug that flew near my ear. "Have you been able to put them together into a cohesive story?"

"No, that's the trouble. There's no arc to it. They're more like vignettes."

"That could work, I suppose."

"No, I want it to be a novel. I was hoping you might be able to help me sort it," she said. "While you're here."

"I'd be honored." I was touched that she'd trust me with her words. It was such a personal journey for writers, and I knew it took great courage to let them out into the world.

"They're light and funny. Literature critics would probably think they're silly fluff. I'm not sure they're any good. If you could tell me, one way or the other, I'd appreciate it."

"Given the subject matter, I'm sure they're entertaining." We continued on through the garden and around the side of the house toward the barn.

"Do you have a beau?" I asked. "Anyone you're interested in?"

"Yes, I like someone."

"Anyone I know?" I glanced at her profile. Her expression was as closed as the tightly bound rosebuds.

"It's not anyone I can talk about," Addie said.

"Forbidden love?" I said it lightly, but she had me concerned. Was this the man making her cry?

"Not forbidden. But unrequited."

A dab of pain in my chest caused my breath to catch. "I'm sorry. We've all experienced that at one time or the other. It's a pity for him. Any man would think he'd married a queen, not to mention getting this family for his own." I was surprised to hear the longing in my voice.

"Not every man," Addie said. "Not the one I want, which is all that matters."

"Do you want to tell me about him?"

"Not today."

"I understand." More than she could imagine, actually.

We walked along the path toward the horse pasture and stopped at the fence. Addie's dress was made of a pale pink linen. The bodice, adorned with crisscross ruffles at the collar, fit snugly around her slender shoulders. The skirts were skinny these days, unlike the dropped waists of the twenties. I quite enjoyed the way fashion had gone to more fitted styles. One didn't have to guess what was underneath. I could certainly see the outline of this particular woman. Like her mother, she was narrowly built and without dramatic curves. Some men might prefer buxom, wide-hipped women, but I liked Addie's graceful silhouette. I could imagine her dancing in the ballet. A white rose twirling and twirling.

I blinked. Wait a moment. Why was I thinking of Addie's figure? No, no, no. I was nearly an engaged man. Anyway, she was too young for me. In addition, Fiona trusted me with her little sisters. I wouldn't betray my best friend, even if I were so inclined. There was six years' difference between us. Not unheard of by any means. But again, she was Fiona's younger sister. I had no business coveting my best friend's sister. What was wrong with me?

"Was Cym right about you?" Addie leaned her torso over the top of the fence. Buttercups kissed the whitewashed boards. In the pasture, horses grazed, tails flicking away flies and bugs. I turned slightly to take in the red barn. I'd thought of this very scene so many times when I was in the city, wishing I could be right here in this spot with the sun on my shoulders and the scent of wildflowers in the breeze.

"Right about what?" I asked.

"Do you have a girl back in New York City?" She spoke so quietly I naturally moved closer to hear her better and caught a whiff of rosewater perfume.

"Ah, right. Lena."

"Lena? That's her name?"

"Yes. Lena Masters." The thought of Lena and all the complications of my life made me uncomfortably warm. I slipped out of my jacket and laid it over the fence post. Then I leaned my backside against the fence and adjusted my hat against the onslaught of late-afternoon sun.

"Who is she? What is she like?" Addie asked.

"She's the daughter of a wealthy businessman. I don't know her that well. Not like I do you or your sisters. But she's beautiful and funny."

"And you're going to marry a girl you don't know that well?"

"It's necessary," I said.

"But why?" Her eyes searched mine for answers.

How truthful should I be? Addie was young and innocent. Would she understand the predicament I found myself in? Perhaps she would. Addie was an old soul. She and Fiona shared the same sweet nature. However, with Addie, there was a fragility Fiona didn't possess. Addie was too good for this world, I thought now, as I stole a glance at her face. She had turned away and was now looking out at the horses, pensive. A tenseness in her shoulders made me want to place my hands on her skin and rub away her worries. Good Lord, what was wrong with me?

I sighed, forcing myself to focus on answering her question. "My family's in deep trouble..." I trailed off, unsure how to describe the mired mess in which I found myself.

"What is it? You can tell me anything. Anything at all. I won't pass judgment on you. That's not my job, after all." She looked upward, in what I suspected was a silent dialogue with Jesus.

"My father wrote to me several months ago," I said, patting my pocket again as if the letter were still there. "He asked me to save them. My family, that is. We're in terrible straits. The estate is close to disrepair, almost inhabitable. Other than a few rooms, everything's fallen to the rats. The staff is gone. They're living day to day, never sure what the next one will bring." I closed my eyes, nodding. The pain of what I had to do wilted me more than the warm sun could ever do. "A marriage has been arranged between her father and mine. A business agreement. If I marry Lena, Mr. Masters will save my family."

She hung her head for a moment. A shudder rippled the back of her dress. "She's rich? This Lena?"

"Very much so."

"Like Papa?" Addie straightened and looked up at me.

"Many times more, I suspect. The Masterses regularly dine with the Vanderbilts. People like that. Rich enough that he could restore my family's estate and everything around it. Wealthy enough to save my father from ruin."

"Do you want to marry her? If it wasn't necessary? I mean, are you in love with her?"

I turned all the way around to look at her squarely in the face. "I'm sorry to say that it doesn't matter either way. Her family can save mine. In addition, he's threatened me—if I don't marry Lena, I'll never work in publishing again. He has that kind of influence." The weight of that fell heavily upon my shoulders. I slumped over my legs, bending in half and pressing my hands into my knees. "I've no other choice."

"Why does Mr. Masters want you? It makes no sense."

I sat down in the soft, dry grass and leaned against the fence, then patted the spot beside me. She sat next to me, her legs stretched out and the skirt of her dress falling at her ankles.

"It's hard for you to understand, given where you live, but in New York, there are those who are in society and those who are not. New money is still shunned, even with the economy the way it is. The elite have snubbed Lena. Her father wants the world to open for her and feels that marriage to me would do so. They're willing to pay for my family's legacy, as if it makes them legitimate. Despite all the wealth, Mr. Masters cares what people think of him and his daughter. I find it strange, but I'm what he thinks will solve that problem."

"Some people have a thirst for importance. Significance even."

"Marrying me, with my pedigree, despite my lack of funds, gives them that. Or so it seems."

"How tragic for all of you."

"Yes. It is, actually." A sadness settled on me. Even all these miles away and under this sky, I could not escape the reality of my life. I was no longer free. Maybe I'd never been.

She was silent. The sound of the children laughing drifted from the back of the house.

A fly buzzed near my ear, and I swatted it away. A need to justify my decision came over me, quite suddenly. I didn't want Addie to think poorly of me or pity me. I didn't know which was worse. "Not everyone gets to choose for love, you know. I don't have the luxury of a choice. I'll marry for practical reasons and not love. It could be worse. She's actually quite a lovely person."

"Barneses have the luxury. Because of Papa. Not only his

wealth but his ideals. Ideals that are not typical. I hadn't really understood that until recently."

"Yes, look at his stance on Li and Fiona, for example. I thought he'd be against the marriage, but I was wrong." I grimaced, the need to defend myself disappearing as quickly as it had come. This was Addie Barnes. She was on my side, just as they all were. I could tell her the truth—allow myself to show her my soft underbelly. "I'd be lying if I said I wasn't envious. When I see what your sister and Li have—it's what I want, too." Like an unexpected storm that rose up inside me, I suddenly wanted to tell Addie the details of my troubles. However, she was too young and unburdened. It hardly seemed fair to tell her about how disappointing my life had turned out to be.

"You could marry me."

I jerked my head up to look at her. She smiled, but there was a somber quality in her eyes. Was she serious? *Of course not,* I told myself. *She's young and beautiful.* I was old and poor. Not a good match, even though I adored her for even thinking of the idea. "You're the sweetest girl to think of it. Saving old James and his decrepit bloodline. But even if I were willing to let you sacrifice your happiness for me, it would never do. The kind of wealth we need is the kind Lena's father has. Even your dear papa couldn't save us."

She nodded, looking crestfallen and so very pretty with the bees buzzing around us and the scent of the wild roses blooming on the other side of the pasture. "I'd do it for you. If I could help, I would."

"You have your whole life ahead of you," I said. "I want you to have love." I smiled, sadder than I'd ever been in my life. "At least one of us should. It'll make me happy to think of whomever it is you choose." *The lucky bastard,* I thought.

Her eyes glistened. She looked away, a myriad of expressions flexing the muscles of her face. "Have you ever wondered what love is?"

"What do you mean?" I asked gently.

"How to explain love in words? As in, what it is to love another? How does love manifest? Is sacrifice the way to truly love another? Is that the way we know we're loved? That a person is willing to give up what they want for the sake of your happiness?"

I nodded, knowing she was right. She was wise beyond her years. I'd always known this to be true, even when she'd been fourteen. It was her eyes. The way they searched a person's soul and saw everything true. I had to do this for my family. This was love in motion, in action. "I've never told anyone this but all my life, I've wanted to save my father. As a little boy, I would see how he hurt my mother with the gambling and drinking. I vowed to save them all if I could. Then maybe, just maybe, he would love me. Now's my chance."

"James, surely you don't mean that?"

"I do, in fact. I've been waiting to do something so spectacular that he can no longer withhold the love I want so badly. I didn't think it was possible."

"I'm sure he loves you. All fathers love their sons."

"I don't know if that's true." The last time I'd seen him he'd told me I was useless to him. Wasting my life with my face in a book, instead of seeking a fortune to save the family. "He loves his drink and his poker games, but my sister and me? I don't think so. He certainly doesn't act as if he does, anyway."

She drew in a breath and pulled her bottom lip into her mouth. I caught a glimpse of her small white teeth as she did so. A stirring in my gut confused me. I wanted to trace the path of a wayward tendril on her cheek with my finger, but I resisted. What was this? This sudden longing for Adelaide Barnes was unconscionable. What kind of disgusting old man was I? She was not for me. She could do so much better. Not that she wanted me, obviously. She was only being a good friend and a little sister.

"Is there any other way, James?" She placed a hand on my bare wrist for a brief moment. "Is Lena the only way?"

"I can't think of another," I said.

Her voice raised in pitch, and her hands gripped each other in her lap. "What if you let them find their own way out? Your father got you into this mess. Shouldn't he be the one who gets himself out?"

I watched her, confused. "Didn't we just decide that sacrifice and duty were what we must do when we love someone?"

"Yes, but why does it have to be so hard?" Addie asked. "I can't bear it. I can't bear to see you unhappy."

"If our theory is true, then my sacrifice should make me happy."

"But it won't, will it?"

I shook my head. "If I were a better person, perhaps it would."

"You're one of the best people I know," Addie said. "Your father and his irresponsibility shouldn't fall on you."

"But it does."

"Yes." She dipped her head, and a tremulous sigh made her narrow shoulders shudder. "I wish…I wish so many things were different."

"Addie, promise me something?"

She looked up, her blue eyes bright with emotion. "Anything."

"Whoever this man is who is making you cry—run from him. Love should never make you cry. Wait for the man who would do anything to be with you. Who would sacrifice for you."

"What if no such man exists?"

I smiled and allowed myself to brush her cheek, just once, with the back of my fingers. "He does. Right now, he's wondering where you are."

"If only that were true." Her fingers found mine, and she squeezed three times. I love you, those fingers seemed to say. Wouldn't that be wonderful? Addie's love would be true and loyal, life-giving. But even as I thought it, I dismissed the idea. Even if she were to love me, where would that leave us? It would not change my duty to my family or their desperate need. My life would play out as I'd always known it would. A loveless marriage. Years of loneliness in a house full of people, just as my mother and father had done. What audacity it had been to think I could escape my fate. My family's fate.

"Do you know what I think?" I asked.

"What's that?"

"I think we should have as much fun this summer as we possibly can. Starting tomorrow. What would you like to do?"

She lifted her face upward, smiling. "We could go on a picnic at the river park. Delphia could join us. She's always interested in a party. All the young people get together on Saturday afternoons. I don't usually go."

"Why not?"

"I'm too busy writing."

"When will I see this masterpiece?" I asked.

"Soon. I think. Every time I think it's ready for eyes other than Delphia's, I change my mind."

"Take advantage of my time here," I said. "I should pay my way somehow for your parents' hospitality."

"Yes, I shall. I promise. Perhaps next week."

I smiled, thoroughly charmed, as I had been from the first time I met my little wordsmith. She was all grown up now. A woman of talent and beauty in equal measures. The man who ended up with her by his side would be a lucky one indeed.

4

ADDIE

All my life I'd thought of myself as a good and virtuous person. Less selfish and self-centered than many of my peers, perhaps even more grateful to be alive because of my near-death experience as a child. However, the next afternoon at the river, I had to face my true self. I was not good. I'd told James a lie. I didn't want only for him to be happy. I wanted him to be happy with me.

Now, we sat on a blanket in the shade of the tall aspens at the river park. The grass was scattered with young couples or groups of friends picnicking on blankets. The water was deep at this particular spot on the river, which made it a great area for a park. Years ago, when I was still a child, my brothers had fallen trees and planted grass to make it a recreational area for whoever wanted to enjoy. For a long time now, it was a popular location for swimming and bonfires on the sandy beach below the grassy bank.

We'd already eaten the fried chicken Lizzie had packed and were now enjoying sweet, plump grapes. Delphia had her back against a tree with her legs stretched out. She held a book on her lap, reading about the history of the queens and kings of England that Papa had found for her. She was fascinated by history, especially that of our father's homeland. We might be Americans, but we also thought of ourselves as British, at least in spirit.

Every once in a while she looked up to ask James a question about English nobility or politics, but for the most part, she remained absorbed in the pages. James was sprawled out on his side, resting his face in his hand. A copy of Sinclair Lewis's latest, *Work of Art*, lay unopened next to him. I sat with my legs tucked under me, reading E.M. Forster's *Howards End*. I'd read it before but had decided to revisit it.

"Do you know all these people?" James asked, drawing me from the story.

"Mostly, yes. From school or church." I told him the names of most of the young people around us.

He seemed especially keen to hear about each one, which struck me as odd. "Why do you want to know?" I asked.

"No reason, other than I'm trying to pick out the chap who has captured your heart. Is he here?"

"I wouldn't tell you if he was," I said.

"But why?" His eyes narrowed as he studied me.

"Because it's private."

"You're afraid I'd do something to embarrass you?" James asked, without a hint of teasing.

"I know you'd not do it on purpose, but your protective nature might get the better of you."

"Fair enough. When it comes to the Barnes women, I cannot be expected to behave rationally." His gaze flickered toward a pair of young men striding across the lawn toward us. "What about them?"

I looked at them carefully but didn't recognize them. I'd never seen them before, which didn't happen often. "I can't say as I do." They were both tall and wide-shouldered and wearing hats like the ones cowboys donned in photographs. "Maybe they just moved here." I couldn't see their faces too well because of the shadow from their hats, but they both had strong, square jawlines. Brothers, perhaps?

They stopped a few feet from us. "Howdy. Mind if we sit here?" A gruff voice came from the slightly taller one.

"It's a public park." I held my hand over my eyes to see them without the sun being in my eyes and gave them a friendly smile. Mama and Papa had always insisted that we be welcoming to newcomers. "You may sit wherever you like."

"Thank you." The shorter of the two took a blanket from a knapsack and spread it on the grass. When they were seated, the taller looked over at us and lifted the brim of his hat to reveal blue eyes with dark lashes. "I'm Mathias Jefferson. This is my brother Boone." He took off his hat and laid it next to him, revealing dark hair, slicked back with pomade.

"Pleasure." Boone took off his hat and nodded toward me. An unruly mob of dark curls tumbled down his forehead. He had the same eyes and jawline as his brother, but he seemed slightly smaller in every way—shorter, slimmer, more delicate features.

"James West." James leaned over to shake hands with each of them. Delphia had glanced up from her book and was scowling in their direction, as if she were irritated to be interrupted from her book.

"I'm Miss Addie Barnes, and this is my sister Delphia."

"Ah, yes. The famous Barnes sisters," Mathias said. "We've heard some tall tales."

Delphia laid her book aside and sat up straighter, obviously interested in what these tales might be. "Please, elaborate."

"You're the younger one, right?" Boone asked Delphia.

"If it's any of your business, which it is not, but yes." Delphia seemed to be taking them in like she might a tall glass of lemonade on a hot day.

"Yeah, you're the feisty one. We heard stories about you in particular."

Next to me, James sat up straighter. He wasn't smiling or

acting like his usual friendly self. In fact, he seemed rather hostile. Why was that? Had he taken a dislike to them for some reason?

"What have you heard about me?" Delphia's fists clenched in her lap, ready for a fight.

"Nothing bad," Boone said, amusement making his eyes dance. "We'd sure like to hear those, though."

Delphia lifted her slim shoulders in a dismissive way. "Maybe."

"We were at your brother's club last night," Mathias said. "He mentioned you two, that's all."

"And then someone else said you were the only two Barnes ladies left." Mathias reached into his bag and pulled out a glass jar of water and handed it to his brother.

"Left?" Delphia asked. "Left for what?"

"Marriage," Boone said.

"Is that all we're good for?" Delphia raised one eyebrow and glared at him.

"No, miss, I expect not," Mathias said. "According to a few of the men sitting around the table, all the Barnes women are beautiful. They were right."

"No sirree, they weren't lying," Boone said. "If you don't mind my saying."

"We do mind," Delphia said.

"I'm sorry to offend," Boone said, flushing. "Your beauty's flustered me."

"Well, I do have that effect on people." Delphia smiled primly.

"Your brother said you're the rebellious one," Boone said. "And Miss Addie's the sweet one."

I grinned. "True enough."

James chuckled and inched closer to me. I might have imagined it, though. "Both ladies have protective brothers and a father with a shotgun," James said, casually. "If you were wondering about that?"

"James," I said, laughing. "Don't try to scare them. My father's a gentleman. He'd never shoot someone."

"That is untested," James said. "You don't know what he might do if a couple of scoundrels showed up at his door looking for one of you ladies."

"We'll keep that in mind." Mathias's eyes had widened, and I could see him thinking through everything James had said.

"Where are you from?" I asked.

"Oklahoma. We're here visiting our aunt," Mathias said.

"Not visiting exactly," Boone said. "We don't know if we'll go back. There's nothing but dust. That's all we had left. Our folks passed away a few months back."

"I'm sorry," I said.

"Thank you," Boone said.

"The farm's gone," Mathias said. "Not much there for us now."

"Our father and his father before him worked that land," Boone said. "We won't have that privilege."

"Do you need work?" I asked. These poor men, leaving their home. Chased out by the dust storms.

"We sure do," Boone said. "You know of any?"

"I'll speak to my father," I said. "If there's any work, he'll know about it."

"We'd sure appreciate it," Mathias said. "This place doesn't seem as bad off as some of the other places we've been."

"We've been spared the kind of troubles you've seen," I said. "But there are some who've needed some help."

"We take care of our own," Delphia said.

I glanced over to see James peering at me as if I were of great interest to him. Our eyes met for a second. A spark flickered in those blue eyes that sent a wave of desire through me. I turned back to Mathias and Boone. "Would you two care for some chicken? Our Lizzie makes the best there is."

"We'd be much obliged." Boone's face looked like a child at

the sight of Christmas candy, I thought, humbled. I took so much for granted.

"Are you sure you have enough?" Mathias said. "We don't want to take your food."

"There's plenty," I said. "It's best if someone eats it up. In this heat, it won't last long."

The next few minutes I spent fixing plates for them. James opened bottles of cold beer for everyone, and we spent a pleasant time getting to know the brothers. We quickly learned that their elderly aunt was one of the women Mama dropped in to check on at least once a week, taking food and making sure she was all right. She was quite elderly and feeble. Mama had worried about her living alone. I told the brothers as much.

"She's our great-aunt," Mathias said. "Never had a husband or children. She was glad to take us in, but we're worried we're making things even harder for her."

"We've started a garden," Boone said. "Big ol' fat tomatoes are ripening. We're hoping to help her more than she's helped us. We got nothing left but her, and she's got nothing but us."

"I'm sure you will," Delphia said, speaking for the first time in a few minutes. It wasn't like her to be so quiet. "That's what family is for."

At this point, James stood and offered me his hand. "Come on, Addie. Let's take a swim. Anyone else want to join us?"

The Jefferson brothers declined, as did Delphia. I leaned close to ask her if she minded being left alone. "Go ahead," she said. "I'll stay here and watch our things."

My bathing costume was on under my cotton dress. The fabric was sticking to my back. I could already feel the coolness of that river on my skin. "Come on then, James."

We walked to the edge of the grassy cliff. A rocky trail led down to a sandy beach. Bathers swam and splashed in the water. I took my dress off and hung it on a birch tree branch. James did the same with his pants and shirt and placed them next to my dress. They were a nice couple, those empty clothes, I thought.

James's muscular chest and shoulders were slightly freckled. His arm and chest hair were lighter than the copper tones of his thick waves. I glanced down at his legs. Muscles and more fuzz. What would it be like to run my nails through it?

I shook my head to dispel my far-from-virtuous thoughts. "You want to jump in or wade?" I gestured toward the hill where mostly children were jumping into the water.

"You want to jump?" He looked a little unsure for a moment. "I've never done it before, so you go ahead."

"What? You haven't? All these summers here and you've never jumped?"

"I'm a tad frightened of heights."

"You are?" I laughed, despite the serious glint in his eyes. "Take my hand. We'll jump together."

He smiled as he took my offered hand. "I suppose I have to conquer this fear at some point."

Holding hands, we walked to the edge of the rocky cliff and waited as two little boys jumped into the deep green water. "You ready?" I asked him.

He'd gone pale. "Maybe not."

I tugged on his hand. "Do you know how many times I've jumped in from here?"

"Hundreds?"

"Probably. Anyway, nothing's ever happened to me. Look at me. Still intact."

His gaze slid over my body. The sun burned hot above us but not hotter than I. "Yes, quite perfectly intact, I must say."

To hide my confusion I took him over to the edge of the cliff. "All you have to do is jump outward, as if you wanted to land in the very middle."

"Jump outward? What happens if you're too close to the edge?"

I laughed. "You won't be. Hold my hand and I'll count us off."

"Fine, yes, sure. I can do this."

"One, two, three." On three, we jumped, hands clasped until we hit the cold water. I lost him as I sank and then swam to the surface. At around the same time, his head popped out of the water. He shook his head like a golden retriever and grinned.

"Isn't it fun?" I asked, swimming closer.

"It was fun." Water dripped down the side of his face as he bobbed slightly in the waves from the jumpers right after us.

I swam up to him, wishing I could feel his wet skin against mine. He was beautiful, this man. His full mouth turned upward into a boyish grin.

"Thanks, Addie. I've been wanting to do that every summer since I first came here."

"You're welcome. You were very brave."

"Not really, but I did it." James took off then for the shore. I followed him. When we reached the sandy beach, we plopped down side by side.

He looked over at me, his head cocked to the right. "Only you could look this pretty after jumping off a cliff."

I breathed in his words as if they were enough to save my inevitable broken heart. For now, he was mine and mine alone. "I'm glad you think I'm pretty."

"Addie Barnes, every man in this town thinks that."

"Even you?"

"Especially me." He reached over and touched a knuckle to my cheek. "The purest kind of beauty—that's what you have. The kind that comes from the inside out."

I ducked my chin, shy but thrilled by his words.

"Don't you let whoever this man is make you feel anything less than that," James said. "Even when I'm not here, you must remember. You'll simply close your eyes and recall how I'm looking at you right now."

I lifted my gaze to his, fighting the conflicting notions of fleeing and allowing myself to be encompassed by him. I chose the latter, giving in to this glorious feeling of being fully seen. "What does that mean? How are you looking at me?"

He peered down at me as if searching the very depths of my soul, a way no other person had ever done, other than my parents and sisters. "With admiration. With humility that I get to be a little part of your life this summer, or at all, for that matter. Men like me don't have the chance to spend time with women like you."

"Men like you?"

"Deeply flawed. Weighed down with the burdens of my family. A man in captivity."

I let his words soak into me as the sun dried my skin. Resting my chin on my knees, I looked over at him. He was sitting with his feet in the water staring blankly across the pond. "I would free you if I could."

For a long moment, he was silent. I held my breath, waiting for him to say something. Finally, he said in a resigned voice, "I know you would, because you're good and strong. Thank you for taking my mind away for an afternoon."

"We'll have more days like today, won't we?" I peeked up at him from under my wet lashes.

"Yes." But he sighed when he said it, like a man on the gallows who knew death would come soon.

When we returned to our picnic blanket, Delphia was surrounded by male admirers. She seemed to care less about suitors or romance, yet boys followed her everywhere we went. At the moment, she was debating the value of the New Deal with Harley and Merry's son Jack. The Depauls had worked for Papa when my older siblings were still young. Harley and Merry now bred horses on their farm and were doing well. Their son Jack was almost exactly my age, with Henry slightly older. Jack was a horseman if there ever was one. He was as wild as a mustang, similar in personality to Delphia, rebellious and wickedly smart. Regardless, they fought about everything and always had.

Henry was more like me, quiet and cerebral, although he shared a love of horses with his brother. He'd gone to university and come home married to a pretty young woman named Lillian. They now helped Harley and Merry run the horse farm. Jack's future was less certain. I knew from my mother that his parents worried about him, wishing he would settle down with a nice woman and have a family as his brother had done. I had my doubts looking at his dark eyes sparkling from sparring with my sister. It would take a woman like my sister to keep up with him.

The poor Jefferson brothers seemed slightly horrified at the disagreement, watching as if afraid one or the other might burst into flames at any moment. On the other hand, my sister seemed to be in her element, cheeks flushed as much from the debate as the heat of the afternoon.

They quieted when we approached. Delphia turned toward us, brushing away a wayward curl with an impatient flick of her wrist. Her eyes narrowed as she looked at me and then James. I could almost hear her brain clicking away, wondering what was between us. She was naturally suspicious anyway, and from the way her mouth tightened, I knew she could see more than others would. Guilt jabbed at me. I had no right to be flirting with James this way. Not when he was promised to another. It was usually Delphia in the wrong, not me. What would she think? Could she see into my heart? My wickedness?

"How was the water?" Delphia asked once we'd sat back down on the blanket.

I was nearly dry and had pulled my dress back on over my suit. "Refreshing," I said, avoiding her eyes. "Jack, you remember James West?"

"Yes, good to see you." Jack held out a brawny arm to shake James's hand. "I ran into Fiona at Johnson's store and she mentioned you'd arrived from back east. You here for the entire summer?"

"Until August. Glad to be here." James's eyes found mine for a split second. "Days like today are the ones that will sustain me during the long New York winters."

Once more, I noticed Delphia watching us. She was too smart. Nothing got past her.

We spent the rest of the afternoon talking and laughing. Delphia brought out the cookies from the bottom of the picnic basket as well as some of Lizzie's homemade strawberry lemonade. The Jefferson brothers seemed to relax and enjoy the company, telling us more about the life they'd fled and their hopes for a new one.

"We might have some work for you boys," Jack said. "Out at our farm. I'll talk to my papa." He pronounced it the French way with a lilt on the second syllable. Harley had immigrated from France as a teenager.

"We'd take whatever you have," Boone said. "We're hard workers and won't give you any trouble."

I smiled to myself. We might not have the most exciting lives, but they were filled with good cheer and friendship. My father had made sure, all those years ago, that our community offered shelter to whoever was willing to work. My chest swelled with pride thinking of him now. Papa's generosity was passing from one generation to the other. He'd helped Harley start his farm as a thank-you for his loyal service. Now, twenty years later, his gifts were being passed on to the two young men from Oklahoma, strangers to us, yet familiar too. Hardworking men in need of assistance, just as Harley Depaul had once received from Papa. That was the way with generosity, I supposed. One never knew the lasting effects of such things.

5

JAMES

A FEW DAYS INTO MY VISIT, FIONA CAME BY THE HOUSE TO INVITE ME into town for an evening at her brother's club. "I'm sorry we've been neglecting you," Fiona said. "But this musical score is taking all of our attention."

"Not to worry. I'm quite content here at the house. Your mother left a stack of books for me. Addie's been hinting around about a manuscript she'd like me to read, but instead, we've been swimming and picnicking. Your little sisters are all grown up, it seems."

We were sitting on the screened back porch in the heat of the afternoon. Most everyone had gone upstairs to rest, but I'd not been tired. I'd just opened up a book when Fiona appeared.

"Yes, it seems to be the way of the world." Fiona sighed and settled back into the chaise next to mine. She yawned and pressed her fingers into the dark circles under her eyes.

"Are you taking care of yourself?" I, too, was spread out on a chaise. My jacket was off and I had the sleeves of my shirt rolled up to combat the heat. A gentle breeze came through the screens of the porch, giving some relief from the hot afternoon air.

"Not too well. Between the boys and work, it's been a busy

time. Some days I'm not sure exactly why I had all of these children."

"It's too late now," I said, chuckling.

"Li wants me to hire more help, especially now that we're doing so well, but I hate to miss anything with them. Time goes too fast. Some days I wake and wonder how it is that I'm a married lady with four children, and other days I can't believe they're growing so fast." She turned her head to look at me. "Is it true about Lena Masters? Are you engaged?"

"What do you mean?"

"It was in the newspaper. I read it with my own eyes," Fiona said.

I sat up, a ball of lead in my stomach. "In the newspaper?"

"In the society section. It was an official announcement of your engagement. I assumed you knew, although I was troubled you hadn't mentioned an engagement to me. You said things were complicated, but I thought you meant with your work."

"It was only just decided," I said, mumbling.

She dug a folded piece of newspaper from her pocket and handed it to me. "I brought it for you, in case you wanted a copy."

I unfolded the paper to read the announcement for myself.

Mr. Maxwell Masters is pleased to announce the engagement of his daughter, Lena Masters, to Mr. James West.

"I didn't know he was doing that," I said, setting it aside. "But we are getting married. As soon as I return home. I got a short reprieve for this visit."

"James, is this what you want? Was this announcement meant to trap you?"

I looked into her eyes briefly before looking out to the yard. Fiona should know the truth. We'd shared so much over the years. She was my best friend. I wanted her to know everything. "Yes, this seals my fate. They know I'd never embarrass Lena by backing out now."

"Do you love her?" Fiona's deep blue eyes studied me with such affection that I nearly choked up.

"She's entertaining. And lovely to look at. I'm hoping to someday."

"James? Someday is not the same as desperately."

"It doesn't really matter if it is or isn't," I said. "You know as well as anyone how I've needed to marry a wealthy woman. There are worse choices than Lena. You'd like her, in fact. She's lively and intelligent. Her father owns the publishing house where I work. Without this marriage, my career is over. It's all been decided. I must simply do what's expected of me. You mustn't feel sorry for me, Fi. I'll be relieved and happy to have no more financial burdens."

She turned away to look up at the ceiling. "If only I could believe you. But I know you, James. You're not the type to marry for convenience. What happened to your idea of love?"

"I could be like the French and have a mistress," I said, hoping to lighten the mood.

"You could, I suppose. But you won't. That's not the kind of man you are."

"You're probably right. It's terrible to always want to do the right thing."

"The right thing? Is that what this is?" She gazed at me again, her eyes inquisitive. My dearest friend knew me well.

"It is the thing that makes the most sense. More so than my desire to be an editor or move to America. None of it has added up to anything. This is my chance to make a lot of people happy, including my mother and my sister. Mostly, my father will have to—"

"Have to what?"

"Love me."

"You've wanted that more than anything else, perhaps?"

"Perhaps."

She sighed but didn't say anything further. What else was there to say, really?

"It won't be a bad life, Fi," I said after a moment. "I'll be rich and free to have my head in a book for the rest of my life. We'll have a family. I'll live an easy life."

She reached over to take my hand. "Don't forget that we're your family, too. You're one of us and always will be. Please, tell me if you need anything. Do you promise me you will?"

"I promise." I kissed her hand and set it back in her lap. "Close your eyes and take a little nap." I patted the book by my side. "I'll just read for a minute and give you a little peace."

She gave me one of her gentle smiles before closing her eyes. "A nap does sound perfectly perfect."

I returned to my book, knowing that an escape into the pages would save me, as it had all my life.

THAT EVENING, when I entered the sitting room dressed for dinner in my best suit, they had champagne on ice, ready to toast my engagement. Delphia and Addie were there waiting as well. My eyes were drawn to Addie, who wore a plum-colored dress that made her fair skin look luminous in the evening light. When had she grown so beautiful? She'd always been pretty, but maturity had brought a new loveliness. A sense of substance emanated from her eyes. A woman was before me instead of the child I'd once known.

I didn't know what to make of it or the feelings she'd stirred in me the last few days. Why was it different than what I felt for Delphia or Fiona? They were beautiful, too. I could see that. I had eyes, after all. But Addie tugged at me in a visceral way. One that made me wish to touch her moonbeam skin.

What was wrong with me? I had to stop thinking this way. I was an engaged man. However it came to be, it was still true. My father and Maxwell Masters had made their move. It was now time for me to come through for all of them.

My father. A memory flashed before me. I'd been eight years

old. Nanny had fallen asleep in her chair in the nursery. My little sister was napping. I took it upon myself to wander downstairs and find a book from our library. To my surprise, I'd found my father there. He'd been slumped over on the sofa, a drink in his hand. Upon hearing me, he looked up with bloodshot eyes. I'd taken in a deep, painful breath at the sight of him. *Sad and defeated.* Those were the two words I'd thought of to describe him. Then I noticed that my mother was there, too. She was in a dark corner of the room, hidden in shadow. A ghost in her own home. She'd been crying. I could see that, even though I was young.

And a feeling inside me had emerged fully formed, whereas before when I was younger, it had been fragmented. I'd not been able to understand it before then, this overwhelming urge to fix him. To fix everything. To make it all better.

"Mother?" I'd said out loud. "What should I do?"

"Nothing, love. Go back to the nursery." Her voice was flat and hoarse, as if she were sick. "Don't dally. Take one of your little books and leave us."

"But I…I could help," I said.

"Wouldn't that be something if you could?" Father downed the rest of his drink and slammed the glass on the table. "You're a worthless, weak boy, aren't you now? You'll grow up to be a taller version than you are now but the same anyway. Useless to me. To anyone."

"Michael, please. He's only a little boy." My mother's voice now shook, not from rage, but despair. Even at that age, I knew the difference.

Father looked at me, his eyes unfocused. "You want to help? When you're all grown up, you can do the smart thing and marry well. I married for love and look what good came of that? Nothing at all. Nothing at all. This life of mine, nothing but a disappointment."

"You've done this to us, Michael," Mother said. "Your carelessness. That horrible itch you have to gamble everything away."

"Mother, what's happened?" I asked.

"Your father took a gamble and it's ruined us," she said, wooden now. The true mark of a person who has given up all hope, I realized later.

I couldn't look at either of them, staring down at my hands that were clasped so tightly together the whites of my knuckles were in sharp contrast to my freckled skin. I wished with all my might that I could fix whatever it was that was so terribly wrong.

"Marry a rich woman, James," Father said. "And save us all. If only I'd been smart enough to do the same."

"If only I'd been smart enough to marry an intelligent man," Mother said. "One who didn't waste the last of his fortune on a gypsy tale."

Even at such a young age, I understood two things. If either of them had their wish then I would not have been born. And secondly, because I was born, I must be the one to save them. For my existence was part of the problem. If I could be a good enough boy, perhaps they would be happy.

Now, I blinked myself back to the present. Alexander was offering me a glass of champagne. Quinn invited me to sit next to her and tell her all about Lena. I did as asked, happy to oblige anyone who showed interest in me, as I'd been doing all my life.

Delphia and Addie sat across from us on the other couch. Alexander took one of the easy chairs. Outside, twilight dusted the world orange. The bubbles in my champagne popped enthusiastically to the top of my glass.

"You're in trouble with us," Quinn said. "How could you not mention the engagement? We would have had a party for you instead of only opening a bottle of bubbly."

"Without the bride, it's rather strange to do so, isn't it?" Delphia asked.

"Yes, yes, of course," Quinn said. "I'm only teasing. James, tell us all about her. How did you meet?"

I stole a furtive look at Addie. She stared into her champagne glass, seeming removed from the world. Actually, she appeared quite sad. Was it my engagement? *No, don't be daft,* I scolded myself. *She's probably bored of me and my silly life and wishes she were out with her young friends.*

"We met at a party at Mr. Masters's apartment in Manhattan. I was with my boss," I said. "It was Christmastime and everything was very festive." I'd been missing my Colorado family that night and had agreed to attend the party to distract myself. "To be honest, I was wishing I was here with all of you."

Addie looked up at me. "You were?"

"Yes, that Christmas I spent with all of you was the happiest of my life."

"You're always welcome here," Alexander said. "Perhaps this year, you and your new wife will join us?"

"When is the wedding?" Delphia asked.

"We haven't decided yet. In fact, the note in the paper was a surprise to me. I hadn't realized a formal announcement was planned yet. We'd only just decided before I left that we would marry upon my return in August."

"What? So soon?" Quinn asked, sharply. Her motherly instincts aroused, I thought.

A bittersweet twinge at her obvious fondness for me pricked at my eyelids. "She's anxious to start our life together," I said.

Quinn peered at me with surprise in her eyes. "I would have thought Lena would want a long engagement with many parties and festivities before having a large and expensive wedding. Isn't that how they do it in society these days? Not that I would know. In Colorado we do it however we please, don't we, dears?"

Her daughters nodded. Delphia darted a look at me, as if she were trying to work out a puzzle.

"My father and Mr. Masters are old friends." Was that true? Friends or enemies or somewhere in between. I knew nothing, other than they'd teamed up together to ruin my life. Not ruin. It was not ruined, I told myself. Just altered. Drastically and finally. "They've asked for us to get married sooner than later. This marriage means a lot to both of them."

"Why is that?" Alexander asked.

"It solves many problems for both of them," I said, evasively.

No one spoke for a few seconds as this sank in. Alexander held out his glass for the maid to fill, all the while watching me. What did he see? Could he sense that I was trapped?

"We didn't want to wait either. Once we decided, we wanted to marry as soon as possible." Quinn sent a pointed look at her husband. "Do you remember, darling? We were very much in love, which made us impatient."

"Oh yes. I couldn't marry you fast enough." Alexander shared a smile with his bride. "By then we knew each other very well, so there was no reason to wait. The children wanted us to marry, too."

"We had a Christmas wedding," Quinn said. "Oh, it was a grand day. Will your wedding be in New York or somewhere else?"

"Mr. Masters owns a home in Long Island as well as his Manhattan apartment," I said. "Whatever Lena wants will be fine with me."

"Good man," Alexander said. "It's best to let the woman have whatever she wants. You're just happy to be there."

"Quite right," I said. If only that were true. I felt an urge to pretend that this was a love match instead of a business arrangement. The idea of Quinn and Alexander feeling pity for me made me inwardly cringe. Fiona and Addie could know the truth, but their parents would be devastated to think of me compromising in any way. They didn't understand that I didn't have the advantage of freedom. I could not choose who I wanted. If I'd been their son, perhaps. But I wasn't. As much as I loved this family, they weren't mine. They were only mine to borrow.

"Tell us more about Lena," Quinn said. "Did you know right away she was the one?"

"She' and I share a similar hair color, although hers is redder than mine," I babbled, unable to think of anything else to say.

"Really? How remarkable." Quinn clasped her hands together, her face alight with joy. "I wonder if that means you'll have redheaded children?"

"I don't know," I said. "However they turn out, I shall be glad to have them."

"Is that all she is?" Delphia's eyes glittered at me from across the table. "Redheaded?"

"No, no," I said. "She's many things. Smart and pretty. Very accomplished."

"In what?" Quinn asked. "Music? Academics?"

"Um, yes. Academics, I think," I said. "Not music." I'd not heard her speak of it, anyway.

"How well do you know this Lena?" Delphia asked.

"Delphia, mind your manners," Quinn said. "We've put him on the spot, that's all. We're sorry, James. It's simply that we're curious to know who has captured your heart at last."

"It's quite all right." I gulped champagne from my glass. If I wasn't careful it would give me the hiccups. I'd been unable to eat after I learned about the announcement in the newspaper. It had made the whole thing real. I'd been able to put it out of my mind while spending time with Addie. Addie *and* Delphia, that is.

"Does this announcement mean you'll have to leave us earlier than you planned?" Addie asked. Was her voice shaking, or was that my imagination?

"I'm not certain," I said. "I'll write to Lena tonight and ask her what she'd like."

"Please make sure she knows we'd love to have her and her father come for a visit," Quinn said.

The idea of Lena here left me feeling strange. I couldn't imagine her here. She would not like it, I suspected. Too much dirt. Was that true? I didn't really know her well enough to know if she would like Colorado or not. That was the truth of it.

6

ADDIE

A WEEK HAD GONE BY SINCE I'D LEARNED OF JAMES'S IMPENDING nuptials. For the most part, I'd avoided him, spending most days volunteering at the library or helping my sisters with their children.

However, on this particular morning, I had no plans whatsoever and decided to brave breakfast, even if James was there. Delphia and I entered the dining room together. Metal bins with scrambled eggs, potatoes, and biscuits lined the buffet. I sniffed the air, taking in the nutty scent of freshly brewed coffee.

Mama and Papa were nearly finished. Papa had his head buried in the newspaper. Mama, strangely enough, wasn't reading. Instead, she stared out the window seemingly lost in thought. Whatever those thoughts were, they troubled her. I could see it in the knit of her brow.

"Good morning," Delphia sang out before heading to the buffet to load her plate with eggs and biscuits.

"Morning, girls," Mama said, jumping slightly. She hadn't heard us come in.

Papa lowered his paper to give us each a smile before returning to whatever article had grabbed his interest.

"Where's James?" Delphia asked.

"He's on his way down," Mama said. "The poor man's exhausted. I made him promise to sleep as late as he wanted."

I put some eggs on a plate and added a few slices of peach and a handful of raspberries. This time of year, we had the most glorious fruit from local growers as well as from our own garden. Usually, I delighted in them, but today everything tasted of dirt.

Papa laid aside his newspaper. "You're both looking lovely. What are you doing today?"

"I'm working a shift at the library," I said. If it were slow, I usually worked on my stories in between patrons.

"I'm headed over to Cym's," Delphia said. "She needs me to look after the girls."

"What's she doing, I wonder?" Mama asked.

"Shopping, I think," Delphia said.

Jasper came in then with a handful of mail in his hands. "I'm sorry to interrupt," he said. "There's a letter for James and something here from the university for Miss Delphia."

Delphia's fork clattered on the table. Her hands flew to her mouth. She looked over at me, fear in her eyes.

Jasper set the letter for James on the buffet and laid the letter from the university in front of my sister. I saw him and Papa exchange a glance. One I couldn't interpret. Was it a commiseration between two fathers who had to let their daughters leave the nest? Or was it an unspoken fear? Would Delphia be disappointed? None of us wanted that. She would take it hard. Like Theo, she'd had aspirations of higher education for years now, pushing herself in her studies. Although she was only sixteen, she'd already finished high school and had applied to attend several colleges in the east. Two had already denied her entrance, saying they did not accept female candidates and especially ones so young. She had one more hope, a college back east, and had been waiting for their letter. This was it. She would know now, one way or the other.

If she got in, then I would be here alone. Florence was

already at university. She wrote often, telling me of her adventures. She didn't ask but I know she wondered why I wasn't interested in attending myself. I figured anything I needed to know was in the books at our library, and I didn't need to be away from home to learn it. Anyway, Florence and Delphia were the adventurous types, and I was not.

Delphia slid the letter across the table toward me. "Addie, you have to open it for me. I can't look."

I took the slim envelope and slid a finger under the seal. *Please God, let her have this,* I prayed silently. The correspondence was written on the thin paper used with typewriters and folded in three. I unfolded it with sweaty fingers and used my quick reading skills to take in my sister's fate. The first sentence said it all.

We are pleased to accept you into the fall semester of 1935.

"It's a yes," I said.

"Marvelous," Papa said, clearly pleased.

"Thank goodness," Mama said under her breath.

Delphia yelped and rose up to dance around the table until she reached me. She picked up the letter and read it for herself, then whooped again and grabbed me into a hug.

"I told you," I said. "I knew you'd get in."

"I didn't. I truly thought this would be the third rejection."

We'd known the odds. They almost never admitted women. I suspected her exams and essays had been better than most of the men who'd applied. She belonged there. I hadn't been sure the men who ran the college would agree. Apparently, they had.

Jasper excused himself, telling us he'd go down to the kitchen to tell Lizzie.

"Papa, you didn't send them money?" Delphia asked. "Please tell me this isn't because you donated a library."

"You asked me to stay out of it, and I did," Papa said.

"Oh, darling, I'm so proud of you." Mama was on her feet by then and held out her arms for my sister. "But I'll miss you terribly."

"I'll only be away for a few years," Delphia said.

The truth of it all washed over me. Delphia, my best friend, was leaving me. What was I doing exactly? Should I have gone to school with Florence? The very idea gave me a pit in my stomach. I didn't want to leave home. This is where I belonged. I'd be an old maid living with my parents for the rest of their lives. I sighed and tried not to cry. *Be happy for her*, I told myself. *That's my job as her big sister.*

James appeared in the doorway. "Have I missed something?"

My stomach fluttered at the sight of him. A cut on his chin told me he'd nicked himself shaving. His hair was slicked back, but even pomade couldn't keep that attractive curl from falling over his left eyebrow.

"I got into college, James." Delphia thrust the letter at him. "Even though I'm a girl, I got in."

"Well done, love." James beamed at her. "They're not going to know what hit them once you arrive."

"I'm going to amaze them with my discipline and cleverness." Delphia jutted out her chin. "Just watch me."

"I have no doubts at all." He looked over at me. "You'll miss her, but she'll be back."

How had he known that's what I was thinking? He often did. But what did it matter? He was leaving me, too.

"Of course, she will be," I said, more stoutly than I felt. "But yes, I'll miss my baby sister."

Mama encouraged James to get breakfast and join us. For the next few minutes, while he filled his plate and one of the maids poured him a cup of coffee, we chatted about Delphia's plans.

"Perhaps the three of us will take you out there." Mama brushed away the dampness from the corners of her brown eyes. "To get you settled."

"You could come to New York afterward," James said. "We could see a show or two. Meet some literary folks for Addie?"

"What a wonderful idea," Mama said. "Something to look forward to."

"James, there's a letter for you, too," Papa said. "Jasper left it for you there."

"Oh, yes, in the excitement, we almost forgot." Mama gestured toward the side table where the letter sat waiting.

James had already set down his plate in the spot next to me but got up to grab the letter. His expression darkened when he looked at the address. "It's from Lena."

Lena. I swallowed the bile that rose to the back of my throat.

James sank into the chair, then lifted the letter from the envelope. I watched as his eyes roamed over the words. When he was finished, he folded the letter and pushed it away from his plate, as if it were something he didn't want to eat.

"Is everything all right?" Mama asked. "It's not bad news, I hope?"

He met her gaze. "No, it's good news. It seems Lena and her father are on their way here. I mentioned your invitation, and I guess they took that as something more formal. They'll be here in a few days."

For the second time that morning, my stomach dropped. Lena was coming here. I would see with my own eyes the woman who had taken my James.

"She said to tell you how anxious she is to meet you and make a good impression." His voice sounded as if someone had placed a brick against his throat. "Lena's heard me talk about you all so much, she feels as if she knows you."

"Excellent," Papa said. "We're delighted to meet the girl who has stolen your heart."

"They know I think of you all as my second family," James said. "Are you sure you have enough room for them?"

"Yes, absolutely," Mama said. "We'll move Delphia in with Addie so Lena can take her room."

"Do you mind, ladies?" James asked, sounding apologetic.

"Not at all," Delphia said. "Anything for you, James."

"I didn't think they would come all the way out here," James said, speaking as if he were thinking out loud. "She says her father is anxious to make your acquaintance, Alexander. He's a businessman, always looking for opportunities. Mr. Masters is very American that way. I hope he won't be too much." James flushed, obviously embarrassed. "I find him abrasive and aggressive."

"If you love Lena, then we shall love her. As far as her father goes, he's nothing Alexander can't handle." Mama tilted her head as her gaze fixed on our guest. "You're not having second thoughts, are you?"

James didn't answer for a second or two. Finally, he hung his head. "No, not that. I didn't expect they'd come here, that's all. I wanted a less complicated summer than that." He looked over at me. "Addie and I had a lot of plans. This was supposed to be a fun vacation for me before I had to go back and face the rest of my life. And I wanted to help her with her manuscript. Lena will take up a lot of my attention."

Mama and Papa exchanged a glance. Did they suspect his reluctance?

"James, darling, won't it be even more fun to have your sweetheart here?" Mama asked.

He blinked, as if she had spoken to him in a foreign tongue. "Yes, yes. Quite so."

"My manuscript isn't important," I said. "Please don't think two seconds about that."

"It is important. You must always remember that your work matters, Addie. I want to give it the attention it deserves."

I wanted to cry right then and there. "That's kind of you, but I know the pecking order. Fiancées are more important than old friends who think they have writing talent."

"Don't do that," James said. "Don't ever diminish yourself like that. You're very talented. I'm proud to help you. In fact, it's my honor."

"You haven't even read it yet," I said.

Everyone else fell away. Our eyes locked. The room seemed to shrink to include just the two of us. In his return gaze, I saw everything that I would miss. All the ways in which we could have enhanced the other's life. It was not to be. I must accept it. But I wanted him. I wanted his voice to be the one I heard first thing in the morning and the last at night.

"I've read enough of your work to know, Adelaide Barnes," James said gently. "I want to have the chance to help shape whatever it is you've written. I want to have a part of it. If you want me to."

"You can still do that," I said, trying hard not to cry.

When I looked away from James, I became aware of the three others in the room. Three people who were now staring at me as if I were sitting there in my underclothes. Had I revealed myself to all of them? Did my secret adoration of James West show on my face? In everything I did? Because it was that way for me. He was inside me, making my heart beat.

I CRIED myself to sleep that night, weeping until there was nothing but exhaustion to take me into dreamland. When I woke, the problems were still there, and my grief was like an elephant on my chest. What childish daydreams I'd had. All these years, I'd let myself believe that by some miracle James would see me as something other than his best friend's sister. But as it turns out, even if he had, it would not matter. He could not marry me. For the first time in my life, it appeared that even my father's vast wealth was not enough. I'd not thought I'd ever want for anything because of lack of money. Yet here it was. If we'd been able to save James and his family, then he could have chosen me for practical reasons and perhaps fallen for me eventually.

I bristled at the idea, though. If I were to have had James as my own, I would have wanted him because he loved me, not because he needed our family money. *What about this Lena?* I asked myself as our maid, Bitty, coaxed my slippery hair into fat curls. I wore it somewhere between long and short, as was the style now, crimping it with a hot iron to give the appearance of waves. Bitty was a master at making both Delphia's and my finely textured hair appear more plentiful.

I stared back at my reflection, horrified to see the puffiness around my eyes and pallor of my skin.

"Miss Addie, would you like me to bring up a cucumber for your eyes?" Bitty asked, standing back to look at her work.

Cucumbers were supposed to take the puffiness out, but other than feeling like cold slugs on my skin, they hardly seemed effective. "No, thank you, Bitty. Nothing a hot cup of tea won't cure." I forced normalcy into my voice, not wanting Bitty to know of my despair. She had her own troubles and complexities and was so tenderhearted she would take it upon herself to console me. Not her job, I reminded myself as I forced a smile. Mama was not pretentious but she'd often told us to keep our sorrows among the family so as not to burden the staff. "Considering what we have compared to so many, we must keep a brave face," she'd said to me once.

Bitty picked up my Max Factor compact. "Nothing a little Max can't make right, Miss Addie?"

"Let's hope so," I said.

Bitty was a strapping girl who'd recently moved to Emerson Pass from Minnesota. She had a wide, pretty face and fair skin dotted with freckles. She was engaged to one of our gardeners, Harry, and would marry him once they'd saved enough to build or buy a cottage of their own. Bitty didn't seem to mind waiting, but I had to wonder. How were they able to resist each other? I watched them with envy at our schoolhouse dances. They seemed to move as one in those moments and nothing else mattered but being together. What would it feel like to be loved like that? I'd probably never know. Instead, I'd have to watch James marry this Lena Masters and be forever taken from me.

I must have sighed because Bitty, who had been about to brush makeup onto my cheeks, stopped what she was doing and narrowed her eyes, taking me in. "What is it, Miss Addie? What's making you sad?"

"Nothing, really. Just a poor night's sleep."

Her mouth went into a straight line, but she didn't say anything further and began to carefully apply the makeup, patting under my eyes gently.

A knock on the door, followed by Delphia bounding into my room, interrupted my wandering mind.

"Good morning." Delphia rushed over to perch on the side of my dressing table. Apparently, she'd been up for hours. She was dressed in her riding clothes and a wide-brimmed hat and smelled of morning sunshine. "I thought you'd never wake this morning. Didn't you hear me pounding on your door earlier? I wanted you to ride with me."

"I'm sorry. I was tired, I guess." I smiled over at her to reassure her I was all right, but my sister was no fool. We knew each other too well for that.

"What's wrong?" Delphia asked, her tone softer than the moment before. "You look like undercooked bread."

Despite my misery, I laughed and caught Bitty's gaze in the mirror. "Bitty was kinder in her assessment of my appearance this morning."

"Never you mind, Miss Addie," Bitty said, bobbing her head, as if I'd asked her a question. "You're always very pretty, even on a bad day."

"Dear Bitty," Delphia said. "I can take it from here. I'd like to talk to my sister before breakfast."

"Is it all right?" Bitty asked me, bringing the hairbrush close to her chest.

"Yes, it's fine. Take a little break," I said.

"I saw Harry out by the stables." Delphia grinned and took the brush from Bitty's outstretched hand. "Take him a little breakfast and give him a kiss."

"Miss Delphia." Bitty blushed pink, then red. "Both of those things are against the rules."

"Phooey. No one cares if you take a roll or two," Delphia said. "And some jam, of course."

My sister was incorrigible. Teasing poor Bitty was one of her favorite pastimes.

"Miss Addie, will you be sure to go down for breakfast?" Bitty asked. "Your mother always asks me if you've eaten."

I smiled. Mama, despite the fact that I was a grown and very healthy woman, still worried about my eating habits. No one could blame her, including me. She'd almost lost me to malnutrition when I was a child. Fortunately for us, my brother Theo was clever enough to figure out that I had an allergy to wheat. Since then, as long as I stayed away from bread and other items made from flour, I was fine. "I'll be sure to have some the moment I get downstairs." I said this even though the idea of food made my stomach twist. What I really wanted was to hide under the covers for the rest of the day.

Bitty nodded and scurried from the room. Despite her embarrassment, I had a feeling she would go out to see her Harry before returning to her next chore.

The moment she was out the door, Delphia waved the brush at me and perched on the edge of my dressing table. "What's wrong with you this morning, sister of mine?" We had the shades drawn halfway to keep the intrusive sunlight at bay, but a sliver sliced across my sister's face. Her blue eyes inspected me like a prison guard. "Don't try to deny it. I can see you cried yourself to sleep last night." She patted rouge on my cheeks. "There, that's a little better."

We'd moved from our childhood nursery into separate bedrooms after Fiona married. Still, we were attached with an invisible thread. No one could read me like my little sister. I'd not told her of my affection for James West. It's the only thing I'd ever kept from her. Why? I suppose I couldn't bear her teasing. Not about him, anyway. Everything else, perhaps, but not this. However, in my miserable state, I was sorely tempted to spill it all here in the morning sunshine.

"If I tell you, can you promise to keep it to yourself?" I asked.

"Of course. That's our sisterly pact." She gestured for me to close my eyes so she could swipe a light pink onto my eyelids.

"Yes, it is." I glanced toward the hallway before doing her bidding by closing my eyes. I waited until she was finished before speaking further.

She returned to her perch, watching me. As much bravado as my sister had, she was loving and kind, especially when it came to me. Perhaps because I'd been so sick as a child, she felt protective of me, even though she was the younger of us. "Addie, what is it?" Her thin eyebrows raised slightly. "You're scaring me."

"I have a secret. A terrible one."

"What did you do?" Her eyes widened in horror. If I knew her, she was probably conjuring up all kinds of sins. Ones she herself would commit. Which gave us a wide breadth.

"I haven't done anything." I tapped my chest. "It's what I'm feeling, not what I've done."

"Yes?" She seemed somewhat relieved. "What are you feeling?"

I spoke just above a whisper. "It's James."

She was silent for a moment. When I peeked up at her, she watched me with a mixture of pity and comprehension on her pretty face. "I had a feeling. Last night, I saw it on your face. I'd not suspected before."

I nodded, too miserable to speak. The truth had stuck in my throat, but I didn't have to say the words. Delphia knew.

"But he's ancient," Delphia said. "Isn't he the same age as our sisters?" When she spoke about "our sisters" she meant Fiona and Cymbeline.

"I don't think of him as ancient," I said.

Delphia didn't say anything for a moment, walking over to the window and pulling up the shade to look out to the front yard. Our rooms were next to each other and faced the southern mountain. She pinched the narrow bridge of her nose, obviously thinking through my predicament. Finally, when she spoke, it was with a question. "I don't suppose he knows of this affection?"

"No."

"And do you have any indication that he feels the same?"

"None whatsoever." I swallowed, trying desperately not to cry and ruin my makeup. "He's going to marry that Lena anyway. He must marry her."

"Must?"

"It's all to save his family from ruin." I explained what James had told me.

"So that's what it is. I knew something was wrong. He doesn't love her. I've known it from the first time he told us anything about her. For one thing, he doesn't know anything about her. They're little more than acquaintances, as far as I can tell."

"It's nothing short of an arranged marriage," I said. "He's told me as much."

Delphia moved back to stand next to me, reminding me of the bobcat that visited the parameters of our fenced yard on full moonlit nights. "How long have you felt this way?"

"I can't remember when I didn't feel this way." I explained in a halting, nearly incoherent way about my feelings, how he made me feel alive and seen. "From the very first, he's captured my heart. I'm too young for him—in his eyes anyway. Or, at least that's what I thought. But I'm starting to believe he might have an inkling of romantic affection for me. If it weren't for this arranged marriage, I might have had a chance. Papa isn't rich enough to save them. Isn't that something? I'd never thought I would say there were limitations to our happiness because of money, but there are."

"What makes you think he has an inkling of affection for you?" She crossed her arms over her chest and wrinkled her brow as if she were a detective and I the mystery.

"Just a feeling more than anything." An image played before

my eyes. He'd brushed away the hair from my cheek in a gesture of intimacy.

Or was that me? I was the one who had reached out and taken his hand. It had been only friendship reflected in his eyes. The affection of a man for the younger sister of his best friend? Or was there more? I could not know. It was not my place to know.

Delphia sat in the other hardback chair with a thud. "Dear James. He cannot possibly choose anything else but to save his family, can he? He's too good."

"Even if it were possible he might love me, yes." This was the truth. Only a miracle would solve all of these troubles, piled as they were one on top of the other.

"What do we do?" Delphia asked. "What can I do?"

"Sometimes we cannot do anything at all. Except accept our fate."

Her eyes flashed, reminding me of our father. She had the same laughing eyes as him and at times, when needed, they reflected grit and ambition, just as his did. They were not the type to accept their fate. They would fight against it until the bitter end. Papa had given up his family's expectations and his lineage when he'd moved to America instead of staying in England and performing his lordship duties. What had been different in his circumstance than in mine? Ah yes. Money. His family hadn't needed him to stay. There was a younger brother happy to take his place as head of the family. In the end, money had been the deciding factor. Just like now. If Papa had more money than this Mr. Masters, then we could save James and his family. Instead, I would have to stand aside and watch him solve his problems without me.

"Whatever you're thinking," I said to Delphia, "it won't work. We can't fix this one. Not even Papa can."

"We'll see about that, won't we?"

"Delphia Barnes, promise me you won't interfere."

She gazed back at me, her expression purposely innocent

looking. As well as I knew her silent thoughts, she knew mine. "Sweet sister, I would walk to the ends of the earth and sell my soul to give you what you need."

Tears sprang to my eyes. Darn it all. We'd have to reapply the makeup, I thought, absently. "Delphia, sometimes loving someone means not doing that very thing we think they need. Sometimes we must let go…we must let *them* go." I rose from the chair to take both her hands. "Please, promise me you won't say anything to him or anyone else. I'm embarrassed and humiliated having you know. I couldn't bear it if anyone else knew."

"You've no reason to be embarrassed. Especially not with me. And anyway, we don't choose who we fall in love with, now do we? As hard as it will be, I'll keep it to myself. But you'll come to me anytime you need to?"

"Yes, I shall."

"No more crying alone. If I serve no other purpose in life, allow me to be the kind of sister you've always been to me."

We embraced, clinging to each other. As different as we were, we understood the other and would do whatever the other needed. If possible. Which, it was becoming apparent to me, wasn't always in our control. Perhaps it never was at all. Regardless, my friendship with my little sister would sustain me through my broken heart. I clung to that notion as fiercely as I did to her.

7

JAMES

AFTER BREAKFAST, STILL REELING FROM THE LETTER FROM LENA, I wandered out to the rose garden to read it again.

Dearest James,

I'm writing with happy news. Father and I are coming to Colorado. I hope the invitation from the Barneses was real, because Father couldn't be dissuaded from making the trip. We both know how much the Barnes family means to you, which means they will mean a lot to me too. Meeting them will give me more insight into you as well as reassure them that their friend is marrying a woman who adores him.

In addition, Father suggested we marry out there, so that they can all witness our vows. It's a sacrifice on my part but one I'm more than willing to make. I'd rather have you happy than anything else, darling. I know it will give you joy to have the Barnes family with you when you say "I do"!

Father and I will be there in about two weeks from today. We've been frantically making arrangements and although it's somewhat hasty, we'll be ready. By the time you get this letter, we will have already gotten on the train. I have butterflies thinking about seeing you. And marrying you. I'm wondering if we should go to the justice of the peace in Emerson Pass and keep it simple. Unless you'd like to get married in a church, of course. Whatever you want is fine with me, as long as it's as soon as possible. I cannot wait to begin our life together.

Do you think Annabelle Higgins could make a dress for me on such short notice? If not, I'll wear one of my best dresses and it'll just have to do.

Would you ask the Barneses if we could stay at the house? If there's no room, then we can stay at the inn in town. Is there an inn? I don't know much about this Emerson Pass of yours. I look forward to learning it all when I get there.

I must dash, darling. We have a thousand loose ends to tie up before we leave for Colorado. I simply cannot wait to see you.

All my love,

Lena

I looked up from the letter to swat away a dragonfly. I'd forgotten that Mrs. Barnes's sister, Annabelle, was a famous wedding gown designer. She'd recently created patterns that could be copied by any seamstress or tailor, making her gowns accessible worldwide. However, often the wealthy came all the way to Colorado just to have her make a custom gown. Only the very wealthy would ever consider such a trip for a frivolous item.

I'd wanted time to think, but the fresh air didn't seem to make any of my thoughts clearer. They were jumbled and confused. Lena was coming here. My summertime respite would no longer be such. She would bring the world with her. What I had thought would be my last few weeks of freedom were not meant to be.

"James." I looked up to see Delphia crossing the grass. "Get your swimming clothes on. We're going down to the creek." She carried a basket with her, probably filled with lunch. Lizzie made sure a person didn't go hungry. Trailing closely behind her were Cym's little girls.

"I don't know," I said.

"Don't you dare tell me you're going to sit around all day

feeling sorry for yourself." Delphia adjusted her straw hat to peer at me from under the brim. "You're here, and we have to enjoy it before we both have to go away. Addie's on her way down. She decided not to go to the library and is going to spend the day with us instead."

"Uncle James, you have to swim with us," Holly said. "We've got sandwiches, too."

"I am awfully fond of sandwiches," I said, scooping Holly up to balance her on my hip. She smelled of strawberries. She snuggled into my neck, her dark curls warmed from the sun. "Give me a chance to change and I'll meet you all down there." I was very familiar with the Barnes family swimming hole, having spent many hours there over the years. Delphia was right. There was no reason to waste my precious days of freedom moping around.

THIRTY MINUTES LATER, I was sitting in the shade listening to the birds tweet in the aspens above me. Delphia and the girls were splashing around in the shallow water looking for minnows. The snap of a twig caught my attention. It was Addie, heading down the slight trail toward us, carrying a stack of papers. She clutched them as if they were of great importance. Her manuscript.

"Have you brought me a present?" I asked as she flopped next to me on the blanket. She wore a red-and-white-checkered swimming suit that hugged her body in ways I wished it didn't. I had to avert my eyes to keep from staring at her long, slender legs.

"If you'd like to take a peek you can." Addie set the stack of typed pages next to me and reached for a bottle of Lizzie's homemade lemonade. "My goodness, it's hot." She wore a straw hat trimmed simply with a pink ribbon. I moved farther into the shade to make room for her on the blanket. I didn't want her pretty skin to burn.

"What made you decide to skip the library?" If I'd been paranoid, I'd have thought she was avoiding me all week, leaving for her volunteer work before I even came downstairs. I looked at her closely, scrutinizing her under the bright sun. Although she wore makeup, I could see remnants of a poor night's sleep in the redness of her eyes.

"I was writing in my room." She tilted her head downward so I couldn't see her face under the brim of her hat.

"What's wrong?" I asked softly. "I can tell something's upset you."

She pulled her legs up to her chest and rested her forehead on her knees. "I'm all right."

"Is it this man of yours? Did he make you cry?" This man she loved needed to be disposed of. Maybe I should talk to Flynn and Theo. They would know who it was and might have ideas of how to get rid of him.

"Who are you talking about?" She raised her head to look at me, her hat going cockeyed.

"This man you're in love with. The unrequited one."

She wrinkled her nose as if she smelled something bad. "Oh, that. Him, I mean. No, nothing with him. I mean, not really."

If it had been anyone but Addie I would have been suspicious that she'd made up this man. The blankness in her eyes seemed strange. Was she fibbing to me? No, of course not. I quickly dismissed the idea. She would have no reason whatsoever to lie to me or make up a man who didn't exist.

"How are you doing?" Addie asked. "The letter must have shocked you."

"Yes, it did." I looked out to the water where the girls were taking turns being tossed into the water by Delphia. "It's inevitable, Addie. I have to accept my internment."

"Internment?"

"Is that what I said? I meant engagement."

This made us both laugh, a little manically.

She sobered, tilting her head toward the sky. Her hat, not held by pins, slid from her head to hang down her back. "James, what if you were to refuse? What would happen to you?"

My initial reaction was to say, *nothing*. I would be free, that was all. Sadly, the truth wasn't that simple. If I ran away, my life would fall apart, perhaps ruined forever. "I would be plagued with guilt for the rest of my life. I'd be fired from my job and probably never hired as an editor again. Since they've already announced the engagement in the paper, it would embarrass her and make me look like a cad. All of which would make me an outcast among New York City's elite society. I wouldn't care about that part, I guess, except I have no idea what I would do for a living. My job is all I have."

"They've trapped you," she said flatly.

"They have. Everything I've worked for would have been for naught. And there's my family to consider. Can you imagine if it were up to you to save this lot?" I gestured toward her sister and nieces.

"I can imagine it, yes. At the same time, I know my parents would never put something like this on me." She placed her hand over her mouth and mumbled an apology. "It's not my place to say any of this. I'm sorry."

"Don't be. It's all true." Her father wasn't a gambler and irresponsible. He was a pillar of society, a self-made man despite the easy route he could have taken by staying in England and becoming Lord Barnes as he was destined to do; he'd made his own fortune in America. I wanted to say, *Lucky for you,* but kept it to myself. She shouldn't be punished simply because she'd been blessed to be born a Barnes rather than a West.

What happens when one walks away from his expected fate as Lord Barnes did all those years ago? I'd have thought it interrupted the order of things and caused harm. But it didn't. Not for him. Instead, it made his beautiful family possible and for them to enjoy this creek where the water ran clear and trout made their home and little granddaughters splashed and squealed with joy.

I simply couldn't do it. I had to save my family. "Tell me about this." I tapped the stack of papers.

"Read it for me, James? Tell me the truth. Is there anything in it good enough for publication?"

For now, I could do this, I thought. A favor for this beautiful young woman whose family had taken me into the fold all those years ago. This I could do.

"I'll start right now."

She breathed in and then out before resting her forehead on her knees and speaking into them. "I hope I won't be sorry I asked."

I draped an arm over her shoulders and gave her a squeeze. "You won't be."

I SPENT the next two hours reading through the typed manuscript. To my delight, it was good. However, it was not what I'd expected. I'm not sure what I'd anticipated, but it wasn't this. They were stories of the Barnes family before Addie even came to be. Of a time when Miss Quinn Cooper had arrived in Emerson Pass as a young woman ready to take on the teaching position at the newly built school and the five little children who so desperately needed a mother. This was the story of their family in the making. A family not of blood but one of heart.

Addie had taken the stories her older siblings had told her and made them into the novel of a family meant to be together. Again, fate, this giant question, I thought. Would I ever understand how it all worked? Was fate beyond our control? Did we simply follow our already fated path? Or did we make our own destinies by our choices?

I was halfway through when Delphia declared it time for lunch. The children, wet and happy, fell onto the quilt, claiming near starvation and dire thirst. While the ladies got them settled with lunch and a cold drink, I helped myself to a sandwich and a beer. The sun had risen higher in the sky, stealing the shade. Delphia made everyone get up so we could pull the blanket back into the cool shadows near the embankment.

I took a long drink from the beer and went back to reading, making mental notes on sections I thought could be expanded or tightened. In general, the writing was engaging and the characters lovable. On the occasion when I'd read a manuscript I particularly liked and became excited about, I felt a tingle at the base of my spine. This was one. There would be a readership for this book. I could help her get it published. Yet another reason to marry Lena.

A while later, I set the last page facedown on the rest of the stack. Addie was in the water with the girls, but she must have sensed I'd finished because she looked over at me. Her fearful, hopeful expression made me laugh.

"It's good, Addie," I called out to her. "I told you not to worry."

She looked up toward the heavens before breaking into a grin. "Thank goodness you think so."

I grinned back at her. "I have some notes, but you've got something here."

"I told you." Delphia, who was coming in fast on the rope swing, let out a whoop right before she plunged into the deepest spot of the swimming hole.

Addie, dripping with water, was making her way toward me. The little girls were quietly playing in the sand a few feet from me, oblivious to the drama around them.

"Can you tell me now?" Addie asked. "Your ideas, that is."

We talked over a few sections I thought could be expanded,

fully immersed in our conversation until we realized Delphia was gathering up the girls to take them back to the house.

"Come on, rascals," Delphia said. "Let's go up to the house and get you cleaned up for your mother." To us, she said, "Stay as long as you like, but stay in the shade."

After they left, Addie relaxed enough to lie down with her head propped up on a towel. Again, those legs caught my attention, and I averted my gaze. *Think of something else,* I instructed myself. Instead of obeying, my gaze traveled the length of her. The curve of her hip was like a well-crafted vase. The sun kissing the skin of her shoulders made me wish I could do so myself. Well, so much for thinking of something else.

"What are you thinking about?" Addie rolled to her side and propped up her face with her hand.

"Nothing really." I lay on my back and looked up at the sky. "Just about my childhood in comparison to the one you describe in your book."

"What was it like?"

How could I describe the large, drafty estate? The endless days of rain. My little sister and her night terrors and nervousness that took all of my mother's energy and attention. Father's gambling problems. Fights so loud they rang out into the night when a house should be peaceful. Dwindling staff as the years went on until we were down to only a few. I'd escaped at eighteen to go to university and then on to Paris, where I'd met Fiona and Li. "I haven't been back in a long time. Not since I was nineteen." I'd gone for one last Christmas before I'd decided that the sadness stayed with me for weeks after I left. "When I think of it, I think of rain and cold, damp days. Yes, I remember the dampness and the scent of mildew on stone. And loneliness. My younger sister was troubled, so my mother was occupied with that."

"Like I was?" Addie watched me with big eyes, clearly wishing to know every detail.

"No, not physically. She had a lot of fears. Terrible, debilitating anxiety. She couldn't go to school or have friends. It was awful for her and my mother."

"You never told me that before." She sat up, pulling her legs under her. "What's your sister's name? You never talk about her."

"She is younger by quite a bit. Elizabeth is her name. She's called Beth."

"How old is she?"

I had to think about it for a moment. "She's your age. I was six when she was born."

"I see." She picked up a stick and traced it around the palm of one hand. "So you haven't seen her since she was twelve."

I laughed. "That's some quick arithmetic. But yes, around then I think."

"Is there a reason she can't marry well and save the family?" Addie asked.

Cringing, I studied a wayward cloud moving slowly across the sky. "She's not well enough to marry, I don't think. My mother says she rarely leaves her room."

She lowered her head. Damp strands of her hair stuck to her neck. "That's very sad."

"It was the last piece to seal my fate." I turned just my head to look at her. "I'll be able to help you with your book if I still have my job. At least there's that."

"I'd rather have you happy than have my book published."

That jarred me. Was that true or just something a friend would say? Addie was a good person, but this was her dream. Would she really give it all away to ensure my happiness? The next thought shook me further. What if it were true that given the chance, she'd sacrifice that for me? And if that were true, what did that mean? Were her feelings for me that deep? That loving?

"Addie, I'd never ask you to do that," I said softly. "But it's nice of you to say."

"You don't believe me, do you?"

"I don't know of anyone who's that good," I said. "To give up such a longing, a dream, for another person—that's an act of great love. One that shouldn't be wasted on me."

"It's not that I'm good." She dug the stick into the palm of her hand. "It's a selfish wish."

"What do you mean?" I sat all the way up, watching her. What was she trying to say?

"I mean that I do not want you to marry Lena Masters and that if I could possibly do anything to change it so you didn't have to, then I would."

"Why don't you want me to marry Lena?"

She lifted her gaze to meet mine. "Do you truly want to know?"

I gulped in a breath. Suddenly I knew. She had romantic feelings for me. I meant more to her than the best friend of her sister. She'd never alluded to such a thing. Not even an inkling. "I don't know if I should—but I'd like to hear the truth."

She turned back to gouging the stick into her hand.

"Addie?"

Her eyes snapped as she raised her gaze to me. "James, I have very selfish reasons for wishing you wouldn't marry her. Or anyone else. Anyone but me."

The truth almost knocked me over. I managed to stay upright, thoughts tumbling like the rapids just upstream from the swimming hole. Addie wanted me?

"But you're young and so pretty," I said. "And talented. What would you want with me? You could have anyone."

"I don't care about anyone else. I care about you. I've loved you from the very first day I ever met you." She hurled the stick into the water. I watched it sail out to the middle of the creek like a small boat. "I know you can't—or won't—feel the same. I didn't mean for you to ever know." Tears gathered at the corners of her eyes, and she swiped them away. "I'm sorry."

"Don't be sorry," I said. "Never be sorry for love." I needed to stay calm, handle her with the utmost care. This was the tender heart of an innocent. The sweet, sweet heart of Addie Barnes was on display before me.

"I can't bear it, James." A sob of misery rose from her and floated toward me. "She's coming to my house. My *home.* Invading my family. Taking you. Not that you were mine to begin with." She wiped away more tears with the backs of her knuckles before I came to my senses and pulled a handkerchief from my knapsack.

"I've not thought of you that way," I said, finally and clumsily.

"Why?" She looked straight into my eyes. "Because I'm too young?"

"Not that, no. I mean, yes, before now. You're Fiona's baby sister. She would not want this."

"How do you know that?"

How *did* I know that? I'd assumed it, I suppose. "I guess I don't know that. She might not like it. She might and most likely would think I was too old for you and too poor. Your sister knows me better than anyone, and that's not necessarily a good thing."

She lay on her back and covered her face with the handkerchief as if it were a tablecloth. Her breath made the thin fabric rise and fall. "I'm so embarrassed."

"Don't be that either."

With the handkerchief still covering her, she asked another question. "Is there any part of you that could see me as anything other than Fiona's baby sister?"

"Addie, you're a beautiful young lady. Special, in fact." I reached out to pat her hand but instead found myself leaning closer. I snatched the handkerchief from her face. Her eyes flew open. "I'd have to be dead not to notice you."

She drew in a breath and let it out slowly, staring up at me. "If it weren't for Lena, would you consider me?"

How honest should I be? I'd not thought of her in this way. Not before this summer, anyway. Since I'd been here this time, however, I'd been unable to stop looking at her. And not in an entirely gentlemanly way. "I can't allow myself to venture into that dreamland. I can't have you."

She nodded and remained lying on her back, the leaves of aspen above us making dappled shadows on her fair skin. Tears escaped from her eyes, but she seemed not to notice them. I picked up the handkerchief from my lap and pressed it to one cheek and then the other. "Please don't cry over me. I'm not worth it."

Addie shot up from her supine position and glared at me. "Do you really believe that? Do you really think your worth is only what you can do for your family? You're more than that. You shouldn't have to take on the burden of your father's mistakes."

"Yes, but the fact is—I must or face the rest of my life guilty and regretful." What could I say that I hadn't already? I was afraid if I said much of anything else, the precarious ground upon which we currently trod would grow treacherous. I must tell her the truth. She deserved that much after opening her soul to me. What was the truth? If I were free, would I welcome her affection?

Yes, you fool. She would be the best thing that ever happened in your whole life.

No, I mustn't think that way, or my selfish nature would take hold and never let go. I would become my father, concerned only with himself without regard even for those he held most dear. That man would not be the man for Addie. She needed someone noble of mind, not of birth.

And so, in the end, I told her again that she was beautiful and so good and pure and that a man much luckier than I would soon arrive in her life. "You'll forget all about me, too, when he comes."

"Yes, I will indeed." She smiled, but it did nothing to convince me that she meant those words. "And you're right, dear James. A man living with guilt and regret would not be a good husband to the woman who made him make such a choice. For this, I should be grateful, I suppose. Being spared from that fate."

We sat quietly for a few moments. A dragonfly sailed in on the breeze, cheeky and so very free, as if to remind me of what I could have had.

8

ADDIE

THAT EVENING AFTER MY CLUMSY DECLARATION OF LOVE, I'D SAID I had a headache and stayed in my room instead of going down for dinner. Mama came up afterward to check on me and, finding me weeping on the window seat, rushed to sit with me.

"Darling, what is it?" Mama's brown eyes searched for answers in mine. I could not hide from her. She knew me, knew my heart. "Have you had a fight with your sister?"

"No, Mama." It was just like her to guess that to be the reason. Delphia and I had squabbled often when we were children, but now we were as close as two sisters could be. Mama knew that a fight with her would devastate me.

She studied me for a long moment. I could not hide from her penetrating, knowing gaze. "Tell me, child, what ails you. Please, darling. It will help to tell your mother. No one understands like your mother." A flicker of sadness crossed her face. After all this time, she still missed her own mother.

"It's my heart, Mama. Broken into bits." I sobbed into my lace handkerchief.

"Oh dear." She went still for a second before her expression turned from confusion to discernment. "Is it James?"

I nodded, too shattered to acknowledge it with words.

"You're in love with him?" Mama asked.

"Yes. I'm so ashamed." I buried my face in my hands.

"Does he know?"

I looked over at her. "Yes. I told him this afternoon. Like a little idiot."

"My poor baby. Don't worry, this will pass. I'm sure it will." Mama gathered me against her chest and stroked my hair. "Didn't he propose to her before he came out here?"

"Not completely. She and her father simply announced it in the newspaper column without asking him."

She gasped. "Why would they do such a thing?"

"To make sure they get what they want," I said. "It forced him to follow through or risk scandal for all of them."

"Very tricky, indeed," Mama said.

"Her father is an ambitious man. James says he's climbed over a lot of men to get to where he is. The only thing that's eluded him is respectability, which James and his family's titles bring to them."

"I doubt it," Mama said. "People who care about such things will not care about James's titles. Not here in America."

"The world James has told me about—this old and new money and who is who—it's not anything we understand. Not here in the west. It must be awfully important for Mr. Masters to go to all this trouble."

"Perhaps you're right." Her brows knitted together in worry.

"There was something in his eyes, Mama, that told me he might be able to love me someday if it weren't for her."

"Yes, she and her father have made it quite impossible for him to make his own choice. The announcement in the newspaper, the demand from his father—he hasn't a chance, does he?" She said this matter-of-factly.

"None whatsoever," I said, as if that weren't obvious to my mother. We both understood the game the Masterses and James's father were playing. He was the ball they batted back and forth, all of them wanting to win. The only one who wouldn't win was our James.

Mama dabbed my cheeks, just as James had done earlier. "Too many tears for such beautiful eyes." She folded the piece of lace into a square and set it on the windowsill. The seat cushions were new, soft and plump under me. One wall of my room had been wallpapered with a floral pattern of bright pink. White wainscoting underneath made the pink that much more vivid. A four-poster bed was the height of elegance. I'd loved the room when it had first been handed down to me after Fiona left. Now, however, it seemed like a prison I'd never leave. I would die here, an old maid who coveted another's husband.

"Listen to me for a moment." Mama placed her hand on my knee. Upon returning from our swim, I'd bathed and changed into a casual cotton dress to battle the heat of the afternoon. Usually I dressed for dinner in evening attire, but since I'd hidden in my room it had not been necessary. "If you and James are meant to be, something will make it possible for you to be together."

"But it's impossible."

"If love is true, God makes the pathways possible. Don't lose faith, dearest. Keep writing. That's the most important thing for you to do. Pour your heart into those words on the page. Can you do this? If not for yourself, for me?"

"Why do you ask that of me?" I was genuinely curious. Did she truly think writing could save me?

"Because when we do the work we're meant to do, other things in our life fall into the exact place they should be. Our only job is to stay faithful to God and ourselves." She smiled her gentle smile, crinkling the fine lines at her eyes into crepe paper. "And to our mothers, who know us almost as well as God does."

"I'll do my very best, Mama. For you."

She gestured toward my typewriter. The last page I'd written was still in there, waiting for a final sentence or two. "Right there. That is as much your destiny as anything or anyone will ever be. Stay true to that, and the right road will open up before you."

"How can you be so sure?"

"Because I'm so much older than you, and I've loved the same man for over twenty years. I found him because of my work and my desire to take care of my mother and sister. I often think of what would have happened to me if I'd not been brave enough to get on that train for Colorado. Everything good came from that one decision. There are times, darling, in our lives that are crossroads, tests maybe, that we must pass through to get to the other side."

"I don't like this test. It's an impossible one."

"You're stronger than you think." She gathered me in for another embrace, and I let myself be loved, taking in the flowery scent of her fragrance. The smell and feel of my mother's hugs would always be among my favorite things. This would never change. I could count on loving her and having that love returned. It was something to cling to in the darkness of this hour, and I did so with all my might.

THAT NIGHT, I could not sleep and tossed and turned until finally deciding to get up and go down to the sitting room. I put a robe on over my dressing gown and ventured downstairs, careful to walk lightly on the stairs that creaked. The hardwood floors felt cold on my bare feet. I should have grabbed socks, I thought as I walked into the sitting room.

This time of night, I didn't like to use my typewriter in my room, as the clang of the keys might wake someone. However, if the mood struck me, I could use Papa's typewriter, so I'd brought my stack of manuscript pages with James's notes down with me.

I'd have loved a cup of tea but didn't want to traipse down the stairs and wake Mrs. Wu or the maids, who all slept in staff quarters down the hall from the kitchen. Mrs. Wu, Li's grandmother, had worked with Lizzie in our kitchen for as long as I'd been alive. She'd tried to retire six years ago and move in with Li, but she hated being away from her room here and the work. No one knew exactly how old she was, but we guessed close to eighty. From what we could tell, she didn't have plans to slow down anytime soon. She was a tiny woman, growing tinier by the day as the years took their toll. Regardless, her mind was as quick as ever. She claimed it was the concoction of herbs she used for her magical teas that kept her young. Whatever it was, Lizzie was glad to have her, especially now that Florence was away at college.

I turned on a few lamps in the sitting room. It was too warm for a fire and the room felt stuffy, so I opened a few windows, careful to make sure the screens were in place. I'd catch it from Jasper in the morning if he found flies or bugs in the sitting room. He and Lizzie had their own cottage not far from the big house, but he felt a great responsibility to keep the estate pristine. He was old-school, Papa said. "You must remember where he's from and what he was trained to do," he'd said to Delphia recently when she was complaining about Jasper being too strict and old-fashioned.

I sat in the chair behind the desk where Mama wrote her correspondence and anything else she needed to take care of in her positions on the boards of both the library and the school. In the lamplight, I read through the notes on chapter 5, written in the margins in James's neat handwriting.

More here.

Tighten this paragraph. Saying the same thing twice.

This brought tears to my eyes.

Can you describe this in a deeper POV?

I traced my finger along the handwriting, thinking of his long, slender fingers. Lucky paper, I thought.

After a few minutes of staring out the window to the moonlit front yard, I stuck a piece of paper into the typewriter and began a rewrite. I'd been working for thirty minutes or so when I heard the front door open from the foyer. I looked up to see James standing in the double doorway of the sitting room.

"What are you doing up?" I asked, standing. Was he all right? He seemed slightly unsteady on his feet.

"I've come from the club with your brother and brothers-in-law. Poker and booze." He grinned and reached into his pocket to pull out a wad of bills. "I cleaned up tonight."

I frowned. Gambling wasn't my favorite pastime for my brothers and brothers-in-law. They usually kept it among them, playing once a month on a night when the club was closed to the public. "Who was there?"

"Li, Flynn, Viktor, and Phillip. No Theo."

Of course. Theo would never be out this late or drinking. He and Dr. Neal took turns being on call.

"What was the occasion?" I asked. I'd not been down to dinner so had not been privy to their plans.

"Welcoming me back."

"Did you have a nice time?" I asked, stiffly.

"Aw, don't be like that. We were just having some innocent fun."

"If one would describe drinking and gambling such," I said, biting my lip to keep from smiling.

His brow furrowed. He walked toward me. "Is your headache better?"

"Yes, but I couldn't sleep. I came down here to work on chapter 5."

"Is that the one where Flynn and Cym get locked in the icehouse?"

I nodded, smiling. "Yes, that's the one."

"It's amazing those two lived to adulthood."

"You're not the first one to say that."

He perched on the arm of the chair. His eyes glittered in the lamplight.

I looked away, embarrassed by his penetrating gaze. What was he thinking about?

"Do you have everything you need?" I asked. "Is your room adequate?"

"Addie, if you saw my hovel in the city you wouldn't have to ask. But thank you. I have everything I need."

He appeared to be focusing on something behind my head. I realized it was the painting of my mother. It had been commissioned when I was only a few years old, but Mama had hardly aged. It was clean living, she always said, when people commented on how young she still looked, even though she was in her mid-forties.

"You look like her. Except for your eye color. There's never been a beauty like a Barnes woman. All of you." He shook his head, as if remembering a distant memory. "The first time I came here, I couldn't help but wonder how it was possible that each of you was as pretty as Fiona. Each of you fierce and smart, too."

"Not me," I said.

"You're the fiercest of all." James crossed over to the desk. He wore a summer suit, slightly rumpled, which strangely enough only added to his attractiveness. "You're the one who lived when everyone thought she wouldn't."

"Theo cured me." I could still remember the night I thought was the end of my life as if it were last week. I'd been twelve that winter. Unable to keep food down, I'd almost starved. I'd stopped eating entirely, so tired of feeling horrible after a meal. I'd wandered outside on a cold, snowy night, delirious and sure I'd heard angels calling me home. Viktor had been the one to find me, having felt some strange urge to head to our house instead of his own that night.

"I can see you thinking." He placed his fingers under his eyes. "Like your eyes have a mouth." He chuckled. "I'm a little drunk."

I caught the faint scent of cigars and whiskey mixed with his spicy outdoor smell that stirred my senses to a boiling point. I'd have liked to put that scent in a bottle and pull it out whenever I wanted. Or would it be too painful to have his essence when I couldn't have him?

"I could watch you all day, Addie Barnes. Just to see those eyes talking to me."

I flushed with pleasure. To hide my reaction, I rattled off a retort. "I've never seen you drinking before."

"Do you disapprove?" He raised an eyebrow. "Have I caused you to change your mind about me?"

"Very much so." I smiled to let him know I was only teasing him.

"It's the devil's drink. The loosener of lips. Your brothers are bad influences. But I had fun. I can't remember when I've had as much fun, actually." He unfastened his tie and sat on the edge of the desk. "Sometimes, Miss Adelaide Barnes, I feel about a hundred years old."

My heart sank at the hopelessness in his eyes. "Oh, James." I sat in the chair, only inches from him.

Our eyes met and remained tethered. I couldn't move, couldn't think. The ticking of the grandfather clock kept time with my heart.

"I shouldn't be in here, should I?" James asked, huskily. "It's inappropriate. You in your nightclothes, me drunk. Scandalous even."

"No one would think anything of it. You're family."

"If they knew what was in here"—he tapped his temple—" they'd have me locked in my room."

My heart now beat faster than that second hand ticking away. What did he mean? What thoughts were such that he should be kept away from me? Surely they couldn't be any more indelicate than my own.

"I should stop talking," James said. "Push all my thoughts back inside me and do the right thing."

I held my breath, unsure what to do next. Part of me wanted

to run away. The other part wanted to move closer, to place my mouth against his.

He chuckled, hanging his head and speaking just above a whisper. Still, the yearning in his voice resounded loud and clear. "Shall we elope, Addie? Leave it all behind? My family would have to make their own way. I could take your name, become a Barnes. Wouldn't that be something?"

"You've had too much to drink," I said softly, the ache in my throat like a pounding fist. "You're talking nonsense."

"I know I am." He looked up at me, his eyes blazing. "But I can't stop thinking about you. Since this afternoon. What you told me, it's—it's made me see everything differently. Isn't that the stupidest thing you've ever heard?"

"Not stupid." Dangerous, I thought. So very dangerous.

"Fortunate," James said. "That's what this is—you being here when I came stumbling home drunk."

"Fortunate?" What did he mean?

"I was thinking about you all night. Li and Viktor were chatting the whole way home about this thing and the other. I couldn't tell you any of what they said because all I could think about was you. Seeing your face, hearing your voice. The way you looked this afternoon in that checkered swimming costume." He drew in a deep, painful-sounding breath. "I must stop."

"Don't," I said. "Say it all. Say whatever it is that's in your heart."

"I shouldn't, Addie, but I will. I have to. Your honesty today—you opened something up inside me. I can't think of how to describe it but for the first time, I could see how my life would unfold if I had the chance to be with someone like you. No, not someone like you. You. Just you. The life we could have—it's the stuff of dreams. Hopeful and alive and buzzing with excitement for the future. That's what it made me feel. How you make me feel. And Addie, hopefulness is no good. Not for a man in my position." His eyes glazed over, unfocused and shiny with unshed tears. He looked down at his hands, and a tear slipped down his cheek.

Without thinking, I reached for him, brushing aside that tear with the side of my ink-smeared middle finger, leaving a mark. He grabbed my hand and held it against his chest for a moment. "I guess I wanted you to know, while I have the courage to say it—if I were free and had anything to offer you, which I don't obviously, but God help me, if I had the wealth and opportunity—it could be you and me. You and me forever. I wanted you to know that it's not just you who feels something between us. It's important that you know that before I go. Before I have to do the honorable thing."

Trembling, and grateful I had a chair under my legs, my skin tingled where he'd touched me. "I don't know what to do now," I whispered.

"There's nothing to do."

I lifted my eyes to his. "What are my eyes saying right now? Are they talking to you?"

"I believe they are."

"Can you hear them?" I asked.

"They're asking me to kiss you."

I touched the tip of my tongue to my upper lip. Here I was in my dressing gown, no makeup, hair disheveled, and about to get my first kiss. Perhaps my last.

He drew me to my feet and wrapped an arm around my waist, tugging me close. His mouth lowered to mine, and then he was kissing me. I was lost to it, to him. Nothing would ever be this good, I thought. Nothing ever again.

9

JAMES

I WOKE THAT MORNING WITH A TERRIBLE HEADACHE AND A DRY mouth. I lay there for a moment, remembering the night in bits, crawling along having fun and then coming home.

A low moan came from deep inside my chest. Oh God, what had I done? I'd kissed Addie. *That's right, you fool,* a voice echoed through my head. *You said all the things you shouldn't have.*

I listened to the morning sounds: a creak of the stairwell, the water running in a bathroom, birds chirping outside the windows. This had been a mistake, coming here. I should have let well enough alone instead of selfishly accepting the Barneses' open invitation for my summer visit. Knowing what Lena and her father had on their agenda, I should have stayed in New York City and left the Barneses uninfected with my nonsense. And what had I done to poor Addie? Telling her those things was inexcusable, but kissing her? I should be punished with a life sentence.

That kiss. I closed my eyes, feeling it all over again. The softness and tentative kisses that had led to something more desperate and raw. For both of us.

What had I done?

She might have hope now, which would break her heart when Lena arrived and everything unfolded as I knew it would.

I would apologize to her. Beg her forgiveness and make sure she knew it wouldn't happen again.

After I bathed and dressed in my white linen suit, I went downstairs for breakfast. Addie was at the table with her parents and Delphia when I arrived in the dining room. My thigh muscles clenched at the sight of her. God help me, she was lovely in a simple blue dress that matched her eyes. Her hair was pulled back, with tendrils framing her face. A trace of my whisker burn showed on her jawline. I'd done that, beast that I was. *A beauty and the beast.* That's what we were, even if I was only a monster on the inside. One no one could see but brought out by too much whiskey.

They all greeted me casually, as if I were always here. As if I belonged. However, Addie wouldn't look me in the eyes. Who could blame her? She was probably as embarrassed as I was.

"Late night, son?" Alexander asked as he unfolded his newspaper.

"Yes, sir." I poured myself a cup of coffee and grabbed two dry pieces of toast. It was all I could stomach for now.

"Did the boys make you drink and gamble?" Quinn asked.

"*Make* might not be the right word." I grimaced, lowering myself into the chair next to Delphia.

"I told them to go easy on you," Quinn said. "You're not used to the wild ways of the west and these reckless young men we have in our family." She tilted her head, watching me with obvious amusement. "Would you like some pain powder for your head?"

"No, thank you, I'm fine." My stomach churned as I brought the cup of coffee to my mouth. Liar, it seemed to growl at me.

"They have booze and gambling in New York, darling," Alexander said, teasing his wife. "I'm sure James is not an innocent at his age."

"I work a lot," I said. "And stay out of trouble."

"So it is our boys that did this to you," Quinn said. "I suspected as much."

One of Delphia's eyebrows shot up as she watched me with absolutely no sympathy. "You do look a little green. Did they get you drunk and take all your money?"

"They did no such thing," Addie said, speaking for the first time. "He won all of their money." She defended me, I thought, even when I didn't deserve it. I let myself enjoy the sensation of her protection for a second. What was this warm feeling she gave me in the pit of my stomach? Love? No, no, no. What was I doing? Selfish, that's what I was.

"Tell them, James," Addie said. "You're no fool."

"Yes, I did take all their money last night," I said, sheepish. "It was luck only, of course. No skill involved."

"I doubt that," Addie said.

"How do you know he won all their money, Addie?" Delphia crossed her arms over her chest and inspected her sister with excited eyes. "He just came down for breakfast."

"I'm guessing," Addie mumbled. "Because James is clever with cards. Always has been."

"Is that true?" Delphia turned back to me.

"Which part?" I asked, stalling for time. This morning was not going well. Now I was lying to Quinn and Alexander right to their faces.

"Are you clever with cards? And did you win all the money?" Delphia asked.

"Yes and yes," I said.

"And how exactly does my sister know all this?" Delphia's mouth twitched with delight. She was an evil little thing with an angel's face. "Did you speak afterward? Before breakfast somehow?"

"Delphia, please." Addie spoke sharply to her sister. "Just leave it alone."

"Fine." For once, Delphia seemed abashed and returned her

attention to demolishing a piece of toast with a generous layer of butter and strawberry preserves.

"It does beg the question," Alexander said. "How did you know, Addie?"

Quinn looked at me, her eyes narrowing. "Yes, how did she know that, James?"

"I *am* good at cards," I said, hurriedly. "Your brothers always underestimate me when it comes to games. As for how Addie knew of my misadventures, she happened to be up writing when I came in last night. My apologies, once again, for disrupting your evening." I directed this last part to Addie, who blushed a pretty pink. A quick glance at Quinn confirmed my fear. She studied both her daughter and me with a discerning gaze that popped from one of us to the other as though she was watching a sparring match. Not much would go unnoticed around here. I had to be more careful.

"Why were you up in the middle of the night, love?" Alexander asked Addie. His low, resonant voice was not harsh in any way, merely curious. Regardless, a chill passed through me.

"I couldn't sleep." Addie shifted a glob of scrambled eggs from one side of her plate to the other. "James gave me some notes on my manuscript, so I gave up and went downstairs so as not to disturb anyone."

This seemed to satisfy everyone. The subject turned to Addie's manuscript. I'd assumed everyone had read it or at least knew what it was about. I'd been wrong. Only Delphia had seen it.

"She won't let anyone but me read it," Delphia said. "I can tell you all that it's quite good."

"Perhaps after a polish, she'll feel less shy," I said. "If she's like most writers she'll want it to be as close to perfect as it can be before sharing it with those she loves the most."

"That's correct. Very astute of you, James." Addie lifted her eyes to mine. As usual, her eyes spoke volumes, thanking me for understanding and coming to her rescue. "I'll let you all read it when I think it's ready."

"Delphia's right. It's very good." I buttered a piece of toast and took a bite, hoping it would stay where it was supposed to.

"It's about us. All of us," Addie said. "The story of our family."

"Really?" Quinn asked. "How exciting."

"Sadly, I'm not in it," Delphia said. "Which is unfortunate because I would be the most interesting character of all."

Addie laughed. "The stories are about the time before we were born." She looked over at her mother, a shy expression on her face. "It's all the stories the others told us growing up—about when they were small and you and Papa first met. I tried to capture the point of view of each of them. They each get a chapter."

"What about us? We have our own stories." Delphia stuck out her bottom lip. "When will it be our turn? I hate being the youngest."

"No, you don't," Addie said, rolling her eyes with obvious affection. "You love being everyone's darling."

"What do you think, James?" Delphia asked. "Will she be famous someday?"

"I don't know about famous. That's up to many things that none of us have much control over, but I can tell you in all honesty that it's very good. Funny and heartwarming. You'll all be very proud to read it."

"Do you really think so?" Addie beamed at me from across the table.

My opinion matters too much to her, I thought. *I'm nobody.* I should never have agreed to read it and inserted myself into her world. She deserved so much better than me and my fumbling ways.

"I never fib when it comes to a writer and their work," I said out loud. "You have something special. You're special." That last part slipped out of my mouth before I could stop myself. Our eyes met and stayed locked for a moment.

"I can't wait to read it," Quinn said. A worried glance over at her husband told me she understood too well what had happened between Addie and me last night, what seemed to be unfolding without my permission minute by minute.

Fiona swept in, drawing all of our attention away from the conversation. "Hello, everyone. I'm sorry to be late but I overslept. Late night."

We all greeted her and waited for her to return to the table with a cup of coffee and a plate of eggs and fruit.

"Where are the boys today?" Quinn asked.

"I've left them with their father. I have several things to take care of today." She darted a look at Addie. What was that about? "I can't stay long, but I wanted to see how James was holding up. I'm sorry I've neglected my best friend." She smiled over at me. "Are you having fun?"

"A little too much," I said.

Fiona frowned. "You *are* looking peaked. I told my husband to protect you from Flynn and Phillip last night. He must not have done as I asked. They're like wild animals when they get a night out."

"Shannon doesn't let Flynn out often," Quinn said. "For obvious reasons."

"Josephine doesn't mind giving Phillip a night for a little debauchery," Fiona said. "Or I Li, for that matter. But I do worry sometimes about what kind of trouble they could get into."

"My only trouble is an aching head," I said. And that I'd kissed an innocent and confessed my obsession with her.

Quinn smiled kindly over at me. "James, ask Bitty for some powder for your head. We have a jar of it in the girls' bathroom." She glanced down at the watch around her wrist. "Oh dear, look at the time. I've got to go. I'm supposed to be in town for a meeting at the library in a few minutes. Can anyone drive me?"

"I'll take you in," Alexander said. "I have some business myself."

"I want to go too," Delphia said. "Jo said there's a new book on the American Revolution I want to read."

"That seems like heavy reading for my little girl." Alexander puffed out his chest and beamed.

"I have to be ready for college, Papa. So I can be the best one there."

"I've no doubt, love." Alexander stood and offered his hand to his wife. "Dearest, are you ready?"

"Yes, I am. Delphia, I'll bring the book home if you'd like. Save you the trip." Quinn put aside her napkin and rose up from her chair.

"Thanks, Mama, but I want to go with you." Delphia reached for the strawberry preserves. "I'm going to have one more piece of toast, though. All this babysitting has me half-starved. Do you know how much trouble those two little girls of Cym's are? They've run me ragged."

"I have an inkling," Quinn said, exchanging an amused look with Alexander.

Alexander chuckled. "Yes, we know all about little girls and their mischief." He gestured toward his wife. "Are you ready, darling, or do you need a moment to freshen up? I can bring the car around."

"Yes, I'll put my hat on and be down in a moment."

Delphia jumped from the table and with a piece of toast in her hand, followed Mama into the hallway. Papa excused himself as well, leaving Fiona, Addie, and me still sitting around the table.

Fiona had helped herself to a cup of coffee and one of Lizzie's sweet rolls. She nibbled a piece half-heartedly before shoving her plate away.

"Are you feeling all right?" Addie asked her sister.

"Yes, just more of the same."

Addie nodded as if she understood perfectly. What was

going on? "Fi, are you sick?" A dart of fear tapped my throbbing head.

She sighed. "No, nothing like that. I think I may be having another baby. I'm going to see Theo this morning."

"How wonderful," I said.

"I've not let myself think about what it means too much," Fiona said. "Or I might dissolve into a puddle right here and now." She looked at me and then over at her sister. "Speaking of which, is something wrong with you two? You both look as if you've been caught doing something naughty. Yes, indeed, you both stink of guilt."

Addie choked and coughed before pressing a napkin to her lips. Her eyes flitted around the room, clearly uneasy. Fiona was right. She looked guilty. Which meant I probably looked five times worse.

"James?" Fiona prodded me with her foot under the table. "What is this?"

I looked into her dark blue eyes. Although I couldn't know for sure, it felt as if all my secrets were laid out in front of her, my soul bared for everyone to see. Fiona would figure me out. She was my dearest friend. How could I have thought I could hide it?

"Nothing at all," I said. "Addie and I were up at the same time last night and talked for a while in the sitting room. We're abashed at having done something inappropriate. The talking alone, I mean. In the middle of the night, that is." This all gushed out of my mouth too fast. Good Lord, I should never commit a crime if this was how I acted.

"Just talking?" Fiona asked, her voice dry as an autumn leaf fluttering to the ground.

"Don't be silly," Addie said. "Yes, we were talking about my work. That's all. What else would it be?"

"I see." Fiona jerked up from the table and headed back to the buffet. With her back to us, she said, "These modern times are changing every day. However, some conventions should be honored. Men and women spending time together unsupervised is not what we want for either of you. It's too easy to be tempted to act in ways you can't tell your mother." She turned around to look at us pointedly. "Ways that could cause a lot of repercussions for a lot of people. You must be careful, for everyone's sake."

I glanced over at Addie. To my surprise, a mischievous smile played on her lips. Those lips, so firm and soft at the same time. How I'd love to taste her again.

"Of course, Fi," I said. "We'll keep that in mind."

"What's this I hear about Lena Masters and her father?" Fiona returned to the table, this time with peaches and berries smothered in fresh cream. "Is it true what Li told me? They're really coming here? How do you feel about it?"

No one could get right at a thing like Fiona. I'd missed her. However, a vision of hens clucking in their coop came to mind.

"I should go," Addie said, rising from the table. "It's good to see you, Fi. But I've work to do."

"Yes, understood." Fiona raised her cheek for Addie to kiss. "You and I can talk later."

How did Addie and Delphia survive their childhood with all of these mother hens? I wondered.

The moment Addie was gone, Fiona focused on me with her full attention. "All right, Mr. West, what's going on between you and my baby sister?"

WE ENDED up out in the garden, walking in the pleasant coolness of the morning. Dew sparkled on the grass and flowers. Blue sky peeked between the trees. None of it did anything to help my head or my churning stomach, made worse by Fiona's direct question of my intentions.

Fiona linked her arm in mine as we strolled along the fence surrounding the yard. "Are you going to tell me or not?"

"There's nothing to tell," I said.

"You're a liar. I know you too well, James West. I could practically feel the attraction between you. I've had my own forbidden love story, you know."

I halted near one corner of the fence, withdrawing from her. Around us, bees were busy gathering pollen from the flowers. Above us, two birds were having either a squabble or a mating ritual. "Has she told you anything? About how she feels about me?"

"No, but I had a feeling. I have a sense about these things, especially when it comes to my sisters. Last summer, her eyes lit up every time you were in the room. Since then, when she speaks of you, it's with a certain reverence. I take it she finally told you?"

"Yes."

"And what about you? How do you feel?"

"More than I thought I did. I'm an imbecile, actually. I didn't see it before. I thought she was too young. Plus, she's your little sister."

"Age differences between men and women aren't that unusual, James. It's not as much of a gap as Li and I have."

"Have you ever doubted your decision?" I shifted to look at her.

"No, never. Li and I are...everything to the other. There was no choice, really, unless we wanted to be miserable. But as you recall, it took some convincing on his part. He didn't want me to suffer because of him. His error was in thinking I would rather have it easier in the world without him than with him."

I draped myself over the fence and peered down into the grass. "There's no point in discussing any of this, really. I have to marry Lena."

She twisted the strings attached to her hat. "Lena's crafty, putting it in the paper. Is that her or her father?"

"They're one and the same," I said. "With a shared interest."

"I don't want Addie hurt," Fiona said.

"I don't want that either. I've been clear with her that I'll never be free. She understands. You know how she is, serenely wise. After this summer, I'll go back with Lena and do what's needed of me, and Addie will stay here and marry some strong mountain man and live happily ever after." My throat constricted at the thought.

"As long as she knows, there's not much you can do about her heart, I suppose. As much as I wish she could be rid of these feelings so easily, we all know that wishing won't make it so."

My feelings, too, I thought. *My stupid, misguided heart.*

10

ADDIE

A WEEK SPED BY WITH JAMES AND ME WORKING CLOSELY TOGETHER on the manuscript. He was careful to stay far away from me. We never touched or even breathed the same air. It was as if the kiss never happened. I would have the moment, though. Forever. No one could ever take it from me.

The morning the Masterses were supposed to arrive, a thunderstorm shook our little part of the world. I suspected God had quite the sense of humor and not much subtlety when it came to story settings. A storm? How appropriate. It mimicked my tumultuous thoughts only too well.

I was in the sitting room working when James came in dressed for the train. He and Papa were going together to pick them up. The guest rooms had been made up by the maids. As much as I wished they would stay at the inn, my mother's good manners wouldn't allow it. "James is our family," she'd said to me last night before bed. "We have to welcome his soon-to-be in-laws."

"Yes, Mama."

"And Addie," she'd said, before I walked into my bedroom, "please, darling, be kind to yourself and stay away from them. It will only hurt worse to see them together. Throw yourself into your work."

I'd promised I would and then gone into my room, flopped on my bed, and cried myself to sleep. Regardless, I'd dressed carefully this morning in a dress I normally saved for parties. This Lena would be dressed in Paris fashion, I felt certain. I glanced out the window at the rain pounding the grass and wished for her hat to be ruined the moment she disembarked from the train. I'd resigned myself to pettiness and jealousy. I didn't have to like it even if I did have to accept it, and I certainly wasn't going to go out of my way to engage with a woman who had trapped James into marriage. I couldn't even muster up an ounce of guilt over my evil thoughts, either. I'd been good all my life, and the only thing I'd ever wanted would be taken from me. A bitterness had crept into my soul. So be it. This was me now, preparing for my life as an old maid.

Despite all this, I smiled at James. The way his face lifted my spirit would never change. Even when he was married to Lena. "Papa will be down momentarily," I said. "Jasper said he was running a few minutes late."

James pulled his watch from his pocket. "We have plenty of time before the train arrives. I wanted to make sure we had a moment alone before I left. I wanted to see how you are."

"I'm fine," I said. "I'm a Barnes. Tougher than we look."

"I know what you're made of." His blue eyes captured mine and wouldn't let go. I had to force myself to look away.

A bolt of lightning lit up the sky, followed by thunder so loud it shook the house. "Goodness," I said.

"God isn't big on subtext," James said.

I laughed. "That's exactly what I was thinking a few minutes ago."

"If I were his editor, I'd say it was a little on the nose."

"Yes." I set my pen back in the ink bottle and stood. I'd been writing longhand, hoping to capture the right words before using the typewriter.

"I wish I knew what to say." He gestured toward the door. "Everything's going to change the moment she walks through that door, and I wish it didn't have to."

"I'll remember that. It's all I'll have, but it's something."

"Thank you."

"For what?" I asked.

"Being you. Grace personified."

Papa entered the room, pulling us from our reverie. He was dressed in one of his best suits. We all seemed to think these Masterses and their fat purses needed to be impressed. It bothered me. Yet here I was in my nicest dress, so who was I to talk?

"James, are you ready?" Papa asked.

"Yes, sir."

Papa's face, lined from his years on this earth, creased further but he didn't comment.

James straightened his tie. "Shall we, then?" He looked over at me and before I knew what I was doing, I'd stepped forward and taken his hand. I said into his ear, "Be brave, dear James. I'll be fine, and so will you."

I looked over at Papa. His expression had softened. He knew what was between us, I thought. Mama had told him. Of course she had. There were no secrets between them. Regardless, they were helpless to save me from myself. There was nothing anyone could do except love me. I took comfort in that love, not only from them but in the adoring eyes of James. He loved me. I knew it. I'd known it since the kiss. I would have to be satisfied with knowing the truth.

After a few minutes of staring blankly at the typewriter, I decided to go downstairs and see how Lizzie was faring with preparing our midday meal. I wasn't sure where my mother or Delphia had gotten to this morning, as I'd slept too late for breakfast. Having endured another restless night with sleep eluding me until dawn, I'd not been wakened to the usual sounds of early morning.

Lizzie and Mrs. Wu were sitting together at the kitchen table, a pot of tea between them. Mrs. Wu, sitting more often than standing these days, was in the process of cutting a pile of potatoes into wedges; Lizzie shelled peas from our garden. When I was a child, the sight of piles of empty pea pods made me sad. They'd been discarded after giving shelter, not even provided the courtesy of providing nourishment to the very people who grew them. One time, I'd mentioned this to Lizzie, and she'd allowed me to eat one of the shells raw while warning me that they would disappoint. I'd had to agree with her. They were tough and flavorless. However, that didn't change my opinion. It still seemed like a waste.

"Addie girl, what brings you down to the kitchen? Can we make you something? Your mother said you missed breakfast." Lizzie's mixture of English and Irish accents were as thick today as they had been almost three decades before when she'd followed my father and Jasper across the seas to make a new home in the States. I'd noticed she seemed forlorn lately. She missed Florence, I'm sure, although she never complained. Sending her daughter to university had been a dream come true, and she wasn't about to do anything to lessen Florence's enjoyment of higher education.

"Thank you, but I don't need you to make anything," I said. "Would you take pity upon me and let me sneak a little something?"

"Yes, dearie. Look in the pantry. There are apples and cheese left from breakfast and a ramekin of berries I set aside for the new gardener. He's young, don't you know, and always hungry." Lizzie pushed a strand of her silver hair away from her flushed pink cheeks. The kitchen was warm this time of year, even in the mornings. She was plump and sweet, our Lizzie, and seemingly tireless. She and Mrs. Wu seemed impervious to age, their boundless energy nourishing a household of staff and family.

"We have a new gardener?" I asked.

"Yes, quite a bonny lad, as my Irish mother would have said, God rest her soul." Lizzie's eyes darted upward to heaven. "His name's Jesse, like the outlaw. Can you imagine a mother naming her son Jesse?"

"It seems a nice name to me," I said.

"He's big here." Mrs. Wu held up her skinny arm and mimicked a muscle. "This Jesse works in his undershirt. Vanity is no good, Addie."

"But who are we to tell him to put his shirt on?" Lizzie asked. The ladies cackled in unison.

"I'm not sure if you two should be allowed in the garden," I said, amused despite my aching heart.

"We must get the peas for dinner," Mrs. Wu said. "We sacrifice for the family."

"Indeed." Lizzie nodded. "What we wouldn't do for all of you."

Laughing, I went to the pantry to forage for the aforementioned apples. When I returned, the ripe scent of a working man greeted me. Near the doorway, a man dressed in overalls and an undershirt stood by the kitchen door. Lizzie had gotten up from the table to pour him a glass of lemonade.

I took a good look at this bonny lad. He was handsome, with caramel-colored hair streaked with golden highlights and bright green eyes. His jawline was strong and there was an air about him of ambition in the firm set of his mouth and glint in his eyes when his gaze meandered my way. *Predator.* This was the word that came to my mind, as they did sometimes, playing before my eyes in the font of my typewriter.

"This is Miss Addie," Lizzie said to him. "One of Lord Barnes's daughters."

Jesse nodded, polite as could be. Yet a shiver ran up my spine. "Miss Barnes, how do you do?"

"Very well, thank you. Nice to meet you, Jesse. You must be doing well. Those are some pretty peas." I gestured to the bowl on the table.

"I've been here only a few days." His gazed fixed on me, with eyes that seemed alight from an inner blaze. "I only picked them. Someone else planted them." He drawled with a Southern dialect that reminded me of muddy, slow-moving water.

I didn't respond. For some reason, I felt that he was taunting me. Mrs. Wu and Lizzie seemed oblivious. This was how a home was invaded with depravity, I thought. Then, as quickly as it had come, I dismissed the idea. He was only a boy, not a panther to be afraid of.

"Where are you from?" I asked Jesse.

"Atlanta," he said. "My mother keeps house for a man called Roman Steele. I was born and raised there, helping her in the kitchen when I wasn't learning about the garden and plants." He grinned over at Lizzie, who had returned to the table. "You let me know if you ever need any help, you hear?"

"We won't, love," Lizzie said. "You'll be busy enough in the garden anyway."

"We're glad to have your expertise, Jesse." I smiled politely before excusing myself and escaping up the stairs. It wasn't until I reached the top of the steps that I realized I'd forgotten my apple. I wouldn't go back down, I decided. Staying away from Jesse seemed more important. I must warn Delphia. Hopefully she wouldn't be charmed by him as Lizzie and Mrs. Wu so obviously were. He was dangerous. I don't know why I thought so, but I did.

Instead of returning to work, I went upstairs to my room. Bitty was on her hands and knees scrubbing the floor. The bed had been made, and newly washed underclothes were stacked on the dresser, waiting to be put away.

She jumped when I came in, as if she were guilty.

"I'm sorry to scare you," I said.

"It's all right. I was lost in thought." Bitty sat back on her knees and glanced out the window. I hurried over to join her, thinking Papa and James would be back with the Masterses. Instead, it was that Jesse making a big show of pouring pumping water into a bucket and splashing it over his head. That undershirt of his clung to the muscles of his chest. Did he know that Bitty watched?

As if he'd heard the question, he looked up then and seeing us standing in the window, waved. I turned away, disgusted.

"Isn't he a pretty boy?" Bitty asked, dreamily.

"You stay away from him, Bitty," I said. "He's trouble. I can feel it in my bones."

"Yes, Miss Addie, I agree. I can spot trouble as well as anyone."

"What does Harry think of him?" I asked, curious.

"He doesn't like him either. Says he's always prowling around in the middle of the night, coming home late and waking Harry up." Jesse and Harry shared the bunkhouse, built for the men who worked for us. Papa felt strongly the men should not sleep in the same quarters as the women who worked in the house. Given Bitty and Harry's love affair and how easy it would be for them to find trouble in the middle of lonely nights, I'd thought it was a good idea. I was even more convinced now that I'd met Jesse.

"Doing what, I wonder?" I asked.

"Harry says Jesse comes in smelling like liquor, so who knows."

I thought about James coming home after a night out with my brothers. "I don't suppose it's our business what he does during his leisure time. It's unfortunate he's keeping Harry up at night, though. Do you want me to say something about it to Mama?"

"No, please don't. We don't want trouble. Harry says Jesse

has a mean streak. He can see it in his eyes. One of those men who acts real nice in front of his employer but turns dark when they're not around."

"You'll let me know if there's any trouble, all right?"

"Yes, Miss Addie. I will."

I put my washed underclothes away, setting aside my worries about Jesse and soon forgetting about him altogether. I had my own problems to think about. Lena and her father would be here any moment. Everything would change just like that.

Bitty finished up what she was doing and asked if I needed anything. I assured her I was fine and that I'd be working until our guests arrived.

Bitty frowned and leaned against her broom. "I'll do my best, but I'm not sure how to work for a fancy lady such as Miss Masters."

"Don't worry, Bitty. Just do what you do for us and she'll be pleased."

"She will?" Bitty's eyes lit up. "I don't want her to think less of us because of me."

I smiled, touched by Bitty's loyalty. "You'll make us seem as if we live like kings and queens."

She beamed with pride. "Thank you, Miss Addie. I try my best."

"I know you do, and we're appreciative of it, too."

"I shall make sure you and Delphia look as nicely put out as Miss Masters. We can't have her showing you two up, can we?"

"I'm afraid it may be a contest we can't win." I explained about the Masterses' wealth and that Lena probably bought the latest dresses from designers in Paris. "But it needn't trouble us. Delphia and I know our own minds and what's important to us. Having the fanciest clothes is not it."

"Yes, but I do love pretty dresses, don't you?" Bitty asked, sounding mournful. She brushed a hand down her plain gray skirt.

"I was thinking more of our intellect and talents. Pretty dresses can't do anything important, can they?"

"No, I suppose not." She looked up at the ceiling, her brow wrinkling, before returning her attention to me. "All the same, I'll take extra care with your hair and makeup these next few days."

"That sounds fine, Bitty. Thank you."

She scuttled away, her skirt swaying to and fro just above her strong calf muscles. She might not have the prettiest dress, but she had a lovely, curvy figure. I went to the full-length mirror to look at myself. Too skinny, like a board. No matter, I reminded myself. I would think only of my work from here on out and care nothing about my appearance. Or that James was marrying Lena. I would be happy for him and his family. I had to be.

11

JAMES

On the way home from the train station, I shared the back seat with Lena. Mr. Masters and Alexander were in the front seat, talking about the train ride out here from the Denver station and how dramatic some of the sights had been and how beautiful it was here. I remembered very well my own reaction to the views that first summer. Today, though, my gaze swept from the terrain to Lena. She peered straight ahead, having told me that riding in cars made her nauseated.

There was nothing at all wrong with her, I told myself. I was lucky to be marrying such a beautiful young lady. She was indeed pretty, with shiny hair the color of a chestnut horse and dark green eyes. A pointy chin and high cheekbones gave her a regal air. She wore a traveling dress in a pale yellow, complementing her tawny complexion, and a floppy cloche hat with a modest blue ribbon.

That cloche hat would not protect her skin here under the Colorado sky. In fact, those types of hats were ridiculous. What purpose did they serve? Nothing, that's what. The hats Delphia and Addie had worn to the swimming hole, wide-brimmed and made of straw, were practical and smart, like the heads they covered. Now, those were hats with a purpose.

Addie. My stomach ached as if I were homesick at the image of her pure blue eyes gazing at me this morning. She'd tried to encourage me even though I knew it hurt her to know where I was headed. She was good. As good as anyone I'd ever met.

This morning, before we left, I'd gotten a letter from my father. His words had not been surprising, full of gratitude for our luck, saying this marriage had been granted to us by the grace of God. *It will be good for all of us, my boy,* he'd written. No, I'd thought. It would be good for everyone but me.

"Darling, it's a little frightening, isn't it?" Lena rested her gloved hand on my knee for the briefest of moments and leaned closer, perhaps to show me a hint of her cleavage. A flirtatious gesture, sensual in nature, that made my head throb. I couldn't do this. I shouldn't have to.

But you do.

"What's frightening?" I asked.

"The mountains. I mean, look at them. How is it possible they're so tall? It's just too-too."

We turned off the main road from the train station, bypassing downtown. In the front seat, Alexander was telling Mr. Masters about the history of the area. "When I moved here, it was nothing but a ghost town of a place. The gold rush was over by then, as I'm sure you know, and the old spot abandoned. A fire had come through and taken out what was left of the town. Everyone had moved on by then."

"This is how you were able to buy all this land, then?" Mr. Masters asked. He was a bulky man with a thick mustache. Despite the heat and time of year, he wore a dark suit. A red tie matched the ruddiness of his cheeks. Trickles of perspiration melted into his sideburns. Occasionally, he dabbed at his face with a handkerchief embroidered with his initials.

"That's correct. Good timing. Isn't that the American way?" Alexander asked.

"By God, yes." Mr. Masters smacked his full lips, clearly delighted with himself. "Indeed, I was in the right place at the right time, but you have to be ready to seize opportunity when it presents itself." He went on to describe to Alexander his investments in various markets.

"And you've been able to weather the depression?" Alexander asked.

"I took advantage of it, bought up stocks and everything else cheap." Mr. Masters picked up his hat and swiped the sweat from his brow. "Is the weather always this humid this time of year?" The rain had ceased earlier, but the air was warm and moist. Flowers along the roadside drooped with the weight of water.

I looked up at the sky from the back seat window. Purple clouds hung low and moody.

"Sometimes," Alexander said. "Our weather's a little unpredictable. You'll see all kinds in the weeks you're here."

Weeks? "How long are you staying?" I asked, leaning forward slightly.

"Your father said he and your mother will come to New York for a visit once we have everything settled."

"Settled?" I asked, unable to keep the tension out of my voice. Alexander caught my eye in the rearview mirror, concern knitting his brow.

"The legal papers drawn up and the wedding, of course," Masters said. "You'll want a honeymoon, I assume?"

"I want to go to Paris and Milan," Lena said. "And buy up every new fashion there is." She giggled. "Is that naughty of me?"

"A little," I said under my breath.

She leaned close again, her breath tickling my cheek as she said into my ear, "I know I'm dreadful, but I shan't say sorry for wanting what I want."

I took her hand in mine before she could let it wander over to my knee. She was like a child, really. More so than I'd realized before spending time with Addie and Delphia. They were roughly the same age and yet they seemed so much more mature than my fiancée. I sighed and turned back to the scenery. We were coming down the dirt driveway toward the Barnes estate. Green pastures were dotted with wildflowers in purples, yellows, and pinks. The red barn came into view as we rounded the corner and then the house made of dark wood and stone. Roses tumbled over the front fence, and the dogwood trees dripped with white blossoms.

"The house is much smaller than I thought it would be," Lena said.

"Dear, mind your manners," Mr. Masters said.

"Yes, Daddy." She grinned and leaned closer to the window. "Oh, how cute. There's a wooden swing hanging from that tree."

I caught Alexander's gaze in the mirror once again. Was he offended? I didn't think so, given the twinkle in his eyes. He was a man who did not need garish examples of wealth. His family and friends came first. His esteem was gained from his family, not how large or small his house was. Yes, one might say he had the luxury to care about love more than money because he had so much of each. It was only a wealthy man who needn't care about the public display of money. Still, it was an admirable trait, one I'd have loved to emulate. But alas, I was weak, in both finances and spirit. My life was doomed, a slow trudge toward the end, full of compromise and sacrifice. If I were a better man, I would be glad to save my family. Instead, I was resentful and morose.

A memory emerged then of one of the first times I'd ever come here. Addie had been pushing Delphia in that very swing. I'd thought how adorable and sweet they seemed. Fiona had come running out of the house to greet me, followed by Li, Alexander, and Quinn. They'd welcomed me as if I'd always been part of the family. "We're glad to see you again. Make yourself at home," Alexander had said.

Now, here they were welcoming my fiancée and her father without question. For me. They were doing it all for me. I held out my hand to help Lena from the car. "Come meet everyone," I said.

"Do I look all right?" Lena smoothed her hands down the sides of her dress.

"You look beautiful," I said, truthfully.

"I'm nervous."

Her fragility touched me. I managed a smile and squeezed her hand. "Don't worry, they're the nicest people you'll ever meet."

We went inside and were greeted by Jasper and Quinn, then taken back to the formal parlor. The heat of the afternoon was in full force, but the dim room felt cool and smelled of the vases of roses set on the grand piano and side tables. Decorated in plush fabrics in burgundy and blues, the hardwood floors gleamed around the edges of an Oriental rug. Bay windows looked out to the green lawn and blooming hydrangeas in purples and pinks.

One of the maids brought tea, and Quinn and Alexander asked polite questions about the Masterses' journey and their life in New York. Lena was quiet but polite. Yet she'd seemed to have shrunk since I last saw her. The bubbly, vivacious girl had been replaced by a more somber, worried-seeming woman. Was she having doubts as well? Did she not want to marry me? Was this solely her father's idea?

She must have caught me looking at her because her face lit up with her best smile. "Do you want to take a stroll outside?" Lena asked, close to my ear. "I could use some air."

Before I could answer, Delphia and Addie entered the parlor. Delphia, dressed in yellow, reminded me of a daffodil, whereas Addie conjured a pink rose. Lena looked artificial and overly made up next to them. I stood, catching Addie's eye. They were red and puffy. She'd been crying. I hated myself for it. I'd done this to her. Made this awful mess. Why couldn't I have just let well enough alone? Pretended that I didn't share her feelings, instead of kissing her like a madman?

"How do you do?" Lena was saying to the girls. "It's simply

aces meeting you. James has talked endlessly about the little sisters."

Little sisters. They wouldn't like that, I thought, bracing myself for whatever Delphia said next.

"That's funny. He hasn't said much of anything about you," Delphia said.

I bit the inside of my lip to keep from laughing. After all, it wasn't funny. But God bless Delphia. She was loyal and fierce. I couldn't help but adore her for it.

"How odd," Lena said. "Since we're officially engaged." She looked at me with a pretend pout on her lips. "Darling, haven't you told everyone how in love we are? How excited we are to be man and wife and live in New York?"

"It's not come up much." We were not in love nor excited to be married, but I didn't contradict her. "Addie and I have been busy working on a manuscript."

Lena's eyebrows shot up. "A manuscript? Are you a writer?"

"I'd like to be," Addie said softly.

"You are," I said. "You write. You have an entire manuscript."

Addie sent me a grateful look. "Thank you, James." To Lena, she said, "I feel a bit of a fraud, but James is building my confidence."

"Well, of course you would. There are many hobbyists, I suppose," Lena said. "Or that's what James tells me about the submissions he receives. Mountains of them, right, darling?"

"A lot, yes," I said, feeling traitorous for saying so. When had I mentioned that to Lena? I must have said something about it at some point. What else had I forgotten I'd said to her?

Delphia crossed her arms over her chest, glaring at Lena. "It's a very good manuscript. In fact, James says he thinks it will be the talk of New York."

Had I said that? Regardless, I liked the momentary uncertainty on Lena's face.

"Oh, that's funny," Lena said. "I always think of writers as someone with an actual published novel." The woman could spar with the best of them.

"Let's sit outside on the porch," Addie said. "We can have a cool drink, Miss Masters, if you're thirsty for something other than our very English tea."

"I wouldn't mind something cold," Lena said. "The train was hot and dusty."

"You poor thing," Quinn said. "I'll have some lemonade and cookies sent out to you."

The four of us traipsed down the hallway and out to the screened porch. The warmth of the day pushed against my face, as if we'd opened an oven door. We all settled around a low table in chairs with cushions. The yard, for once, was empty of children. Only a few croquet mallets remained scattered around the grass.

"Do you read?" Delphia asked Lena. "Books? Magazines? What're you interested in?"

"I'm not much for reading. I prefer parties and dancing. I'm an accomplished dancer, aren't I, darling?"

"Yes, very much so." This was true. I'd first noticed her at the party because of her dancing. She'd been doing the Charleston with a young man and laughing. I'd been drawn to the joyousness of her movements.

"Not very much for books?" Delphia asked. "James's wife not interested in books? What a strange match you are."

Out of the corner of my eye, I saw Addie's foot tap Delphia's. A warning to be nice, I thought. I needed one too.

"We have loads in common," Lena said. "Loads and loads." This was said with more aggression than the words suggested. "You don't yet know me but you'll see as time goes on that James and I are perfectly matched. A love match, as they say in England."

"Really? Like what?" Delphia sat up straighter and stared at her guest. The glint of a warrior shone in her eyes. To her, Lena was a threat to her beloved sister, therefore she was ready for a battle.

Lena looked over at me, the left side of her mouth curling upward for a moment, reminding me of a rabid dog I'd seen once as a child. Her voice was sharp and flinty when she said, "I had no idea both of Fiona's baby sisters were so knowledgeable about you, darling. What other secrets do they know about you?"

"James's love of books is hardly a secret," Delphia said.

Next to her sister on the love seat, Addie picked up her glass of lemonade, the sides of which were dripping with condensation. For a split second, I thought she might hurl the whole thing either on her sister or Lena, I couldn't decide which. Instead, she took a dainty sip while looking directly at Lena. Sizing her up, I thought. She might not be as outspoken as Delphia but nonetheless, she saw the truth about people. Could she see the good in Lena as I had? Her zest and thirst for life?

An image of my pale and listless mother came to me. She reminded me of a pillow that had lost its stuffing, leaving only the thin cover. She was not like the women here; she'd had no idea how to fight for what she wanted. Mother was a victim of a love match that had turned terribly wrong in the end. Men like my father did what they wanted without concern for others. She could do nothing but watch helplessly as the life she'd thought she'd have faded into nonexistence. My mother was powerless, as was I, against my father's demons.

"James, darling, have you told the girls about the wedding?" Lena asked.

"The wedding?" Had it been decided?

"Our wedding." Lena laughed without mirth. "What else would I be talking about?

"I didn't know there was anything to tell," I said as calmly as I could. "Have you decided what you'd like?"

"Yes, you said I could decide, right?"

"Whatever you want, yes," I said.

"Aren't you too good?" Lena turned to Addie and Delphia.

"May I ask—why the rush?" Delphia asked without waiting for permission.

Lena's eyes flashed but her tone remained light. "Can you blame me for wanting to get him to the altar before someone else decides to snatch him up? I'm sure I'm not the only girl who dreams of being Mrs. James West."

"I don't think so," I said, avoiding Addie's gaze.

"There might be one or two. Right under my nose." Lena's eyes slid toward Addie. She was a lot of things, but stupid wasn't one of them. "I can see you've been busy out here on the frontier these last few weeks. Fortunately for all of us I got here when I did. I'd not realized how pretty you two were. And Addie, you must be in the market for a man yourself."

"Not particularly," Addie said.

"Well, as long as you know you can't have mine, then we can be friends." Lena hiccupped out what was supposed to be a frivolous giggle but instead it sounded like a small dog's bark.

"You've nothing to worry about. My sister and I are women of honor." Delphia pressed closer to her Addie. "We don't take what doesn't belong to us."

Addie had turned the color of the light pink hydrangeas pressing their heads against the screened porch. We were not honorable. I wasn't, at any rate. She was a casualty of my aggressive kisses. Now she felt bad. She shouldn't—it was my fault. I was the one who had forced my kiss upon her.

"Lena," I said quietly. "Tell them you're only teasing."

"Oh my goodness, yes, of course, I'm only teasing. I know the sisters of James's best friend would never weasel their way into his life when they know he's getting married in a few weeks." Lena's eyes bugged slightly. Beads of perspiration dotted her nose.

Addie set down her lemonade and touched her graceful fingers to her temples. "I'm feeling poorly. It's a headache from the heat, I think. Please forgive me, but I must go lie down."

"I'll go with you," Delphia said, glaring at Lena. "We're sharing a room since we have unexpected guests. Uninvited ones, at that." She said the last part under her breath, but we all heard it.

Lena made another one of her pouty faces. "I'm terribly sorry to have put you out of your room, Delphia. When we asked if we could stay, we had no idea the house was so…small. We're accustomed to the estates of our friends in the east."

Delphia opened her mouth, obviously summoning a retort, but Addie gave her a look that only sisters could exchange, and she shut it again.

"We'll see you both at dinner," Addie said. "I hope you'll be comfortable in your room."

"Thank you. I'm sure I shall," Lena said.

I watched the two sisters leave the covered porch and disappear into the house. No sooner had the door slammed than Lena turned to me. "How sad for her. She's obviously in love with you. Poor little lamb."

"What are you talking about?" Sweat very suddenly dampened my palms.

"Addie Barnes. She's smitten with you. Surely you can see it?"

"No, we're close friends, that's all. I'm helping her with her manuscript, as I said."

"I know it's on the up-and-up, darling." She smacked a hand playfully against the lapel of my jacket. "I could hardly blame her for having a crush on you. You're irresistible."

I smiled, pretending to be pleased with the compliment. Inside, however, I was a bundle of nerves. How had Lena known of Addie's feelings? Could she see mine as well?

12

ADDIE

THE MOMENT WE WERE IN MY ROOM, DELPHIA FLOPPED ONTO THE made bed and tossed a throw pillow against the wall. "Can you believe her? Saying our house is small and that you're a hobbyist. I hate her.""

If I hadn't been quite so miserable, my little sister would have made me laugh. "If I were in a war, I'd want you by my side." I unpinned my hat and left it on my dressing table. With my fingers, I fluffed my hair back into shape, wincing at the sore spots where the pins had pulled at my scalp.

"The heat's unbearable." I tugged my shoes and stockings off my damp skin and placed them neatly in the wardrobe before helping myself to a glass of water from the pitcher on the dresser.

"This is a war, Addie." Delphia sat up, glaring at me. Not in the same way she'd just done with Lena but in a sisterly way, exasperated but loving at the same time. I'd heard about secret codes during the war. My sister and I had them, too.

"It's a war I can't win. Even if I convinced him to marry me instead, he'd eventually become resentful for ruining his family." I sank into the window seat and bent my knees, holding on to my bare legs under the skirt of my dress as if I might fall from grace otherwise. Outside, the flowers wilted under the heat, tucking their heads in repose.

She tugged off her shoes and hurled them toward the fat chair in the corner of the room. They bounced off the cushion and fell onto the floor. "This is maddening." Delphia sprang up from the bed and began pacing around the room in a circle. When we were small, she'd done the same thing, pretending a tiger was chasing her. "What are we supposed to do? Accept this?"

"What else can we do?" I rested my chin on my knees and fought tears. "We have to pretend that I don't care. I can't let her know how much it hurts. At least I'll have my pride." I looked over at my sister, who now leaned her back against one corner of the four-poster bed frame.

"Pride? Isn't that what you're always lecturing me about? 'Don't be so prideful, Delphia.'" She mimicked my breathy voice.

I sighed, the headache I'd feigned taking hold now. "Will you deny me even that?"

She scrunched up her face, clearly remorseful for making me feel worse. "No, you may have your pride. I understand perfectly well."

This made me smile a little. "Thank you."

"I wish there were something I could do. You know I don't like to be helpless." Delphia came to sit next to me on the window seat, placing her feet so they met mine.

Bookends, I thought. I would always have my sister. And the others, plus Mama and Papa. I had to remember this when feeling sorry for myself. I was blessed with love. "I understand, but in this case, we have to accept that not everything we want is what we will get."

"What if it were only his job he'd lose?" Delphia asked. "Would he run from her then?"

"Yes, I think so. It's his family he's worried about, more than anything."

"Has he told you that?" Delphia asked.

"No, we haven't spoken as if there were things to weigh and sort through in this decision, because there aren't. He must save his family." I lifted my chin from my knees to get a better look at her. "What if it were me or Mama and Papa? What if you could save us? Wouldn't you do so, no matter the cost to yourself?"

She huffed, crossing her arms over her chest. "I hate it when you're right."

"I wish there were a way out of this," I said. "But there isn't. I've been all around it and back again in my mind. I shall be like Emily Dickinson, pining away for the man I loved all my life. Writing from a place of despair."

"I can't bear it. I simply can't. Not when you fought off death. Not when you're so good. I'd take the broken heart myself if I could. I don't care for love anyway."

Her sweetness brought on the tears I'd managed to keep at bay all afternoon. I laid my forehead on my knees and allowed myself to cry. Delphia took me in her arms, and I wept into her dress until it was nearly soaked through. All the while, she stroked my back and whispered that she would fix it, that everything would be all right in the end. But I could tell that even Delphia, who thought she could will the outcome she wanted simply because she was clever, didn't believe it to be true.

WITH DELPHIA'S HELP, I managed to dress for dinner. After a cold compress on my eyes, the swelling reduced enough that I could make up my face. My sister did my hair for me, coaxing it into obedient waves.

Li and Fiona, as well as Cym and Viktor, were joining us for dinner. I was glad of it, knowing the conversation would be lively and distracting. I'd not be required to speak and thus could pretend in front of my family and the Masterses that I was quite fine.

We were descending the stairs together when Cym and Viktor arrived without their girls, who were staying with the nanny for the evening. Jasper was with them, having rushed to the door. I could only imagine the competitive streak the snooty Masterses had evoked in him. He would go out of his way to be the perfect English butler this evening. I had a feeling downstairs in the kitchen Lizzie and Mrs. Wu were putting together a meal for the ages.

Cym looked stunning in a sleeveless purple gown that emphasized her trim waist and wide shoulders. Although she claimed to be retired from ski jumping now that she had the girls, she still trained every day with Viktor. She said there might be a time when her muscles would come in handy again. There had been just a smidge of wistfulness in her voice. Who could blame her? She'd had the world record for longest jump when she retired after finding out she was pregnant with her second child.

"Hello, dear sisters." Cym gave us each a kiss. "It seems like ages since I've seen you."

"We've been busy," Viktor said. "Your sister's inventory is nearly wiped out, despite this depression."

Viktor had decided not long after he and Cym married that banking wasn't for him. His parents had owned a tailor shop all his life, and he'd admitted he missed having a product to sell instead of only counting money. In hindsight, we were glad of it, considering what had happened to the banking industry after the crash. Together, Cym and Viktor had opened a sports shop where they sold skis made by our brother-in-law Phillip, as well as clothes for various outdoor activities like fishing and skiing. Not just for men but women, too. Cym had insisted on that. Viktor's father and mother now supplied much of the inventory, having hired helpers to create from their patterns. Although Mr. Olofsson still made custom dresses and suits, more and more of the business was focused on producing sportswear.

"You both look lovely, as always," Viktor said, kissing each of our hands as Jasper disappeared down the stairway to the kitchen. "But I must say, Delphia, you seem distressed. What's wrong?"

"You won't believe everything that's going on around here," Delphia said in a loud whisper. "These people who have invaded—they're horrible. Viktor, do you think our house is small?"

"Don't be ridiculous." Viktor lowered his voice to match Delphia. "No one could call this house small." He gestured around the dark foyer with its gleaming walnut wainscoting and dark beams. "And beautiful. I can still remember the first time I ever came here, I thought I'd come to a palace."

"See there," Delphia said to me before turning back to Viktor. "This houseguest of ours said it was small. Can you believe the gall?"

"Miss Masters said that?" Cym said, lowering her voice. "Why would she say such a thing? Is she awful?"

"I'm afraid so," Delphia said.

"Addie, what do you think of her?" Cym asked.

"She's fine. A city person, that's all." I looked down at my hands and forced myself to keep my mouth from trembling. *I mustn't cry again*. Not when I'd finally gotten the puffiness to go away.

"She's jealous of Addie." Delphia glanced down the hallway toward the parlor. "I bet it's eating her alive right as we speak."

"Jealous of Addie?" Viktor said, narrowing his eyes. "Why would that be?"

"Because Addie's four thousand times prettier and smarter than…that woman," Delphia said. "And James is taken with Addie. That much is obvious, even to Lena Masters."

"Yes, I thought I picked up on a spark between you two," Cym said, glancing at me. "Is there one, Addie?"

"Addie's mad for him," Delphia said dramatically but still quiet enough that no one but the four of us could hear.

"Delphia, please." I should never have told her the truth. The entire family would know it before the night was done. "That was supposed to be kept our secret."

"Is it true?" Viktor turned to me, compassion in his light eyes.

I nodded. "Yes. But nothing can come of it. We must never speak of it again. For James's sake, if nothing else. He's tortured enough."

"Oh, darling." Cym took both my hands. "Are you all right?"

"It's nothing, Cym. Truly, we should go in. They're all waiting." My voice quivered, so I shut it tight.

Cym dropped my hands but remained close. "You poor girl. Is it true what Mama says—he's being forced into marriage because of the financial problems in his family?"

Viktor shook his head sadly. "Nothing good can come from gambling."

"Unless it's poker with your brothers," Cym said, teasing him, but immediately sobered, perhaps at the sight of my wretchedness.

Viktor put a brotherly arm around my shoulders. "Listen, kid, you must never give up hope. Not when love's involved."

"We would need a miracle," I said. "He's honorable and has given his word to all of them."

"Yes," Cym said. "Loyal and steadfast."

"Well, we'll see about that, won't we?" Delphia asked. "True love could win in the end."

"Mama's waiting," I said, desperate to get out of the foyer and on with the evening. The sooner we started, the sooner it would be over with.

Cym took a second look at me and gave me an extra squeeze as we entered the parlor where my parents and the Masterses were already waiting. James had not yet arrived. Jasper, on duty for the evening, gave Cym, Delphia, and me glasses of sherry and a whiskey for Viktor.

Lena was in the corner of the room speaking with Mama. She wore a splendid gown in dark blue, which complemented her russet hair and complexion. A diamond necklace draped just above her collarbone and large sapphire earrings sparkled in the evening light. She glanced our way, her eyes harder than they'd been earlier.

"That's her?" Cym asked in my ear. "She looks like a red fox."

"That's what I think, too," Delphia said. "A fox without a tail. That we can see anyway. Maybe there's one under that ugly dress."

"The dress isn't ugly," Cym said. "If we were to be truthful."

"Sometimes I don't care for the truth," Delphia said.

At the moment, I didn't either.

"Well, she's no match for you, Addie," Viktor said. "No wonder she's jealous of you."

I flushed from the compliment, feeling better in the presence of steady Viktor and my strong-willed sister. When together, they seemed to exude a sense of invincibility. Since they'd teamed up, there was nothing they couldn't do. I longed to be in such a partnership with James. I sighed. What did it matter if Lena were jealous or not? James belonged to her now.

Jasper had returned with a tray of champagne, which he placed on Fiona's baby grand in the corner of the room. It would have been a beautiful evening, other than my despair. The weather had cooled and the ripe humidity had been replaced by fresh, dry air. Jasper had opened the doors and windows to allow the breeze to cool the room and bring in the scent of the wild roses and honeysuckle that crawled along our whitewashed fence.

We turned as Fiona, Li, and James entered the room. My sister's hair had curled attractively around her face from the heat. Li had taken off his jacket and had it slung over one arm. James's fair skin was pink from the warmth of the evening, giving him the appearance of great health and athleticism. His eyes were red-rimmed, though. Red and haunted.

His gaze fell to me first. Of everyone in the room, he found me. It should have given me comfort but it didn't, for I knew what was to come. I smiled at him, hoping to give him courage for what would surely be a wretched evening. He smiled back at me and drew in a breath that made his chest visibly rise and fall before heading toward his fiancée.

Fiona and Li went to meet Lena and her father, as they should. Still, I couldn't help but feel hurt that they hadn't come to say hello to me first. This was an irrational wish. They could see me any old time. Their beloved James was marrying. They would want to meet his bride and her father.

As for me, I had Delphia on one side and Cym on the other, like shields. It would have to be enough, perhaps for the rest of my life.

I WAS SEATED between Fiona and Cym for dinner, their husbands on either side of them. The table was adorned with the best china and silver. Candles burned between small, short bouquets of hydrangeas.

Papa, at one end of the long table, and Mama at the other welcomed everyone. "We say prayer in this house, no matter how many are at the table," Papa said to Mr. Masters. "Would you care to say it for us tonight or shall I?"

"You do it, please. I have a feeling you're better acquainted with him than I." The corners of his caterpillar mustache twitched. Did they not pray in New York City?

Papa bowed his head, as did the rest of us. "Dear father in heaven, thank you for this food we are about to enjoy and thank you for bringing our esteemed guests from so far away and for James, who has given our family much joy. Please keep us all well and guide us in the direction of your will. Amen."

A chorus of amens was followed by one of the maids bringing in the first course, a cold cucumber soup. This was one of Lizzie's specialties, using the cucumbers from our own garden. I ate mine without my usual enjoyment, wishing the night were over so that I could be in my room with Delphia.

James, who was seated across from me, would not look at me. He seemed to be playing the good fiancé role this evening, I thought, bitterly, as he whispered something in Lena's ear. She cackled at whatever clever thing he'd said. Much too loudly. *Trying too hard*, I could almost hear Delphia say.

Mr. Masters had engaged Mama in a conversation about education. From what I picked up, he seemed to think it should be afforded only to the rich and middle class. Mama, too polite to argue with him, simply nodded between spoonfuls of soup. She looked stunning, as she always did, slim and elegant in an off-white gown. Her hair was up tonight, arranged by her maid into a chignon on her long neck, as she'd worn when she was the young bride at this table instead of our matriarch.

On the other side of the table, Delphia had been seated between Mr. Masters and James. She seemed small between the large, wide-shouldered men, and wore an expression of turmoil tinged with mischief. I could only imagine her thoughts. Hopefully there would not be a frog in Lena's bed tonight. Our older siblings had done that and other naughty things to the various nannies that poor Papa hired for his unruly brood in the years before Mama had come to them. I had captured a few of those times in the pages of my manuscript. They were the stories of my siblings, really. Passed down to me, the family storyteller. If there was no other reason to write them, it would be to at least have them on record for generations to come. Would I have any of my own children? Anyone to pass the traditions of our family on, or would I become the eccentric aunt who remained with her parents? I almost groaned at the thought.

Just then, a racket outside the dining room windows drew all of our attention. I could scarcely believe my eyes. Our mama pig, Daisy, had escaped from her pen and was snorting her way among the flower beds where the purple foxgloves grew tall and pretty.

"Daisy, no," Delphia cried, jumping to her feet. "She could eat the foxgloves. Someone needs to stop her."

"What's all the fuss over foxgloves?" Lena asked no one in particular.

"They're poison to pigs," I said.

"Why would she eat them, then?" Lena asked.

"She loves all flowers," Mama said. "She's ruined more than one of our beds over the years. That pig is a menace."

"Aren't we supposed to eat pigs?" Lena said. "Why is he running around like a dog?"

"Daisy's a she," I said, irrationally enraged by her lack of pig knowledge. "And a mama. We don't eat mama pigs."

"Good Lord, what a sight," Mr. Masters said. "She's enormous. What does she eat besides flowers?"

No one answered him. We were too busy worrying about what to do about Daisy. She hadn't seemed to notice the foxgloves, sniffing around near the dahlias instead.

"She's tearing up the flower bed," Mama said. "Alexander, what should we do?"

Papa was standing by then, looking greatly amused.

"We have to save her." Delphia looked to Cym, who nodded, as if it were perfectly normal for a flower-loving pig to interrupt the soup course.

Delphia darted toward the door, with Cym following closely behind. They loved Daisy, troublemaker though she be. This was not the first time she'd somehow burrowed her way out of her pen on a summer evening looking for a treat.

Before they were out of the dining room, the new gardener, Jesse, appeared in the window frame, running fast toward Daisy.

"The gardener's got him," Papa said to my sisters. "No reason to ruin your dresses." He pointed toward the window.

Mama exclaimed at the sight of Jesse. "What in the devil?" she asked, her eyes wide.

It was not the attempt to save Daisy that caused Mama's alarm but rather his lack of attire. Jesse wore no shirt at all this evening and was dressed only in a pair of dungarees with suspenders hanging down his backside. The copious, robust muscles in his shoulders and chest rippled to grand effect.

Just as Daisy was making her way toward a particularly juicy-looking foxglove, Jesse flew through the air, wrestling the unsuspecting pig to the ground. They rolled around like boys in a schoolyard for a moment, before Jesse rose to his feet and reached into the pocket of his pants, pulling out a peach.

"Daisy loves peaches," I said under my breath. "That should do the trick."

I was right. Daisy seemed to have forgotten completely about the foxgloves and was now snorting her way toward Jesse, who was backing up slowly.

"Who is that?" Lena asked.

I glanced at her. What tone was that? Admiration? My goodness, it was. And the way she was looking at him! As if she would like to eat the peach in his hand and lick the juice from his skin. How could she when James was sitting right next to her? This woman was very tacky. No manners at all. No wonder she wanted James's pedigree. She needed Jasper to give her some lessons on etiquette.

"Our new gardener," Papa said. "What's his name, darling?"

"Jesse," Mama said. "We hired him in the last week or so."

"Why does he wear no clothes?" Fiona asked.

"He usually has clothes on," Mama said drily. "Perhaps he was in the bath and grabbed his pants?"

His hair *was* damp. Instead of a bath, I guessed he'd been down at the creek taking a swim. Who could blame him in this heat?

Delphia and Cym rushed from the doorway to stand by the window. "Good girl, Daisy," Cym called out, as if the naughty pig could hear her through the glass.

"She's a lot of things," Mama said. "But good isn't one of them."

"Poor old Daisy," Viktor said, laughing. "But look how good

she is now." Daisy was now obediently following Jesse toward the barn. He dangled the peach at his side, which explained the obedience.

James, who hadn't yet spoken, joined him in laughter. "You'd never get this kind of entertainment in New York City."

"I would have to agree," Mr. Masters said. "This is the most unusual dinner I've ever attended. Well done, Daisy."

13

JAMES

AFTER THE PIG INCIDENT, DINNER WAS CONSIDERABLY LESS EXCITING. Stories were told around the table of other escapades of Daisy the pig. The old girl got around between her litters of babies. I'd have enjoyed the evening immensely if it hadn't been for the sorrowful look in Addie's eyes. I was a terrible person. Not only had I betrayed Lena but I'd hurt Addie. I couldn't forgive myself for either of my actions.

Later, Lena asked me to take her around the property. Mr. Masters, apparently oblivious to the situation, suggested that Addie and Delphia accompany us. "We don't want you two lovebirds getting into trouble alone," he said.

Delphia raised an eyebrow and asked wickedly, "You mean if they ran into a bear?"

"Not exactly," Mr. Masters said, sounding alarmed. "Should we be worried about that?"

"Only wayward pigs," Delphia said. "Tonight anyway."

A few minutes later, the four of us walked out toward the barn. Lena was on my arm but the sisters walked a few feet ahead, shoulders occasionally rubbing. They were not pleased to accompany us but knew it was impossible to decline. Alexander, who had looked worn out from entertaining Lena's father, had seemed inclined toward bed. However, Mr. Masters would want his after-dinner drink beforehand. I hoped, for Alexander's sake, that the evening would not go too late.

As hot as the afternoon had been, tonight was glorious. Temperatures had dropped, and the sky was the deep purple of twilight. I'd taken off my jacket and felt comfortable in my shirt-sleeves.

"It's a different life out here, isn't it?" Lena asked in a pensive tone.

I glanced at her. She seemed different tonight than she had when she first arrived. Calmer and less inclined toward putting on airs. Maybe the mountain air was having an effect on her. Stranger things had happened, I supposed. "Yes, it's quiet. No one to worry about."

"What do you mean?"

"What people think, I guess. People don't care about society and all that here."

"It would be terribly boring, wouldn't it? No one to show my pretty things to?"

"Is that what you like about it?" I asked. "Being the center of attention?"

"I do enjoy it, yes. I can't imagine any other life. Here, for instance—what would I do all day and night?" She squeezed my arm tighter. "You would never want to move here, would you?"

I gazed up ahead to make sure the ladies couldn't hear us. "I'd have liked to, once upon a time."

"But what about your work?"

Crickets chirped in accompaniment to our shoes on the gravel. A rustle in the long grass that ran along the horse pen rustled. Some kind of creature. Probably one of the rabbits I'd seen scurrying around. The reasons for fenced gardens, Quinn had told me. Deer and rabbits didn't care about Lizzie's needs in the kitchen. They ate whatever they could get.

"James?" Lena asked, prompting me to answer her question.

"I don't know what I want anymore," I said. "All of it seems far away when I'm here."

"But what would you do? Isn't publishing what you love?"

"Yes, I suppose I do. It's lost some of the luster for me. Perhaps because I've had some successes. Maybe it's enough. I don't know."

"You sound like a lost little boy," Lena said softly. "Father won't like it."

"Your father is getting what he wants. He can't control my thoughts."

"Father will control all of us before this is all over."

We came upon the barn. A light hung over the side door. Delphia and Addie had already gone inside, probably to check on Daisy.

"It smells awful out here." Lena plugged her nose.

"That's the smell of the horses and other animals. I love it." The smell was nostalgic to me. It meant I was with the Barnes family and could let go of the burdens that weighed me down for a few weeks of the year.

"If you don't like it, you can go back to the house," Delphia said.

Lena let go of her nose and lifted her chin. "I shall stay with my fiancé."

Several chickens plucked at the floorboards looking for grain and bugs. Others sat in their roosting nests and gave us wary glances with one eye and then the other. At the other end of the bar, Daisy, safely back in her stall, was fast asleep. Apparently, her escapade had worn her out.

"She's going to have a litter of babies," Delphia said. "If we can keep her from poisoning herself."

Lena leaned over the top of the pen to get a better look. "Is it always so disgusting in there?"

"There's nothing disgusting about it," Delphia said. "Did you know pigs are actually quite clean animals?"

A movement on the other side of the barn drew me away

from inspecting Daisy. From the shadows came the young man from earlier. He was now wearing a shirt, I noted. Thankfully.

"Hello, Jesse," Addie said. "Can we help you?" Her tone was cooler than I'd ever heard it. She didn't like him. Why?

"What brings you out to the barn, Miss Barnes and Miss Barnes?" Jesse asked. He had one of those mouths that lifted more on one side than the other. Unfortunately, his crooked smile did not detract from his good looks. He'd not ceased looking at Delphia, virtually ignoring the rest of us. I should probably warn Alexander there was a predator in the henhouse, so to speak.

I'd keep an eye out myself. If he went near her, he would have to answer to me as well as the other men in this family.

"This is James West," Delphia said. "And his…friend, Miss Lena Masters."

"How do you do?" Jesse nodded in our direction.

Lena stepped forward. "My father and I are visiting from New York City. Have you ever heard of it?"

"I'm an American, Miss Masters. I've heard of New York City. The state, too." Jesse adjusted his newsboy hat over his now-dry hair. He had a thick Southern drawl. Maybe Georgia? "You ever heard of Atlanta?"

"Of course," Lena said in her haughtiest of tones. "I had geography in school. The scene for many a battle during the Civil War, if I recall?"

"Yes, Miss Masters. You Yankees know all about that, I'd bet."

"I'm well educated, so yes." Lena scrutinized him through narrow eyes. She'd taken a dislike to him almost immediately, maybe because of his accent. I'd heard her comment to her friends that the young women all sounded "dull and dumb" in the South. "What brings you out to the Wild West?"

He lifted an indolent shoulder. "Can't say that's any of your business, Miss Masters."

Lena's mouth opened and then shut, then opened again.

"Why not? Aren't you the gardener? Don't you have to answer a question if a guest asks you?"

"I don't recall that in the instructions." Jesse met her gaze, obviously unruffled by Lena or her arrogance, then looked over at Addie and Delphia. "Miss Barnes, is that part of my duties?" He grinned. This man was unafraid of losing his position. Good for him, I thought. At least one person in this barn was in charge of their own destiny.

Lena huffed, anger emanating from her in waves of heat. I could feel it just standing next to her.

"I'm not aware of what you and Mama talked about," Addie said, firmly. "But we treat all guests as well as staff with respect."

"Yes, Miss Barnes." Jesse picked a piece of hay from his shirt. "I guess I better know my place from now on. I meant no harm."

"We treat you with respect and expect the same from you," Delphia said. "It's not hard to understand."

"You got it." One side of his mouth twitched, not in amusement, I didn't think, but malice. I resisted the shiver that wanted to run up my spine.

Delphia, who should have been looking either scared or angry, had an entirely different look to her. Calculating, perhaps? As if his presence had prompted a thought. *Please don't let it be attraction,* I thought. This was not the man for Delphia.

Lena squeezed my upper arm with such strength I actually winced from pain. "I should like to return to the house now, thank you very much."

Jesse took off his cap and nodded toward us. "Pleasure to meet you, Mr. West, Miss Masters."

"You as well," I said. "Good luck with your work here."

"Thank you kindly," Jesse said.

All the way back to the house, Lena was quiet. This was unusual. I could safely say that during the time I'd spent in her company, none of it had been silent.

When we reached the steps to the back porch, Lena stopped and turned toward the barn, now hidden by trees. "He's the most arrogant, ridiculous man I've ever met. I shall talk to Father and have him suggest to Lord Barnes that they get rid of him at once."

"Lena, please don't. This isn't your concern. Mrs. Barnes runs the house and garden as she wishes."

"Does she know how insubordinate he is?" Her eyes caught the light shed from the porch. "How rude? Is it safe for either Addie or Delphia to be alone with him?"

"They can hold their own. Plus, they look out for each other. Always."

"It must be nice to have someone love you that much. Sometimes I wonder if my mother had lived if she would have loved me like Mrs. Barnes loves her girls?" She sighed and turned back toward me. The sadness in her voice surprised me. Was she lonely despite all her friends?

"You have a lot of friends." I hesitated, suddenly wishing to make her feel better, to feel loved. I should love her. If we were to have a marriage, I must learn to love her. I must look after her. Was it only my attitude keeping me from doing so? "And you have me."

"I have a lot of acquaintances who would drop me if we were to become suddenly poor or if there was scandal of some kind. As far as you, do I, James? Do I really have you? Or is your heart here with the Barnes sisters?"

One sister, I thought. Such a traitorous fool I was, even to myself. Hadn't I just promised myself I would give Lena a chance? "I love the entire Barnes family like they're my own. You've known that."

"Yes, which is why I've come all this way to meet them. I wish they liked me better."

"Give it a little time," I said. "They're not used to people like you, that's all."

"People like me? What does that mean?"

I chose my words carefully, not wanting a quarrel. "You're a city girl and they're from the country—indeed, from this wild country. You can hardly expect them to care about the same things you do."

"How diplomatic of you, darling." Her voice returned to normal, full of self-confidence that bordered on arrogance. Underneath that was a motherless girl, I reminded myself. A girl with a father who cared only for money and power, certainly over love.

"You asked me earlier what I wanted," I said. "What about you, Lena? Do you know?"

"I want Father to be happy and pleased with me." She was quiet for a few seconds. "And I want someone to love me with their whole heart. I've hoped that would be you but here, with these people, I'm starting to think that isn't true."

"Is this what you want? I've never asked you that," I said.

"I want to please Father. And because he wants me to marry you, I shall, and I'll be happy. You're a wonderful man. I know that to be true, even if I don't know you well."

"I'll try to be happy, too," I said.

She squeezed my hands. "You may kiss me, if you like."

I should kiss her. We were going to marry. Soon, she would be in my bed every night. I was a young man. This was something I should want, in fact, look forward to, yet the idea left me cold. Regardless, I leaned closer and kissed her gently on the mouth. She wrapped her arms around my neck and kissed me back. An experienced kisser, I thought. Not like Addie had been —soft and unsure yet teeming with passion. No, this was not like kissing Addie at all. I likened this to kissing a pretty doll. A man would expect to find pleasure in the company of such a beautiful woman instead of likening her to a cold and porcelain toy. There was nothing wrong with her. It was me.

I loved Addie.

Why? Why did it have to be Addie I loved instead of this woman standing in my arms? It was when I disengaged from her and looked behind us that I realized we were not alone. Delphia and Addie, clutched together as if they were in a windstorm, stared at us. They had obviously just come from around the corner of the house, perhaps thinking of taking in the night air before retiring. Addie's eyes were wide and horrified. The way mine would have been had it been her kissing another man.

I jumped away from Lena as if she were on fire.

"That bad, darling?" Lena asked.

"No, of course not," I said under my breath. "We have company." I gestured with my chin toward Delphia and Addie, who were now backing away, the shadows of the night eating them up, taking them from me. In the next second, they were gone.

I sat on the steps, hard enough that I winced as my backside thunked against the hard wood.

"I know why you're marrying me. I may be spoiled, but I'm not an idiot."

"I don't understand why you want this," I said. "You could have anyone. Maybe someone who you loved."

"I'm sorry you love someone else and not me." Lena encircled a post with one arm.

"It's not what you think. I'm helping her with her manuscript, that's all."

"Don't start our life together lying to me, James."

"I didn't want it to happen," I said. "It was so unexpected."

"I figured as much. Don't look so sad. How could I expect you to love me? You hardly know me. Anyway, I've lived my entire life in a house without love. Why not continue that into my adulthood?" A sad smile played at her mouth. "Maybe in time, you'll learn to love me. We can still have a good life. A family. Children. We can be the missing piece for the other, James, if we can fall in love just a little."

"Missing piece?"

"The love we seek. The love we never received from our fathers. That's what this is about, isn't it? When one really examines it closely? There are worse reasons to marry than to prove our worth to our fathers." She glanced away from me, biting her bottom lip. "Father told me if I don't do this, he's tossing me out onto the street."

My mouth fell open. "Are you serious?"

"I'm afraid so. He wants this, and I am powerless." She sat next to me and rested her head against my shoulder. Her complexion mimicked the color of the moon that had come to rest above the line of aspens in the distance. "Once Father decides something, there's no turning back. Pleasing Father is what I want most in life. It's my only ambition. The only one afforded to me. I have no one else."

I stewed in that for a moment. Was it true? Was she as much at the mercy of our fathers as I?

"So we must make the most of…whatever this is between us?" I asked.

"We can be a comfort to each other," Lena said. "It doesn't have to be terrible."

"Maybe we can fall in love eventually?"

"Perhaps. People like you and me, the son and daughter of reckless men, are at their mercy. The sooner we both accept that, the happier we'll be."

We sat in silence. A cricket started up singing, then abruptly stopped. An owl hooted somewhere in the forest.

"You're right, we should go home to New York City," Lena said. "Get out of here."

"Yes, we should." I sighed, letting my shoulders droop. Would the torture stop if I were away from Addie? Was it possible that I'd ever stop thinking about her? "I'm tired. May I walk you to your room now?"

"Yes, you may. We must be quiet walking up the stairs. I don't want Father to know we've been out here alone."

A twig snapped from somewhere in the yard. A deer or rabbit, most likely. How I wished to be that free. To roam the moonlit garden with no one's destiny but my own to worry about. Instead, I stood and held out my hand to my fiancée and led her into the house.

14

ADDIE

THE MORNING AFTER I SAW JAMES KISSING LENA, I WOKE BLEARY-eyed and sadder than I'd ever been in my life. Delphia, who had held me as I wept, didn't stir as I quietly got out of bed. In the bathroom, I washed and dressed in a casual day dress. The house was quiet, but our rooster was doing his best to wake the entire household. When I went downstairs, no one was about, other than the noise of the staff in the kitchen below. I needed to work, I thought. Distracting work that would take my mind off my troubles.

One of the maids had already set a pot of coffee in the dining room. I helped myself to a cup and went into the sitting room to the desk and typewriter. Instead of writing, I simply stared at a blank page. My eyes were too foggy to read James's notes in the margins. A tear rolled down my cheek and landed on the ink, blurring it further. How could I go on? Not like this.

Perhaps I should go away? Do something with my life, other than pine away for James the rest of my days. Should I revisit the idea of university? Perhaps I could study literature and work on becoming a stronger writer. I looked around the sitting room at the hundreds of books that lined the shelves. Books were here. I could read anything I wanted.

I gave up on working and took my cup of coffee over to sit in an easy chair that faced the front of the house. Sunlight flooded the front yard. Bunnies and birds scurried about looking for their breakfast. I breathed in the delicious aroma of coffee, then took a sip. The coffee was hot and perfectly bitter. Delphia preferred hers with loads of sugar and cream, but I liked it this way. After the cup was empty, I set it aside and closed my eyes, listening to the sounds of my family and our guests beginning to wake. The maids were up and down the stairs, serving coffee and breakfast to whoever wanted to eat in their rooms.

A sound in the doorway made me jump. It was Mama, fully dressed and looking as fresh as the morning dew. "Addie, what're you doing up so early?"

"I couldn't sleep."

She came to stand next to me, drawing my face upward with the tips of her cool fingers. "You've been crying?"

"Yes, I have. Feeling very sorry for myself. Imagining living like Emily Dickinson."

She chuckled as she took the chair next to me. "I hate to see a daughter of mine weep when the Lord has brought such a wondrous day as this."

I nodded as tears came, burning the insides of my eyelids. "Oh, Mama. I don't know what to do with myself."

"Dearest Addie." Mama's face crumpled as she took in my pathetic countenance. "It must be so hard to see them together."

"That's just it. He doesn't love her. He loves me."

She jerked back. "What?"

"Yes, he's told me as much."

Mama didn't say anything for a moment. "Dear, good James, taking the burden of it all upon himself even though he loves you." She looked at me, sharp this time. "And you're absolutely certain he feels the same way about you?"

"Yes, I'm sure. But I can't make him choose between me and them. Not that he would anyway. He's too loyal, Mama. His mother and sister need him. They've done nothing to deserve all of this."

Mama had paled. Her hands trembled slightly as she tented them into a prayer-like gesture. She rose to her feet and went to one of the bookshelves as if to choose something to read but then turned and came back to me. "There must be something we can do."

"There isn't, Mama. We can't simply take what we want with no thought of the consequences. You and Papa have taught me that. For that matter, the whole reason you came here was to save your mother and sister. It was a great sacrifice, and yet you didn't hesitate."

"I didn't have a choice."

"Neither does James," I said. "No matter what James chooses, someone gets hurt."

"I wish it didn't have to be either of you," Mama said. "I wonder what Lena feels about all of this?"

"I caught them kissing last night." I swallowed the bile that rose up from my empty stomach. I'd not been able to get the scene out of my head. All night long it had played before me.

"Oh, my darling girl. I'm sorry." She placed a hand on my cheek. "You poor, poor girl."

After a moment, I withdrew from her to look out the window. The sun filtered through the thicket of trees, a golden and hopeful peach gossamer blanket. "I can't stand it—seeing the two of them together. Not after what we've shared." The kiss we shared. I kept that to myself, knowing Mama would not be pleased. I flushed just thinking of how my whole world had expanded in those stolen moments between us. I'd not known before what it meant to feel passion. No wonder all of my siblings had gone to whatever length they needed to ensure their love would last. Even Cym, who my mother had said was the most practical of all of us, had succumbed.

"Has he kissed you?" Mama asked.

I dipped my head. I'd never lied to my mother in my life, but what could I say that didn't make James sound like a cad? Cheating on his fiancée? "If I tell you the truth, you mustn't think poorly of him. I practically begged him to kiss me."

She let her forehead drift to her hands. "Addie, of all my children, I'd not have thought it was you who would behave scandalously."

"I know, Mama. I'm sorry." I looked up at her, fighting more pesky tears. "Please forgive me. I know it's only an excuse, but have you ever wanted something so desperately that all sensible thought flew from your mind? All I wanted was the chance to know what it would be like to kiss him. Only the one time. One kiss to last the rest of my life."

She was quiet for so long that I thought I'd truly angered her. I braced myself for the tongue-lashing I deserved. Instead, when she raised her gaze to look at me, a light in her eyes told a different story. The fire I saw in them reminded me of Cymbeline. "You must fight, Addie. You must fight for the man you want."

"Fight? Mama, how could I possibly? Think of his family."

"They'll find a way on their own. It's not for him to fix. Children should not be asked to do so. It's our job to take care of you, not the other way around."

"What about Lena?"

"People like Lena and her father do not need our concern. They always find a way to rise to the top, no matter who they trample on the way up.""

"They do?" I stared at her, desperate for her to be right.

"Since the beginning of time, my love." She placed both hands on my knees and looked me in the eyes. "You must not run from your destiny. If you and James are in love, then you must find a way to make it work."

"Regardless of who we hurt?"

"I believe that if it's meant to be, then choosing love always makes everything and everyone else fall into the places they belong as well. Lena and her father will be fine. That's obvious.

As far as James's family goes, they will have to adjust to a new kind of life. If his mother and sister would like to move to America, we will take care of them. The father and his sins will have to be dealt with on his own. I won't have a man in my house who gambled away the life of his wife and children."

"You'd do that? What would Papa think?"

"My darling, since the moment you were born, your father has wanted only for you to be happy. He would do anything in his power to make it so, including offering a home to our new in-laws."

"I don't know what to say."

"Talk to James. I'll speak to your papa. If you and James decide that you'd like our help, then come to us. We'll work something out. But James will have to decide on his own whether he can go against his father's wishes. It is not an easy thing to do, especially for a man like James."

I nodded, knowing it was true. But for the first time since I'd learned of James's engagement, I felt a glimmer of hope. Would he choose me? Would he choose love or duty? All my life I'd thought they were the same things, but now I could see that without love there could be no sustainable duty. One could not be dutiful only for the sake of virtue. A man could not behave as James's father had and expect that the world would then adjust to his sins, including his own children.

I COULDN'T FIND James all that morning. By the afternoon, I'd learned that he had gone into town to see Theo about a pain behind his right eye. He'd not mentioned this to me. Was it only the tension of the last days that had caused it, or was he ill? *Please, God, not that. Not after everything.*

After lunch, Papa called me into his study. I could see by the look in his eyes that Mama had already spoken to him.

"Addie, love, come sit with me."

The study was dark and cool. Shades were drawn by this time on a summer afternoon to keep the heat out. I sat in one of the armchairs and waited for him to join me.

"Your mother has told me of your predicament," Papa said. "I'd like to hear from you, though, before I talk to James." He peered at me. In this dim light, he looked young except for the strands of silver that had taken over the glossy brown locks of yesteryear.

"What would you like to know?" I asked.

"I'd like to know what you're prepared to give up for the people you love."

This had not been what I'd expected him to say. I wasn't sure what the right answer was, but I blurted out the first thing that came to mind. "I'm prepared to give my life, I suppose." I thought of my sisters and Mama. If it came to that, I'd gladly take whatever hardship if it meant they would not suffer. "If one of my sisters needed me, I would walk to the ends of the earth to find them."

"I hope we never have to test if that is true," Papa said.

His eyes were so somber that I trembled in nervousness. I'd not seen him this way before, at least not in my presence. My sisters had told me of his dismay and anger when he learned of Flynn's illegal activities back during Prohibition. "Have I done something wrong?" I asked.

His brow creased, but his eyes softened. "No, not at all. You've fallen in love. It so happens he couldn't be a more difficult choice. If we could control our hearts, then we would."

"I'm sorry, Papa. I tried not to love him. For years now, I've pushed it all away until I saw him again and then all the feelings would come crashing around me. I couldn't avoid it, as much as I wished it could be anyone else. I've tried to stay away from him and resist this temptation."

"That didn't work too well, I take it?"

"No, Papa. It most certainly didn't." I smiled despite my consternation, remembering the long, happy days we'd spent together. "We had the most glorious summer together until Lena came here. We could no longer escape the truth of our situation. I had to accept that he would not be mine. He'd never been mine. I've tried with all my might to accept it as it is. To take comfort in knowing that it is me he loves, even if we cannot be together. Still, it's a bitter, bitter pill. As you say, the heart cannot always be counted upon to obey our commands."

"Your mother wants to offer a place here for his mother and sister. Is that what you want?" Papa asked.

"I want James, no matter what it takes."

"All right, then, we'll see what can be done." Papa held out his arms, and I went into them just as I had as a child when I'd thought he could fix anything. Maybe he still could?

15

JAMES

At his office, Theo walked me out to the lobby. He'd given me an exam but found nothing amiss, diagnosing the pain behind my eye as simply a response to stress.

"Get some rest," Theo said. "And take this with some water. Should relieve the pain away pretty quickly." He handed me a small paper bag with powder in it. He cocked his head, seeming to size me up in a different way than he had in the examination room. Although he and Flynn were identical twins, now that I knew them I could easily tell them apart. Theo was scholarly and austere. He wore wire-rimmed glasses, and his white coat made him seem very doctorly indeed. On the other hand, Flynn had the look of a man who spent a lot of time outdoors, strong and windblown.

"Thanks, Theo," I said. "When I woke up this morning I thought I might be dying."

"What's going on out there at the house anyway?" He pushed his glasses further up his nose and peered at me. "You look like a man who hasn't slept for a week."

"I've not been sleeping too well. I have a lot on my mind. The wedding. Lena's father. Demands from my father." Such simple words to describe such a troubling and complex dilemma.

"You have a lot to contend with, no doubt," Theo said. "Women planning weddings can take a lot out of a man." He gave me a reassuring smile, oblivious to my inner turmoil. "Soon enough, all that will be over and you'll get to the good part." He clapped a hand on my shoulder. "You're a good man, West. I wish you could be part of our family forever, but once you marry, Lena's family will be yours, too."

"There's only her father. I wonder, sometimes, what Lena would be like if her mother were still living. She died when Lena was an infant. Raised by a cold man…" I trailed off. Why was I still talking? Theo didn't need to know all this. "My point is, Lena can be a handful."

"Yes, I understand. Without a mother, Lena's missed the love and nurturing she needed. That will appear in your marriage from time to time. No way around it. Our wounds from childhood remain, unfortunately. You'll have to love her unconditionally and support her, even if at times she may overwhelm you."

"Is that how your marriage is?" If so, this surprised me. He and Louisa always appeared as close as two people could be. In addition to raising two children together, she was part of his medical practice, delivering most of the babies born in this community as a midwife who had trained while assisting her husband.

"Louisa experienced a lot of trauma as a child. It haunts her at times. When it does, I'm there to love her."

Didn't Lena deserve to be loved this way? What kind of man was I to deny her? If only it were as simple as willing myself to love her instead of Addie.

DRIVING HOME in one of the Barnes cars, with the piercing pain still behind my right eye, I winced against the sunlight. I got out of the car. Delphia sat on the wooden swing, the tips of her toes in the grass rocking to and fro. I lifted my hand in greeting.

She jumped down from her perch and came charging toward me.

"James West, we're going to have a little talk."

I sighed. The other eye began to ache. "I know what you're going to say." I held up my hands in defense.

"Listen to me. My sister loves you and yet you're too foolish to make this right. You kissed her, James. And then she saw you kissing Lena. She's broken. You've broken my sister."

I hung my head. Shame inundated me. I'd handled all of this so poorly. "You're right. About everything. I got wrapped up in the little world Addie and I made together this summer. It was wrong because I wasn't free. I knew I wasn't."

She let out a puff of air. When she spoke next, her voice softened. "To be fair, Addie knew your situation as well. She's as much to blame as you. But, James, what are you doing? You can't marry that little fox. It's all wrong."

I leaned against the side of the car and pulled my hat further down to cut some of the glare of the relentless sun. "Delphia, I'm sorry I've hurt Addie. You can't imagine how much. But I have responsibilities." To my alarm, tears flooded my vision, and my voice cracked. "I've made promises to them all."

"Oh, goodness. Don't cry. I can't stand it." Delphia placed her hand on the sleeve of my jacket. "I'm going to fix this."

I couldn't help but chuckle as I wiped my eyes. "You can't just will things to happen."

"I know. However, actions speak louder than words." With that, she trounced off, skirts swinging side to side.

I ripped off my hat and swept a hand through my hair, overwhelmed with the complexities of my life. If only Delphia were right and she could fix it all. Alas, I knew this was not the way of the world. Those of us without power remained thus. Single women and men with no fortunes were among the most powerless.

I WAS WALKING past the study when I heard Alexander's voice calling to me.

"James, is that you?"

I poked my head around the door. Alexander was at his desk in the dark-paneled room. Two chairs, where he and his wife often sat in the evenings, were perched in front of the fireplace. Because of the heat of the afternoon, it remained unlit. Windows on either side of the hearth allowed the afternoon light in, giving the room a golden tinge. Remnants of Alexander's pipe smoke lingered near the ceiling and reminded me of cherries. "What can I do for you, sir?"

"Come in, if you can. I'm about to have a whiskey. Would you care for one? Or a brandy?"

"Whiskey's fine, thank you."

He gestured for me to sit in Quinn's usual chair. A slight indentation in the cushion hinted at the slender form of its usual occupant. "Where is everyone? It's so quiet."

"My wife's taking a nap before dinner. She's been working tirelessly over at the church soup kitchen. We've too many unemployed, James. It breaks my heart to see it in my town, but I'm unable to think of what to do to save them. The women in my family seem to be better at that than I." He went to the door of his study and shut it firmly.

"Fiona mentioned the mill closed." It was not only my family suffering in these times. I must remember this when I filled with self-pity. However, my father's gambling had brought them to the brink of poverty long before the depression began. He had no one to blame but himself. Whereas the hardworking men at the mill were struggling through no fault of their own. They'd been able to feed their families because of their toils. Now? They were like me, at the mercy of others.

"Yes, for now. I hope it'll return once this damned depression is over. Whenever that will be." He handed me a tumbler of whiskey and sat. The chair groaned under the weight of its tall occupant. "It's been a struggle for me to see what's happened to residents in my own town and have no way to help them, other than to sponsor the food kitchen at the church. Not enough, mind you. I should be doing more by opening some kind of business that employs those no longer at the mill. But what would it be? I've prided myself on providing opportunities for anyone who wished to live here. I am no longer able to do so."

"You will again. Once the world economy returns to robustness." I said the words but didn't really know if they were true.

"James, may I speak frankly?" Alexander turned slightly to get a better look at me.

"Of course, sir." I braced myself for what was coming. He knew. The whole family knew.

"I think of you as one of our family. All the summers you've spent here with us—the friendship you share with Fiona—well, that makes you one of us."

"Thank you, sir. I think of you all as family, too."

"It seems to me you're making a great sacrifice for your father. One that no man should expect from his son."

I looked into the fireplace, noticing for the first time the tile behind the grate—patterns of swirling blue against a white background. "I don't know what else to do."

Alexander glanced toward the doorway, as if he expected an intrusion, and lowered his voice. "James, are you in love with Addie?"

I downed the rest of my whiskey and rested the back of my head against the chair, looking up at the ceiling. A polished wooden beam made of walnut ran down the center. Alexander had spared no expense when he built this home. Each decision made with care. "I'm afraid so. More than I thought possible." My gaze traveled over the knots and growth rings. Like this family, I thought. Intertwined for eternity. I wanted to be a part of their family tree.

"I've had more fun with her than I ever have," I said when Alexander remained quiet. "The truth is—she's become my entire world. She's all I think about. All I want. Spending time with her feels like home." I turned to look at him, inwardly wincing and expecting to see anger coming from him. Instead, his eyes were soft and compassionate.

"Son, that's when you know she's the one you should grab hold of and never let go. When I fell in love with Addie's mother, I fought it, too. She was much younger than I and had her whole life ahead of her. I had my children and all the complexities that come with them. Even worse, they'd fallen for her, too. I thought I might have set us all up for broken hearts. Instead, she loved me back and we formed a partnership. One that's lasted for two decades and going strong. All that to say, despite my doubts, I would have done anything to make her mine. Fortunately, I didn't need to make sacrifices in order to have her. Your situation is different in that way. I know it's not an easy choice, the one you must make between the woman you love and your family."

"I've not wanted to fall, sir, but it's proven impossible not to. There's something about her that I find irresistible." Recalling our kiss, I blushed, half expecting a lightning bolt to rip through the ceiling. "She's…we have a lot in common. She's everything, sir. Everything to me." How could I describe this growing sense of her living within me, as vital as the blood that pumped through my veins? "But what do I do? If I let myself have her—I wreck the lives of so many."

"You must decide what you're willing to give up and who you're willing to hurt to get what you want," Alexander said, not unkindly but with the slightest edge in his tone. This was his daughter he was talking about, after all. "What it is you want from this life. Who you want by your side through the good and bad times. And what you're willing to give up to get it."

"Yes, sir." I clasped one hand over my knee, squeezing the skin under my pants.

Alexander's brows knitted together. A streak of silver in his hair caught the light. "Has Fiona ever mentioned her real mother?"

"Not often. She thinks of Quinn as her mother."

"She was very young when Quinn came to us. Only three. Her mother, my wife Ida, died when she was an infant."

I nodded. Fiona had told me the tragic story of her mentally ill mother. She'd perished in a snowdrift, having wandered out of the house in the middle of the night. "Yes, I remember."

"I loved Ida, but she was troubled. Because of the children, I have no regrets, of course. I'd do it all over again to have them. However, she made my life miserable while she was alive and then left me with five children to raise alone. I don't know what would have happened to us if Quinn had not arrived in our lives. I don't want you to suffer the same fate. It's not too late to back out and choose another path."

"I can't. Not without hurting my family."

"Your father made his choices. As hard as that is to understand, that's what they were, choices. Albeit reckless ones."

I stifled a bitter laugh. A hummingbird came to the window and hovered for a moment before flying off in search of nectar.

"Let me ask you this again," Alexander said. "What are you prepared to give up for the people you love?"

"I'm giving up Addie. It's killing me, but it's what I have to do." This was about my family. Saving them. Wasn't it? "I don't know if I can live with the guilt of passing up the opportunity to keep my family from poverty. My mother—she deserved better—deserves better—than being reduced to living with distant relatives. And that would be a good scenario. The truth is, there is no one. Where would they even go?"

Alexander's voice rose. "A man should not ask it of his son." He splayed his hands over his thighs and leaned forward slightly. "I can't stay silent any longer. I'm going to say this bluntly, so forgive me. You must not go through with this. If you love Addie, then make this right between you."

"All my life I've been trying to please my father. This is the only thing I've ever been able to do that will make him look favorably upon me. If I were to betray him, well, he's not a forgiving man. It would be the end of everything I've known."

"You'll have Addie. And us. The whole lot of us." One corner of his mouth twitched into a half smile.

"I'd have no work. No way to support Addie or help her with her writing aspirations."

"She can find her own way if that's necessary," Alexander said. "Your contacts in New York won't completely dry up, I assume?"

"No, sir. However, Mr. Masters will make sure I never work again. What about Addie's book? If she were associated with me, we could never find a publisher for it."

"There are ways around it," Alexander said. "Pen names and such. Isn't that right?"

Strangely enough, I'd not thought of that before now. He was right. No one would need to know it was her. "Yes, that's correct."

"I can't tell you what to do, but I can assure you that there is work here in Emerson Pass. Perhaps not the kind you assumed you'd have, but good work. You could teach at our school or work for me. Anything you want, here, is yours. Your mother and sister are welcome here, too. They could live here with us."

"Live here at the house?"

"Why not? We have room for them. Soon we'll have an empty nest of a home. What's two more when we have so much?"

I stared at him, stunned by his generosity and the absolute love he felt for his daughter. Inviting strangers into his home, purely for the sake of Addie. What would it feel like to have a father like that? I would never know, regardless of my decision.

"We could use a good English teacher," Alexander said. "Especially for the older children. They need to know how to write."

Could I really teach school here? Would I enjoy it as much as I did editing? Perhaps. I could make a difference in a community.

Would that be more relevant than editing books? I couldn't know for sure. But I would have Addie and the rest of the Barnes family. My mother and sister would have a place to come to.

"How do I do it?" I asked. "Tell him, that is. My father will not make this easy. I don't know if my mother would come here." She would send my sister, though. That I felt certain of. My mother would never want my sister to suffer because of her pride.

"Tell your father the truth," Alexander said. "You love someone else, and it's his mess to clean up anyway."

I stared back at him. "It makes me feel sick to my stomach."

"Think about walking out of here without Addie. How does that make you feel?"

"Like death."

"There's your answer." He was quiet for a moment, getting up to pour us both another small whiskey. When he returned to his seat, Alexander took a good look at me before setting my glass on the table between us. "One other thought. It occurred to me in the middle of the night that we should question the motives of Mr. Masters."

"Sir?"

"What's Masters getting out of this? Have you ever asked yourself that?"

"He wants my pedigree," I said.

"It has to be more than that for him to force his daughter to marry a man she doesn't love."

"Like what?"

"Scandal of some kind," Alexander said. "Has it occurred to you that you may be a decoy?"

"A decoy?"

"Ask Lena to tell you the truth about why they're rushing all this. There's more to it than you know, I can guarantee it."

For the second time, I stared at him. What did he mean exactly?

"Son, it's helpful to look at this from all angles. What, truly, are Masters and Lena getting from this?"

"Does it matter?"

"It might, depending on the truth. Ask her, James. That's all I'm saying."

I nodded, pretending to agree but feeling bewildered by this latest suggestion. What could possibly make Lena and her father want me, other than what they'd said?

16

ADDIE

I SPENT MOST OF THE DAY DOWNSTAIRS WITH LIZZIE. IT WAS MRS. Wu's day off and with the extra guests, she needed more help than usual. Craving a distraction, I was happy to help when Mama suggested it. My mother was one who figured the best way out of heartache was to get to work. Lizzie kept me busy through most of the afternoon. We worked side by side in the hot kitchen with Lizzie giving me instructions on what to do and when. I was able to turn my thoughts off and let my hands and body follow Lizzie's commands. Working with her gave me a sense of purpose, especially because I knew how much she missed her daughter. I missed Florence, too. We chatted and gossiped, just as we'd done when Florence still lived at home.

"She's got a beau," Lizzie said, referring to Florence. "He's studying to be a doctor. My Florence married to a doctor. I'd never have thought it possible."

"She'll make a good doctor's wife," I said. Florence was smart and very capable. For that matter, she would be good at anything she chose to do.

It was nearing teatime when Delphia came into the kitchen through the back door, wearing overalls and a mischievous look on her face. What was she up to? No good, most likely.

"May I borrow you, Addie?" Delphia asked. "I need help in the barn."

"Sure." I wiped my hands on my apron and then untied it. "What is it?"

"The chickens," Delphia said. "Their roosting boxes need cleaning out, and I'd like you to help."

I took a better look at her. Sure enough, there were several pieces of straw in her hair. "Isn't that Jesse's job?"

"He's busy." Delphia poured herself a glass of water from the pitcher Lizzie always had on the counter.

"Are you up to no good?" Lizzie asked, echoing my thoughts.

"Why do you two always think that?" Delphia asked, her voice rising upward in pitch.

"No reason," I said, winking at Lizzie before following my sister outside and up the stairs that led to the yard.

We walked in silence toward the barn. When I asked her how she'd gotten the task of the chicken coops, she put a finger to her mouth to shush me. "I don't feel like talking. I'm in a pensive mood."

A pensive mood? I laughed softly, grateful for the distraction from my problems. What had gotten into her? I didn't think any more about it because I noticed the car James had taken into town was back parked under the covered structure where Papa kept our cars. Was he home? Was he with Lena? Kissing her again? My stomach roiled at the thought. I hated her. I hated myself for loving James.

Delphia opened the door as if she were trying to sneak into the house late at night. I gave her a quizzical look but followed her through the doorway. My eyes took a moment to adjust in the dim barn from the bright sunlight outside. When the room came into focus, the first thing I noticed was that the chicken boxes looked tidy and freshly adorned with hay. What was it that Delphia needed me for? Irritated that she'd taken me away from assisting Lizzie, I turned toward her. She pointed upward.

Noises were coming from the hayloft. Human noises. Voices talking softly. Sighs. Murmurs of endearment? That's when I saw them through the slats of the hayloft. Lena and Jesse sat side by side, his hand cupping her cheek. For a second, my brain couldn't understand. But then I knew. They were having an intimate moment. Exactly how intimate, I couldn't be certain.

I brought my hand to my mouth to stifle a yelp of surprise. Too late. The noise came anyway.

Silence came from the hayloft. Straws of hay drifted downward through the slats. Then Lena's face appeared. Before I could react, Delphia yanked me toward the door and out into the bright sunlight.

Dizzy, I leaned against the wall of the barn. What was happening? Had Delphia known they were there? Of course she had. Why else would she have brought me out here? Or had she orchestrated the whole thing somehow? "What did you do?" I asked my sister, who was looking quite pleased with herself.

Delphia scowled. "What did I do? It's what Lena's done."

My suspicions were correct. She'd known they were there and had wanted me to see them. "What did you do?" I asked, repeating myself.

She tugged on my hand, pulling me away from the barn toward the house. "I simply put temptation in her path. A test. Jesse was a willing participant. As you've said a lot the last few weeks, money has power."

"You paid him?" I stared at her, aghast.

"Yes, although I got the feeling after I'd already suggested payment that he would have done it for free. Apparently, this is not their first clandestine visit."

Before I could answer, Lena came running out of the barn. Her hair was disheveled and her dress wrinkled. Mascara made dark smudges under her eyes and on her cheeks. Had she been crying? Or was that the result of whatever they'd been doing in the loft?

"Stop!" she yelled out to us. "Wait!"

We did so, lingering near the fence of the horse pasture. When she got closer, I could see streaks of tears in addition to the smeared makeup on her dusty face.

She breathed hard, stopping in front of us. "You can't tell anyone. Please, I'm begging you."

"Why, Lena? Why, when you have James? Why would you do such a thing?" I asked before I could stop myself.

A flash of impatience sparked in Lena's eyes. "For heaven's sake. You're such a child."

"I'm not," I said. "I'm a woman who would never compromise myself the way you have."

"You can't marry James now, can you?" Delphia asked, triumphantly. "You'll have to tell him you're no longer the marrying kind."

"Is that really what you want?" Lena asked. "For the man you both seem to care so much about to have his future and that of his family ruined?"

As much as I hated her, she was right. This did nothing but hurt James. Either way, he would be hurt.

"That's exactly what I want," Delphia said. "You and James don't love each other. You're making a mistake that will make you both miserable."

"It's not about us," Lena said, voice rising. "It's about our fathers. Don't you see? We may not have much in common, but we share the most important attribute of all. All our lives we've been trying to get our fathers to love us, to approve of just one thing we've done. That is something you two spoiled brats could never understand."

"Spoiled brats?" Delphia said through her teeth. "How dare you call us that." She shoved Lena.

I gasped. "Delphia."

Lena shoved her back.

Before I could fathom what was happening, they were rolling around in the grass, hands and arms flailing about as they tried to swipe at the other.

"Delphia!" I shouted. "Stop!"

Out of the corner of my eye, I saw James running toward us. The ladies were now in the dirt and gravel of the driveway still wrestling like baby bears.

"James, please do something before someone sees," I said.

"What's gotten into you?" James leaned down and grabbed Delphia by the waist, hauling her away from her opponent and setting her on the top rung of the fence.

I knelt to help Lena up, giving her my hand. "Are you hurt?" I asked.

"Just bruised probably." Lena sank onto the ground near the fence. Tufts of wild grass framed her face. "I'm sorry, James. I've made a mess of things."

"What are you talking about?" James looked at me. "Addie, what's happened?"

"It's not my place." A heaviness had overtaken me. My sister may have meant well, but she had no business interfering in this way. All of it had become so ugly. What had Lena been thinking? Jesse was not a good man. Why would she ruin everything with James? Her whole life had been unfolding in the most glorious way, and she'd sabotaged it.

I glanced at Delphia. She was staring at the ground, legs dangling over the fence. For a moment, I was taken back to our childhood. There had been more than a few times she'd gotten herself into scrapes and worn the same stubborn expression. However, she'd been young. A nearly grown woman should not be acting this way.

I gestured for her to follow me. James couldn't seem to figure out where to look, his gaze darting from one to the other of us, clearly baffled.

I approached, grabbed the sleeve of his jacket, and whispered in his ear. "I'm sorry, but it's not my place to explain any of this. Come find me later if you need to."

His eyes were full of questions, but I turned from him. He and Lena would have to decide what to do. It was between them. Whatever he decided, I would be there. *But not this way,* I thought. This was all wrong.

"Delphia, follow me, please."

"What if I don't want to?" Delphia asked, pouty.

"Now."

Delphia jumped off the fence, clearly unhappy with me and my stern tone. I didn't care at the moment. I wasn't happy with her, either.

I DIDN'T LOOK BACK to see what was happening between James and Lena. Instead, I marched Delphia toward our front door. When we were out of earshot, I turned to her. "What were you thinking?"

"I was thinking of you." She blew a lock of hair from her face with a puff of breath. What a sight she was. Dirt was smeared on her cheeks and forehead. Her hair was completely out of its pins and hung unruly around her head. "She's a snake, and I proved it. Now you and James can be happy together."

"What you've done is made everything worse." I dropped my face into my hands. "Poor James. What's he supposed to do now? Not marry her?"

"Yes, what other outcome could there be?" Her face wrinkled in agitation. "I thought you'd be happy."

"I want what's best for James. I am not what's best for him."

"I don't understand."

I let out a long sigh. "Sometimes I could just shake you. He feels he has to marry her, and now she's not only being forced upon him, he has to marry her knowing she was with another man in a very compromising position. It's embarrassing for everyone."

"But he won't marry her. Don't you see?"

"This changes nothing. Everyone will go on as if it didn't happen."

"You're wrong." She stalked away from me, headed toward the house. When she got there, Jasper yanked open the door. "What have you done, Miss Delphia?" He sounded annoyed and not at all amused by her humorous appearance. *Not the first time,* I thought. Delphia had been trying his patience for all sixteen years of her life.

Mama came running into the foyer. "Darling, what's happened to you? Are you all right?"

"She's not hurt." I rolled my eyes. "Unfortunately."

"I'm angry. Furious. At her." Delphia pointed an accusatory finger in my direction. "I was trying to help my sister and all I get is a scolding."

"I think you two better get upstairs," Mama said. "I'll be right behind you."

17

JAMES

WHEN ADDIE AND DELPHIA DISAPPEARED INTO THE HOUSE, I turned to a teary Lena. "What bloody happened? Tell me the truth. For once, just say what you mean. Why were you and Delphia fighting?" Even as I asked the question, I knew the answer. Delphia and Lena had been fighting about Addie and me. Tensions must have finally gotten out of control.

Lena started to cry, falling down into the soft grass and curling into a ball as if she were trying to climb into a shell. Rocking back and forth, she babbled incoherently through her sobs. I couldn't quite make it out but I thought it was something about the gardener. "It wasn't what it looked like."

"What wasn't?" Sweat trickled down my back. I watched Lena crying as if I were not really there but someplace up in the sky looking down on both of us. Shaking my head, I joined her on the ground and put my weight against the fence. The fall grass cushioned me in an embrace.

"I was with that Jesse in the loft and the girls came in and thought it was a liaison." She swiped at her dirty face.

"Was it?" I held my breath.

"No, it wasn't. You want the truth? It was Delphia. She set me up. Jesse told me Delphia paid him to ruin me. She wanted me to get caught. She wanted to make it so I couldn't marry you after lying with one of the staff. All for Addie. So she could have you instead of me. But it's not what happened. He listened to me, that's all. Tried to comfort me." Her dress was torn at the seam, exposing her thigh.

My head, as if I were a puppet with no control over my own body, fell to my hands. I swallowed, feeling as if I might vomit. This was all too complicated to comprehend. Delphia had done a wicked thing. In the name of love. That's how she would see it, anyway. Her sister wanted me, and Delphia wanted Addie to have what she wanted. Therefore all would be forgiven. Delphia did not understand fully how many people could be hurt by her actions. "What happened? Exactly," I asked, my throat dry. "Are you telling me the truth? Nothing happened between you and this Jesse?"

"I'm telling you the truth." She sobbed into her knees, her entire body shaking. "I walk around all the time feeling as if I'm weighed down by a boulder. No one can see me, James. No one ever sees me. No one cares what I want or what I think. My father only cares about money and reputations. He has everything planned out for me. He always has. But I can't please him. I'm never able to please him, and I'm so tired of trying. You won't believe it, but that boy in the barn actually listened to me."

"I see." I felt pity for her. I did. Because I did not love her, I could feel such things. If it had been Addie with another man, I would have wanted to murder him with my bare hands. Instead, I understood. I knew Lena longed for love and yet was being forced to marry me. Finally, with all these thoughts darting around in my mind, I lifted my gaze to meet her eyes. "Lena, what do you want? It's not me, is it?"

"No," she whispered. "I don't love you, and you don't love me. I've known that, but I went along with what Father wanted, as I always do."

"Look at us," I said. "Both trying our hardest to please cold men. Your father uses you for his own devices, as does mine."

Lena wiped her cheeks, smearing the dirt. "What else are we to do? There's no life for us otherwise. You can get another one. Me? I have nowhere to go. No one to turn to if my father decides to toss me away with the trash." She started to sob again. "I'm more trapped than you are."

I rubbed my eyes. "I won't have work if your father doesn't get what he wants from us. This changes nothing, really. Not if I want my father to—" I stopped myself before finishing the sentence.

"If you want your father to love you. Isn't that what you were about to say? Isn't that what this is all about for both of us?"

"There are practical reasons, too."

She sighed and scooted closer to me. The grass brushed up against her cheeks, but she didn't seem to notice. "I'm sorry, James. I'm sorry you can't love me. I'm sorry about forcing you into this. I'm sorry we ever came here." She started to cry again. "You love Addie. I know you do."

"I do. Desperately."

"Oh, James, you poor darling. This must be horrific for you. Forced to marry me and walk away from her. I can't have it. There has to be a way out."

"Lord Barnes has offered to take in my sister and mother," I said. "But that would mean betraying my father. I would not be able to save him."

She blinked and looked up at me from eyes smeared with mascara. "Listen to me, James. You must do what's right for you. Save yourself and let your father fend for himself. I'll tell Father you've changed your mind. He can't force you to marry me. I want you to be free."

I stared up at the blue sky, gathering my thoughts. A fluffy cloud floated just above the line of trees, as carefree as could be. An image of my father took the place of the cloud. His hard eyes stared back at me. *You are worthless,* they said. "What about my father?"

"To hell with him."

I drew in a breath, shocked to hear an expletive from her. Although considering what had happened earlier, this was hardly the most outrageous event of the day. "And you? What will become of you?"

"I'll have to face it. Finally face it. I do love you, James. Not the way I should to spend the rest of my life with you. As your friend, though, I want you to be happy. Isn't that something? I'm not as selfish as we all think I am."

"I care about you, too," I said gently, pity washing over me. "You're not selfish."

"I am. I wanted to be saved from my fate, but it's not fair to you."

"Your fate? What do you mean?" I thought of what Alexander had said earlier. "Why is it you and your father were rushing this marriage?"

She touched the collar of my shirt. "I love someone else, too."

"You do?" Sparks of shock sputtered through me. "Who? Why aren't you marrying him? I don't understand."

"He's a poor man. A nobody. Father won't let me marry him." She wouldn't look at me, staring at the ground. "I kept hoping I could forget him and fall in love with you. I did try, you know. But then when I saw you with Addie, I remembered exactly how it feels to love someone you can't have. I've been desperate, that's all." She drew in a long and shaky breath. "I'm in trouble."

"Trouble?" I repeated, numbly. What kind of trouble?

"I'm going to have a baby."

A baby. And then it all made sense. The hurry and the pushing. Lena was pregnant with the man's baby. Her father needed her to marry someone right away to hide that the baby had been conceived out of wedlock. How had I not seen it? All of it was so obvious to me now. "That's what this is about? Your father wanted to buy your way out?"

"That's correct. Thus, the rush. He didn't want anyone to

know I was already pregnant. You were the perfect choice because you were desperate in your own way."

The shock of what she was telling me made it impossible to think of what to say.

"I'm sorry, James. Truly, I am."

"I'm sorry, too. Sorry for your situation and your broken heart." This poor girl. No wonder she'd agreed to this. I was her savior. Now I was letting her down, as I would my dad. All for Addie. "Is there anyone else who could take my place?"

"I suppose there will be. Men will do a lot for money."

"Will you be all right?" Such a lame question. She wouldn't be all right.

"I'll be peachy, darling." She looked up at me for a second before turning toward the fence, her gaze on one of the horses. "Go to Addie. Tell her you love her. Tell her you'll do whatever it takes to have her, even betray your father. I'll tell Father when he returns—from wherever he's been—that I've changed my mind." Was it relief in her voice? Resignation? I couldn't decide. "Whatever Father does, he will do. I'll be very brave, James, and tell him that you don't want his money and that men like you always choose love."

Could I be as brave? "Lena, how will I do it? How do I write to my father and tell him his one chance out of all of this is gone?"

She looked me square in the eye. "You have to. This is your life, James. He made his. Lord Barnes will take in your mother and sister. Your father will continue on as he always has."

"Making one selfish decision after another," I said.

"That's right."

"I'll not abandon you," I said. "If your father casts you aside, I'll help you find a new way. A job, perhaps? You could stay here in Emerson Pass with us. You could send for this man of yours. Start a new life. Alexander will help you."

Her eyes brightened for a fleeting moment before dimming

into a hue of hopelessness. "No, I don't think that will work. He'll not be able to take care of us. Not the way I need him to."

"What will you do?" I asked.

"I have a plan, don't you worry."

My chest ached. "I wish there was more I could do."

"Ah, James, such a sweet man," Lena said. "It's not your job to save everyone, especially not me. You're a good and kind person. I'm better for knowing you."

We were quiet for a moment. I took her hand, examining the cuts and bruises. "We'll need to tend to these."

"It doesn't matter," Lena said. "None of it matters anymore."

"What do you mean?" I didn't like the listless tone of her voice.

She gave me a wide smile, one that I knew was fake. "Nothing at all. I'll find a way. People always do, you know."

I stood and held out my hand. "Come on, let's get you inside and cleaned up."

Lena took my offered hand and rose to her feet. "Don't look at me that way. I can't stand your pity." She tossed her hair before throwing her arms around me. I held her for a few seconds before pulling away.

"You'll be fine," I said.

"Yes, indeed."

18

ADDIE

UPSTAIRS IN MY BEDROOM, MAMA PACED BACK AND FORTH BETWEEN the bed and chair. Delphia was on the window seat, her face redder than I'd ever seen it. I glanced behind her to the outside. James and Lena were headed toward the house. He held her hand as they crossed the gravel driveway.

What did it mean? My heart sank as the reality of that gesture between them worked its way fully into my mind. He was choosing her and his family. Despite Lena's behavior today, he would make her his wife and solve everyone's problem but mine. If it came down to it, I suppose I would have done the same and chosen my father's wishes over everything else. I could not blame him, yet I did. I'd wanted him to choose me. To give up everyone and everything for me. How could I be so selfish? Love made a person do things one never imagined they would.

Hot tears gathered at the corners of my eyes and escaped down my cheeks. I turned away from my mother and sister, hoping to hide my distress. It was over. I would have to figure out a way to go on, starting with convincing everyone I was fine.

"Addie?" Mama asked, pulling my gaze toward her.

"Do you see?" I asked. "He's choosing her. What happened

today means nothing to him." I swallowed a sob that rose up from my belly.

"The evil fox," Delphia whispered. "How does she do it?"

"It's not about her," Mama said. "Not at all."

"You have to change his mind," Addie said. "One of you could, you know. I tried."

"Yes, speaking of which, am I understanding this properly?" Mama asked Delphia. "You gave him money to take her up to the loft? To try to prove that she was not worthy of James?"

"She was happy to go," Delphia said. "I saw the whole thing. She was all fluttery and ridiculous. He said silly things that made her giggle. It was enough to make me lose my lunch."

"Delphia Barnes, never in my life have I been as surprised or repulsed by the actions of my child. And I raised Cymbeline, if you recall."

Delphia looked crestfallen, but she remained combative. "I thought you'd all be pleased. We'll be rid of the fox, and Addie can have James."

Mama sank onto the edge of the bed. "Poor James."

My sister crossed her arms over her chest, huffing. "It may not have occurred to either of you that they were already headed that way, even before my nudge. I saw him sniffing around her yesterday like one of our animals in heat."

Mama paled and clutched the collar of her dress. "Delphia, you are too much. Goodness, you're going to send me to an early grave. You do realize there have been seven of you? I'm tired. The hardest of you seems to have come last."

Delphia frowned, then burst into tears. "I thought I was doing good. For once. I truly did."

I couldn't stand to see her cry and went to sit next to her, taking her into my arms. "We know you meant well."

"I want everything for you. All the happiness you deserve." Delphia drew away, swiping her dirty, tear-stained face. "Why should that awful Lena get James?"

"You're not God," Mama said to Delphia. "You don't decide

these things for others. *He* is the judge and decider of fates, not you."

"Maybe God was working through me," Delphia said in a small voice. "Did anyone ever think of that?"

"God would not have used treachery and deceit, my dear daughter." Mama sighed and sank into the armchair. "Not even for Addie and James."

"Well, what then?" Delphia asked. "How was I supposed to make sure my sister gets what she wants—what she deserves?"

Mama touched her fingers to the sides of her face and tapped. "You've added to an already complex problem."

"You admit it is a problem, then?" Delphia asked. "That Addie should be protected and looked out for?"

"I understand your motivation, darling." Mama clasped her hands on her lap and rocked back and forth. "However, we have more of a mess than we had before. If Mr. Masters discovers today's activity, he may react with great anger and vengeance. Not to mention James. He's trying to save his family despite what he desperately wants, and now he has to untangle yet another situation he hasn't made for himself."

"He wants Addie," Delphia said. "He's in love with her, Mama. And she with him."

"Yes, dear, I understand that," Mama said, sounding weary.

"Then how can you sit there calm as can be and watch Addie's heart break?" Delphia asked.

"Let me tell you something, dearest," Mama said. "There is no greater hardship than watching your child's heart break. I'm quite aware of Addie's feelings, and I want more than anything for her to be happy. However, you mustn't interfere with something like this. Lives hang in the balance. It's not for a sixteen-year-old girl to solve."

"But no one was doing anything," Delphia said, her voice high-pitched. "I will not have it. It simply won't do."

"Delphia, it's sweet of you to want to help," I said. "But this has to be James's decision. He is the one who has to wake up and look at himself in the mirror every morning."

"Yes, and it's an impossible choice." Mama was quiet as she lifted her face to the ceiling. "A boy wants his father's approval, perhaps more than anything else."

"Not love. Not that," Delphia said. "You're wrong."

"Delphia Barnes," Mama said.

"I'm sorry." Delphia looked down at her hands. "It's just too hard to sit by and watch as the love of your sister's life marries someone else. What would you have done for Annabelle?"

"It is an excellent point," Mama said, less sharply than before.

"What will happen now?" I asked, as if either of them had an answer.

"We must think of solutions to the problems we've caused," Mama said, with a pointed look at Delphia. "I'm afraid for Lena. If her father disowns her over this, then we must offer to take her in and shelter her."

"Shelter? At our house?" Delphia's mouth dropped open before she shut it hard enough that her bottom and top rows of teeth clapped together.

Mama nodded at Delphia. "Your interference in this has made her our responsibility."

"It's like a fox living in a henhouse," Delphia said.

"In this particular case, you're the fox, darling, not Lena." Mama's mouth lifted in a grim smile as she rose up from the chair and looked over at me. "Your father told you of his offer?"

I nodded, scarcely able to breathe. Was it possible? Dare I hope?

"As your father promised, we're willing to take James's mother and sister into our home," Mama said. "This will be disruptive to all our lives, but we're willing to do it if that's what James decides he wants. However, the hold his father has over James is tight. You must remember that, Addie."

"Yes, Mama," I said.

"He may not be able to walk away," Mama said.

I teared up, thinking of my dear Papa and his love for me. What he would do for his daughters seemed to have no limits. "Mama, it's so kind of you and Papa."

"We'll do whatever we can to help you," Mama said. "We remember very well what it's like to be young and in love."

"I love him, Mama. So very much. Regardless of my feelings, though, I want him to have a good life. If he makes any other choice but to help his family, I fear he will not. Guilt and regret will plague him all his days. What kind of foundation would that be for a marriage?" I fluttered my fingers toward the window. "Anyway, it appears he's made his choice." I winced, remembering the way he'd held her hand. *I'd still have my work,* I told myself. *My family, too.* There would be many happy days ahead, just none of them would be with James.

"Looks can be deceiving." Mama came to me and kissed the top of my head. "You must have faith, my darling. God knows what he's doing. Whatever is right for you and James—it will unfold as it should."

"How can you be so sure?" Delphi asked, still sounding sulky. "Thus far he's made a real mess out of things."

"Delphia Barnes, you are never to take the Lord's name in vain or speak of him that way." Mama's gaze remained fixed upon the couple outside the windows, and her tone didn't match the sharpness of her words. "Not in my house."

"I'm sorry, Mama." Delphia bowed her head and covered her eyes with her hands.

Mama knelt and gave me another kiss, this time on the cheek. Her cotton skirt cascaded around her as if invisible fairies had placed it just so. My mother, the queen, I thought. To be obeyed and revered.

"Adelaide, darling, look at me." Mama raised my chin with her cool fingertips. "I know you're hurting, but you must never despair. Whatever comes will be the right thing for all of us."

I nodded, as if I believed her. I knew differently. James had made his choice, and it was right for everyone but me.

"Delphia, you will stay here until supper and stay out of trouble," Mama said.

"Yes, ma'am," Delphia said.

My mother left, closing the door behind her. Delphia turned to me and held out her hands. "I'm sorry. I'm very sorry."

"It's all right." I nestled against her and let the tears flow. "As long as you're here, I can bear it."

"I will always be here." She stroked my hair and let me cry.

19

JAMES

In the sitting room, one of the maids dabbed at a cut on Lena's hand. I looked up to see Quinn standing in the doorway. She walked over to where we were sitting on the couch and told the maid to leave us. "I'll take care of this, thank you." She took the damp cloth and peered down at Lena's cut. "This is just a scratch, really, but it's best to clean it."

"Thank you," Lena said. "Mrs. Barnes, I'm sorry for all the trouble I've caused."

Quinn set aside the damp cloth. "It's all right. It seems the Barneses have disrupted your life as well. On behalf of Delphia, I'm sorry. She'll be apologizing to you separately."

"She doesn't have to. I know why she did it. I'm not worth worrying over."

Quinn cupped Lena's face, her eyes searching. "Young lady, you must learn to love yourself, even when it seems impossible to do so." She dropped her hands back onto her lap. "These circumstances are not entirely your fault."

"They are, though. I'm going to have a baby."

Quinn blanched white. For a moment, she seemed at a loss for words. "All the rushing? It's because of the baby."

"James knows now, and we're calling off the wedding," Lena

said. "He loves Addie, as you probably know. There don't seem to be many secrets around here. I'll leave as soon as I can, Mrs. Barnes. You won't want my kind to stay for long."

"Who is the father?" Quinn asked, glancing over at me for the first time.

"Not James." Lena told her about the man she loved and how her father had forbidden them to be together. "When I told him about the baby, he came up with the idea of marrying James."

"What does your young man have to say about all of this?" Quinn asked.

"Carl doesn't know. I couldn't tell him before I left, because my father fired him and kicked him out."

"He worked for you?" Quinn asked.

"In the garden. He knows how to grow the most beautiful roses," Lena said, with a slight smile. "He can make anything grow. It's rather miraculous, actually."

"Is there a way to tell him?" Quinn asked. "Shouldn't you give him a chance to know the truth and then decide what to do?"

"I don't know where he is but, yes, I could probably find him. He can't take care of us anyway, even if Father would allow us to marry. The whole thing's hopeless."

"You love this man? Carl?" Quinn asked.

"More than anything in the world." Lena's eyes grew glassy, and her voice took on a childlike quality. "He's funny and brave. I'll never love anyone else. I'm quite sure of it. I wish it were all different. All of it."

"We do not ask for love, yet it comes anyway," Quinn said. "Sometimes in the most inconvenient package. Almost never, actually, is it in a pretty box with a perfectly tied bow. Who we love is not always who we thought we would or what people want or expect of us."

"Yes, I didn't want to love him. It just happened. One day, everything changed. The flowers were brighter." A single tear ran down the side of Lena's face. "I'd rather have never seen how red the roses or pink the hydrangeas and lived in peace without this most impossible love."

"You poor child," Quinn said. "Whatever shall we do?"

I leaned against the back of my chair for support, completely exhausted, knowing that I, too, had fallen in love with an inconvenient person.

"How can you be so kind to me?" Lena asked Quinn.

"It's not that I'm kind. Not really. It's that I'm happy and blessed, and when one has all that I have, it is easy to be generous to others."

"I'd like to be generous," Lena said. "But all I can feel is shame and desperation. When I tell Father that James and I will not marry, he will be done with me. He has no use for anything or anyone not perfect. I'll have no place to go. Do you think if I had a mother, I could be saved? Maybe I wouldn't have done what I did."

Quinn pulled Lena into an embrace, stroking her hair. "The motherless never learn how to mother themselves," she murmured. "Anyway, you're not alone. You have us now. Stay here as long as you like. We will figure out a solution to all of this."

I was weeping myself by then. The compassion of Quinn Barnes was something to see. If I hadn't witnessed it with my own eyes, I would have doubted it to be true. Perhaps she was more connected to God than the rest of us, I thought, as Lena sobbed into the comfort of Quinn's arms.

"Come along with me," Quinn said to Lena. "Let's run you a bath and get you a cup of tea. Most things seem bearable after one or both."

Quinn glanced back at me before she guided Lena toward the stairs. "Wait for me in the sitting room, please, James? I'll only be a moment."

"Yes, ma'am," I said.

Wiping my eyes, I sank back into the cushions of the chair. A sheath hung over the windows, filtering the afternoon sun. I let my eyelids shutter, exhausted by the emotions of the day. I no longer knew what to do or think. As much as I'd have loved to simply walk away, Lena and I were connected now. She was my friend. I wanted her to find happiness. I wanted her to be safe. Would Quinn and Alexander's generosity extend to an unmarried, pregnant woman? It would cause a scandal, even here in Emerson Pass.

A commotion coming from the foyer interrupted my temporary respite. Jasper entered the sitting room, his tie slightly askew and a lock of his silver hair escaped from the thick pomade. I'd never seen him flustered and not thought it was possible. He came close to me and spoke softly into my ear.

"Mr. West, Mr. Masters has arrived back from his business, and he's brought your father with him."

I had no time to comprehend fully what was said because my father and Mr. Masters appeared in the sitting room, followed by Alexander.

I'd not seen my father in two years. He'd aged considerably. His shoulders seemed to have permanently slumped, and his white hair was so thin I could see his shiny pink scalp underneath. He wore a fine suit but it hung too loosely, as if he had recently lost weight. I was so taken aback by his arrival that I could only stare dumbly at him.

"Aren't you going to say hello to me?" Father stuck out his hand, and we shook.

"What are you doing here?" I managed to ask.

"Your future father-in-law was kind enough to send for me. He wanted us to meet properly and discuss Miss Masters's dowry before the wedding. He tells me you've decided to marry here in this wild country before returning to New York. Your mother will be sorry to miss the wedding, but perhaps we can have another party in England next year."

"No reason not to do it here," Mr. Masters said as if anyone had asked. "Among your second family. Time is of the essence, son. Your father and I have many business plans, which we'll discuss over the next few days." He turned to Alexander. "Your wife won't mind hosting a little wedding party, will she?"

Alexander glanced over at me, a look of alarm in his eyes. "We'll do whatever it is that James wants." His mouth formed a thin, straight line and a muscle in his cheek pulsed, as if he were holding back what he wanted to say.

"When did you decide to come to America?" I asked. "How did you get here?"

"Well, think of my surprise when the letter arrived from Maxwell with the tickets," Father said. "I took a boat and then a very tedious train. We thought it would be delightful to surprise you."

"I'm surprised," I said. "I'm certainly surprised."

"You're looking well, son." My father clapped me on the shoulder, to give the impression we were close. I knew him too well to be fooled. I caught a hint of alcohol on his breath. Apparently, they served drinks on the tedious train.

I murmured a thank you. Panic was rising in me, tightening my stomach. The pain behind my eye had returned. How could I tell them the wedding was off? Writing a letter was one thing. Telling my father the truth face-to-face was another thing entirely.

"What's a man need to do to get a drink here in Colorado?" Father asked, flashing what had once been a charming smile. I'd seen him use it to manipulate people all my life. It had more appeal when he was a younger man.

Jasper, who had been lurking in a corner, leapt into action. "Sir, what may I get you? It's nearly teatime if you'd care for something to eat as well."

"A brandy will do quite nicely," Father said.

"For all of us," Alexander said. "Thank you, Jasper."

I waited until Mr. Masters and Father had taken a seat before doing so myself. My mind was reeling as it acclimated to this new set of information. The trip on the ocean liner would have taken at least five days and maybe longer. Mr. Masters must have sent him first class on the best ocean liner if he had arrived so quickly. But why? Was Masters worried I'd change my mind? Had he sensed my reluctance and brought my father over to ensure my obedience?

Yes, I thought. I understood now. This was a dirty game these men were playing. Mr. Masters had sent for Father and told him the wedding would be here. All to force us into it before Lena or I changed our minds. I had news for them. It was too late.

Do it. Tell them. You must.

Alexander sent me a sympathetic gaze. I wanted to take him aside and ask him what to do. How would he handle this obvious manipulation? It wouldn't work, though, even if I could ask him. He would not be able to advise me, because he wasn't a coward. He wouldn't be afraid of his own father as I was of mine. Otherwise, he would never have set out for America. I'd run away from my home and family instead of toward something, as Alexander had done. He'd made a purposeful change in his life. God help me, if I didn't head for something, for once, it would be the end of me. Or someone. I must head toward Addie.

I accepted the glass of brandy from Jasper and took too large a swig and coughed.

"Are you all right, James?" Alexander sat near me on the couch and reached over to pat my back. I had a sudden picture of what he would have been like with his sons when they were small.

"I'm fine, thank you," I said. I must gather my thoughts and present them with the truth. But the words didn't come. They were stuck somewhere in my cowardly throat.

Quinn arrived then, her heels clicking on the floor before she reached the edge of the carpet. Her gaze seemed to take in the situation with immediate clarity. How she knew the stranger in her sitting room was my father, I couldn't say. Regardless, it was obvious she understood perfectly what had happened.

Introductions were made. My father was practically dripping

with charisma. Although he'd aged, his mind seemed as quick as it always had. He knew how to get what he wanted from people. In this case, he seemed to intuitively know that Quinn Barnes was no wallflower, no wilting rose. She must be charmed.

He kissed her hand and twinkled at her, almost flirtatiously. "If I didn't know better, Mrs. Barnes, I would have taken you for one of your daughters."

She granted him a small, tight smile. Father didn't seem to notice her coolness. Or if he did, it did nothing to deter him from his mission. After Quinn sat next to Alexander in the spot I'd just occupied, Father returned to his seat. I took the chair closest to Quinn, wishing she had a miracle in her dress pocket to save me from my father's wishes.

Father told Quinn what he'd already told us about the passage and train ride and added how excited he was to see this part of America and thank you so very much for taking care of his wayward son all these years. "His mother and I shake our heads at his notions. First France and then America? All of it paid for by his American benefactors, no less. Some men have all the luck, isn't that right?"

"It's been our pleasure to have James in our home." Quinn's hands were clasped tightly in her lap. "Quite simply, he's our dear friend. There's nothing we would not do for him. Furthermore, he's hardly wayward. His success had been because of hard work and fortitude. He's never been a man seeking assistance without offering something in return."

"What exactly has he offered you in return for your hospitality?" Father's tone remained robust and lighthearted, but I knew the venom underneath. He loved to put me down, embarrass me in front of others. Especially since he could sense the warmth between the Barnes family and me. My father was a drinker and a gambler, but he was smart when it came to people and sizing up how to manipulate them into giving him what he wanted. For a moment, I almost felt sorry for Mr. Masters. He had no idea what he'd unleashed when he brought my father into his life.

"We thought James was not good for much," Father said. "I kept watching to see him prove us wrong, of course. As fathers do."

"You must not have looked carefully enough," Alexander said. "Because it's quite obvious to most everyone who meets him. Perhaps there's something in your own makeup that didn't allow you to see what was right in front of you."

"I can't imagine it but will have to take your word as truth," Father said. "How extraordinary."

"James is rather extraordinary." I'd never seen Quinn's pretty eyes hard, as they were now. Her voice had taken on a coldness, as well. One that would chill most men's blood. My father's veins were too full of booze, I supposed, to freeze.

Father tapped his temple. "As a child, he was thick, you see. Nothing seemed to penetrate his dim-witted mind. We didn't think he'd make it to adulthood."

"Yet here I am," I said under my breath.

"Why would you think that way?" Alexander asked. "Was he ill?"

"No, not at all. I meant that he seemed too dim-witted to keep out of trouble." Father laughed, as if we were all in on the joke with him when, in fact, he'd alienated us all. Even Masters seemed shocked by his behavior toward me.

"Addie was sick when she was a child," Quinn said. "We thought we might lose her. It's the most terrified I've ever been. And I had two sons fight in the war, so I've known the horror of almost losing a child, and it's no joking matter." Quinn was hoping to shame him. However, she underestimated my father. He was not ashamed of his behavior. In fact, he never was. Perhaps that was the crux of the problem. Without regret or remorse, how does one grow and learn from their mistakes?

"His mother thought him weak of character," Father said. "But I never gave up hope that he would grow into a fine young man."

"Mother thought I was weak?" I asked, sitting up straighter. The pain in my head grew worse by the minute.

"She liked to coddle you. Treated him like the king of England, that she did," Father said to Alexander before he looked over at Jasper and tapped his glass for another.

Jasper, bless him, didn't blink. His composure had returned, it seemed. He poured a new glass for Father, presenting it to him on a tray.

Father took the glass and continued on with his prattle about my deficiencies. "Always with his nose in a book, this one. Thought he was too good for the rest of us, I dare say."

"That's not true." I tugged at my collar, hot. "I never thought that." Books were more interesting than my parents and their endless drama. I could escape inside the pages of a story and forget, even if it was just for a moment, the cold dankness of both the house and my parents.

"All of our children loved to read," Alexander said. "As do my wife and I. You can see by our library here. Did you know our oldest daughter started the library here in town?"

I lost the thread of the conversation, sinking further into myself. My father could make me shrink like no one else. In his presence, the ghost of the little boy who had so desperately wanted his love returned. He knew this, too, and played on it to get what he wanted from me. He knew I was marrying for his sake. Yet he would withhold that love anyway. As much as he needed saving by Mr. Masters, he couldn't bring himself to treat me decently.

I hated him.

20

ADDIE

In the bedroom, I sat with Delphia by the window in silence, straining to hear what was being said below us in the sitting room. Mr. Masters had returned from his errands in town a few minutes ago and had brought someone with him. A man we didn't recognize.

"Who do you think he is?" Delphia asked, whispering.

"I can't imagine."

The man had appeared older than Mr. Masters, with white hair and a nice suit that seemed too big for him. He needed Mr. Olofsson to make his clothes, I'd thought, absently.

"What's happening down there?" Delphia jumped up and began to pace around the room. "Do you think he's a business associate of Mr. Masters? But why would he come here?"

I didn't answer, having no idea.

"Are you still mad at me?" Delphia asked, sitting next to me once again.

"I couldn't be mad at you for long, could I?" In truth, I wasn't angry at her, more disappointed. Yet I understood why she'd done what she did. It was strange, really. When one loved another person as much as I loved my sister, one could separate their mistakes from the entirety of their being. Even though she'd made a messy situation even worse, I loved her with the same intensity that she had for me.

Her voice trembled. "I am truly sorry. I thought I was doing a good deed."

I squeezed her hand. "I know."

A knock on the door startled us. I sped over to open it and found Lena standing there. She'd cleaned up and put on a new dress. A soft yellow linen that looked nice with her hair. One would never have known she'd been rolling around in the dirt with my sister such a short time ago. However, although she was clean and put together, she visibly shook.

"May I come in?" Lena asked.

"Yes, of course." I opened the door wider to let her pass by. A quick glance at Delphia told me that she had not softened. Scowling with all her might, my sister.

"I came to say I'm sorry," Lena said. "For everything, but also to tell you that the man with my father is James's father."

My mouth fell open. "How…how is that possible?"

"My father's brought him from England."

"Whatever for?" I asked.

"To make sure James does what he wants him to," Lena said. "Why else would he have gone to all the trouble?"

"Why does your father want this so badly, anyway?" Delphia asked. "What does it give him? I truly don't understand."

Lena held on to the corner of the four-poster bed. "There's a reason."

"What is it?" Delphia's voice sharpened into a blade. "What have you been keeping from James? From us?"

I watched Lena carefully, taking note of the way her chest quivered when she took in a deep breath as well as the splotches on her neck. Her eyes were red and swollen. She'd been crying. The kind of crying jag you think will never stop. I knew all about those.

"I'm no longer keeping anything from James. I've released him. Set him free. Like a butterfly from a cocoon."

"What nonsense are you saying?" Delphia asked. "Speak plainly."

"I'm going to have a baby," Lena said. "It's not James's baby. Father wanted me to marry as quickly as possible so that no one would know. That's why we've been in such a hurry. We haven't long before I start to show."

For once, Delphia was struck silent. I staggered backward into a chair.

"Earlier today, Jesse and I were only talking," Lena said. "The man I love is back home, and I would never fall into the arms of another just for the fun of it. That's where you underestimated me, Delphia. You see, I'm in love with my Carl. That's the name of my baby's father. He worked for my father. In the gardens. He's not even a head gardener, merely a young man who brings flowers and plants to life with his hard work. He was responsible for the flowers outside my window. That's when I first saw him. He was leaning over, planting a petunia. When he saw me watching, he grinned, as if we had a private joke. That smile warmed me in a way I'd never been warmed before. In a way that made me realize I'd been cold all my life."

"Oh, dear," Delphia said.

"I went to Father and begged his forgiveness. He said the only way I would avoid being kicked out to the street was to find a suitable husband. That's where James came in. I knew him from parties and such. We'd been out a few times. I knew about his family's financial situation. When I told Father all of this, he immediately darted off a correspondence, offering Mr. West money in exchange for a quick wedding." She sat in the other armchair and curled over her legs, sobbing for a moment before gaining enough composure to continue her story. "That's why we had to put it in the paper. We needed James to commit. All was well until he insisted on coming out here to see you all. He didn't say so, but I know he thought it would be the last one he ever enjoyed."

"You poor thing." Delphia's eyes were wide with sympathy.

"This is terrible. What about your flower grower? Does he know all of this?"

I, too, filled with sorrow on her behalf. Now that I knew the truth, it was easy to understand why she'd acted as she had. I could only feel terribly sorry for her and her predicament.

"No, I didn't tell him about the baby. My father insisted upon that," Lena said. "Carl was the first person I've ever been completely myself with, but I knew that if I told him about the baby he would do whatever it took to look after me, and where would that have gotten us? Father is a formidable opponent. Today, though, I told James the truth. Seeing him with you, Addie, I knew what I had to do. I couldn't be that selfish. Not when he wants you and you love him so much—I can see it between you—these feelings you didn't want but came anyway, just as they did for me and Carl. I can't bear for either of you to feel the way I do. I wouldn't wish it on my worst enemy. Your mother—she was kind to me just now. She offered me a place to stay if Father disowns me. Even with the scandal I would bring to Father and to all of you."

"She doesn't care," Delphia said. "She's too kind. Right, Addie?"

"I'd have thought she would," I said, truthfully. "She has high moral standards."

"Yes, one would think this would be too much for your saintly mother," Lena said. "And I wouldn't blame her if that were true. Who would want me in their home? I bring only heartache to anyone who cares for me. When I went back to my room, I thought about what your mother said, and I knew what to do. I think I've known all along. It's what I should have done when I first knew about the baby. Instead of dragging poor James into all of my troubles. All of my mistakes."

"What did she say?" I asked. "What advice did she have?" My mother often surprised me with her wisdom and her imaginative ideas for solving even the most complex of problems.

"That the motherless seek love from other sources. Or something of that nature." Lena took a handkerchief from her dress pocket and dabbed her cheeks. "But I didn't seek love. It found me. I didn't want it. I would rather be dead than feel this kind of pain. Being apart from Carl—it's too much. I cannot raise a child without him. I've no place to go and no way of taking care of myself or a baby. I don't want to live anymore. And so that is what I will do. It's the only thing I know to do. I wanted to tell you all the truth before the poison does whatever it is that's going to happen to me."

I leapt up and knelt at her feet. "What are you talking about? What did you take?"

Lena closed her eyes. "Just something to put me to sleep. A little something the doctor gave me for my nerves in combination with the pain powder I found in the bathroom. I took all of it, so that should do what I want it to." A smile twitched the corners of her mouth. "That's all I want. To never wake. To be at peace at last and let all of you have the lives you're supposed to have. I'm only in the way."

The truth of what she was saying stunned me for a moment. Only for a second though. After the initial shock, I realized I must remain calm and assertive or everything could go terribly wrong. Irreparably wrong.

"Lena, what was the medicine that you took? The one for your nerves?"

"I don't know what it's called. The doctor gave it to me so I can sleep at night. I have the most dreadful time sleeping."

"Opium," I heard Delphia say behind me. "They hand it out like candy in the cities."

I wondered how she knew this but didn't have time to think about that now and turned to my sister. Delphia's eyes were wide and frightened. I remembered the last time she'd looked like a scared moon, all round and pale and suspended in space—the night I almost died. I'd never forgotten it.

Mrs. Wu and her magical potions. The thought slid into my mind with such ease that I wondered why I hadn't thought of it straight away. She made herbs and other dried plants into tea. She'd saved Theo with one of them when he was a boy. When I was sick, she'd made ones that soothed my stomach. She claimed her daily concoction of herbs and dried flowers was the secret to her long life.

By the time Theo got here, it might be too late, but Mrs. Wu was downstairs. "Go downstairs. Call Theo or Dr. Neal and tell them what Lena's taken. Then, go down to the kitchen and ask Mrs. Wu if she has an herb that will make Lena vomit. We have to empty her stomach. Then, get Mama—as discreetly as you can—and tell her to come up here."

Without a word, Delphia raced out of the room, as fast as Cymbeline. My sisters, the athletes. Now, we needed my brother the doctor. Or Mrs. Wu. And God. Perhaps a combination of all three.

Lena had slumped onto one side of the chair. Now she brought her legs up as if they were weighed down with rocks and curled into a ball. Her eyes were closed and she *did* look peaceful, I thought. If that had been her aim, it seemed to be working.

What should I do? "God, what do I do?" I whispered.

Get her to the bathroom and keep her awake.

I was not as strong as either of my athletic sisters, but I was still a Barnes woman. I'd traipsed through meadows and swum in the creak and cleaned horse stalls. I could do this.

I wedged an arm around her waist and brought her to the edge of the chair. Her head lolled from side to side, but she was still awake. If she fell asleep, it might be forever.

I took her by the shoulders and shook her. Her neck seemed to have lost all muscle. "Listen to me, Lena. You have to get up. Walk around with me."

"I'm too sleepy. You go ahead." She mumbled this under her breath. Did she know it was me or where she was? Or what she'd done to herself?

I scrambled to my feet and I yanked her up with enough

force that she opened her eyes. She peered at me and let out a soft whine, no louder than a kitten who had her tail stepped on. "Addie Barnes. Too pretty to compete with. Too perfect for James." Perfect? Did she mean perfectly suited or too perfect for James? Never mind. It didn't matter. I must keep her from dying.

Holding on to her waist, I dragged her around the room. "Tell me a story," I said. "About Carl. What's he look like?"

This seemed to perk her up a little because she answered me. "His face is browned from the sun and his neck, too. Sometimes I see a little glimpse of his skin under his collar and I like to touch him there. His skin is almost always warm, like a blanket by the fire. Do you know what I mean?"

"Yes, I do. It's probably you who makes him warm," I said. "Because he loves you."

"He does love me. He begged me to run away with him. But where would we go, I said? He has all those people to take care of, and I have no money of my own."

"People?"

"Yes, all the money he makes goes to his mother. All these sisters and brothers, like you. They're hungry, he says. They need him. Just like James, he has to take care of everyone." She wasn't completely making sense but at least she was talking, still fighting for life.

"You are going to be fine," I said. "You're going to be, and then we're going to find Carl and help him and his family."

"You'd do that?" Lena asked, slurring her words.

The door opened and my mother and Lizzie burst into the room. Lizzie carried a tray with a teapot and a cup. Shortly thereafter, Mrs. Wu appeared, winded from the hike up two floors. Small and shriveled with a slight stoop to her shoulders, but her dark eyes were as bright and vigorous as they had always been.

"Good girl, Addie love," Lizzie said. "Keeping her upright."

Delphia arrived, also breathless. "I've called Theo. He's on his way but he said to go ahead, Mrs. Wu. That he trusts you."

"Yes, yes. We brought tea," Mrs. Wu said. "For stomach. Make her throw up."

"I knew you'd have something." A surge of hope filled me. "We have to save her. She's going to have a baby."

Mama exchanged a look with Lizzie and Mrs. Wu that only women who had been friends for over twenty years can do. A silent language between mothers who together had raised seven Barnes children, Li and Fai Wu, Florence Strom, and the Depaul boys. I had a sudden memory of all of us down at the creek for a picnic. I'd been about four, I think, and we were all there together. All the ruffians together, laughing and splashing about in the water, eating Lizzie's picnic food as if we were half starved. For that afternoon, everything had been perfect. No one was sick. No one had had their heart broken. We had not yet sent my brothers off to fight in a war halfway around the world. It must have been such a joy to our mothers that day to have us all there, safe and happy.

"A baby?" Lizzie said under her breath. "Not with James, then?"

"No. She's in love with one of her father's gardeners." Delphia said. "Mr. Masters knows. And that's why she needed to get married so fast."

Mama plucked at the front of her blouse as the truth of it all fell into place. "Yes, once I learned the truth, well, it made sense. All the rushing and manipulation." Her brown eyes darkened a shade as she touched her fingers against Lena's cheek. "You poor darling girl. All alone."

The life seemed to be seeping from Lena. Without warning, she slumped against me. Her body weight almost knocked me over. My sister rushed to the other side of Lena and together we held her upright.

"Take her into the bathroom," Mrs. Wu said. "Near toilet, but we will need a bucket, too."

"I'll get one," Lizzie said, speeding ahead to grab one from the hallway pantry.

"How will we get her to drink it?" Delphia asked Mrs. Wu.

"We will spoon it in her mouth if we must," Mrs. Wu said. "This tea is very strong."

What was this potion that made people empty their stomach? Someone really needed to get Mrs. Wu to write these things down, but that would have to be addressed another day. How did she have it down there, ready for use? I'd have to ask her about that later.

Between my sister and me, we managed to get Lena into the bathroom. As gently as possible, we had her sit with her back against the bathtub. Lizzie returned to us with a bucket in hand. Our Lizzie might be round and soft, but she was quick on her feet.

Mama knelt on the floor next to Lena, speaking softly to her, telling her how good the tea would be for her and for the baby. "Just open your mouth like a little bird."

Lena, as entranced with Mama as we all seemed to be, obeyed. Mama lifted the cup to Lena's lips and tilted it just right. *Mothers know how to do these things,* I thought. Nurse the sick, comfort the brokenhearted, love unconditionally even when we'd made terrible mistakes. Motherhood made a woman strong, more capable than she ever thought she'd be.

"Will the tea be good for the baby?" Delphia blurted out. "Or will it cause her to miscarry?"

"It is all right," Mrs. Wu said. "Not for getting rid of baby."

Good God, there was something that did that? This whole day had been quite educational. I think I preferred naiveté after all.

Lena swallowed the entire cup of the potion. Mrs. Wu gestured for Delphia and me to leave. "Leave this to us. We take care of her and fix her up for whatever happens next."

What would happen next? Delphia and I locked eyes before filing out of the bathroom. Once back in our room, we fell into each other's arms. My sister was shaking like an aspen leaf in the autumn, and I soothed her, even though I was also overcome with the day's events and the unanswered questions. What about Lena and the baby? What about the poor boy she loved? Would Mr. Masters toss them aside like trash? All of this would have to wait. For now, we had to save her life.

What about James and me? With his father here, how could he do anything but his bidding? They'd surrounded James like wolves. Would he be strong enough to tell him what he truly wanted?

Yes, I thought. He would be. He would do it for us. For me.

21

JAMES

I SAT LISTENING TO THE THREE MEN WHO HAD SUCH INFLUENCE OVER my life discuss politics and business without really hearing them. Alexander, although polite, was not his usual jovial self, and mostly nodded or answered a question if asked. I could tell that the situation with his daughter and me weighed heavily upon him. As it did me, of course.

The revelation that Lena loved another man hadn't fully sunk in when we were speaking earlier. But now, as I sat here, I thought about how tortured she must have been. Forced to leave him behind when all she wanted was to stay with him. Or was this man a scoundrel like Jesse? Had he rejected her, too? No, that wasn't what she'd said. Her father forbade her to continue on because he was poor. Masters couldn't let his daughter have what she wanted. I couldn't understand why. It wasn't like my family, who needed a good marriage to save them. He was cruel and unfair, claiming to love his daughter but only if she did what he wanted.

The clock in the corner of the room ticked away the seconds and seemed to say: tell him, tell him, tell him.

However, something was happening upstairs that kept me silent. Whatever it was had dragged Quinn from the conversation. Delphia hadn't looked at me when she'd come into the room, breathless and red-faced. She'd gone to her mother and whispered something in her ear. Whatever it was she said had caused Quinn to jump to her feet so abruptly that a vase rattled and would have fallen over had I not snatched it up at the last second.

As much relief that Lena's confession and absolution had given me, the worst of it was yet to come. I had to tell our fathers. My stomach clenched at the thought. They could not force me, I told myself. It would be only my guilt that would hold me back. I thought of Addie's face when she laughed or when she was pensive, waiting for the next sentence to come to her, and such a longing filled me that I could no longer stay silent.

My mother and sister could come here. They would not be on the streets. My father would have to find another way.

"Excuse me," I said, interrupting Masters, who was talking about the evil of taxes on the rich. "I have something to say."

All three men turned to me. Alexander's eyebrows raised before he gave me a nod of encouragement. I took hold of it with all my might. I would be part of this family. Where I belonged. To whom I belonged.

"What is it?" Father asked, sharply and with his usual impatience whenever I spoke.

"I'm not going to marry Lena. I'm in love with Addie Barnes. I can't in good conscience marry another. Lena knows. She doesn't want to marry me, either. We've spoken and decided to call off the engagement."

"Well done, son," Alexander said quietly. His eyes sparkled with goodwill. He was on my side. I must take courage from it. Right now, however, my insides quivered. I thought I might be sick.

"You must be mad." My father turned the color of a boiled beet. "It's already done. We've decided. Worked it all out."

"This is ridiculous." Masters lurched out of his chair with

such violence that I thought he might punch me. "It's not up to you, young man." Despite his threatening countenance, his voice sounded controlled and even. Yet I knew the anger simmered just under the surface ready to burn me at any moment. "We've made an agreement. One you cannot decide, upon some whim about some twit of a girl, to disregard. My daughter's reputation is at stake."

"Twit of a girl?" Alexander said. "That's my beloved daughter you're talking about."

"Whatever she is," Masters said, "is no concern of mine. It's my own daughter I'm trying to save here."

I took in a deep breath, gathering courage. *Addie.* I must do this for us. "Lena and I want to marry for love, and we don't love each other. You know as well as I that she loves another."

This time the pot boiled over and Masters shouted at me, spittle flying through the air. "That's a bald-faced lie. She adores you. You're all she's ever wanted."

"Even if that were true," I said, "would you really want her to marry a man who doesn't love her?"

"I don't give two figs about love," Masters said, still shouting. "Money runs the world, not love."

"Not in Emerson Pass," Alexander said, calmly. "Here love wins. Always." He stood, facing Masters head-on. "I mean you no harm, Maxwell." He turned to my father. "Nor you, Mr. West. I'm sincerely sorry for your troubles. However, I'm afraid I'm going to have to ask you to leave my home. James loves my daughter, which makes him part of my family. And I always protect my own."

"That's what I'm doing, you blasted idiot." Masters glared at Alexander. "My daughter's in trouble. I need James to marry her. He must marry her.

"Do you see, Father, what's happened here? Masters was using me to hide the fact that his daughter got into trouble with one of the staff. They'd announce after the honeymoon that we were having a child. No one would do the math too carefully." I turned to Masters. "'The baby came early,' you'd tell everyone as you handed out cigars. Meanwhile, your daughter would be miserable. I would be miserable. Both of us trapped because you won't let her marry the man she loves."

"What if I were using you to cover up my daughter's terrible mistake?" Masters shook with rage. "Your father needs financial rescuing. You want to keep your job. Lena needs a husband. We all get what we want."

"Why do you care?" I asked, bold now. "Why not just let her marry this man, poor or not? What does it matter to you? That's the part I don't understand. It's not as if you need the money like my dear old dad here."

"It matters because I would be humiliated in front of all the people who so badly want to keep me out of their world. If I allow her to marry the gardener—what does that say about us?"

My father's voice trembled. "Please, James, you have to do it. For me. For your sister and mother."

"You'd have me marry a woman pregnant with another man's child?" I asked.

"If it saves us, yes. You, my son, could save us with this one unselfish act. You'd be the family hero." Father's earlier anger had changed into a simpering cajoling. He would be nice to me until he got what he wanted. Not this time.

"You must save yourself, Father. You got yourself into the mess, and you must get out of it."

"You'll never work in publishing again," Masters said. "Your precious book career—all will be lost. Is it really worth it? This idea of love?"

I closed my eyes for a brief moment as images of the last month played before my eyes. Addie on the swing. Addie laughing by the creek. Addie's tear-filled eyes when she admitted her feelings for me. Kissing her soft mouth, feeling the way her body yielded to me. "I would walk to the ends of the earth for Addie Barnes. I'd even turn my back on my family and the career I love to be with her. At first, I couldn't imagine being responsible for the downfall of my family. This career I love—I've worked so hard to get where I am—it will hurt deeply to lose it. But none of that matters. Because now I know that without her, nothing has any meaning. Without her, I would be lost, regardless of how convenient your money made everything, Mr. Masters." I glanced at Alexander. "I belong here anyway. It's been my home since the very first summer I came here with Fiona and Li. I'll find another career and make a family with Addie." I faced my father, making myself look him in the eye even though his anger frightened me. "Father, I'm sorry for your troubles. I truly am. I wanted to save you. I thought more than anything I wanted to be the hero in our family story. For that matter, all I've ever wanted was for you to love me and be proud of me. There was this hole where you should have been. It's filled now with someone else. I have Addie's father now. He doesn't make me beg for approval or understanding. He sees me for who I am, who I want to be. He *notices* me and respects me. I never knew what that was like until I came into this house."

I was saved from further reprimand from Father when a noise at the front door proved to be Theo, carrying his medical bag. From the hallway came the sound of footsteps and then Quinn's voice. "Darling, thank goodness you're here. Lena's in the bathroom upstairs."

Out of the corner of my eye, I saw Theo and his mother dart past the doorway of the sitting room toward the stairs.

"What is wrong?" Masters asked Alexander. "Why is he here?"

I couldn't hear his reply because of the buzzing between my ears. What had Lena done to herself? She'd been hopeless, I realized now. There didn't seem to be any solution to her problem. She simply wanted to end her suffering. She'd thought we'd all be better off without her.

"You did this." Masters lunged for me, but I was too quick and jumped up and out of his way.

"No, you did this." I pointed a finger at him. "This is all

because of you. She loves him. Why can't you let her have him? Wouldn't it be better than having her kill herself? And the baby? Think about the baby."

Mr. Masters paled and staggered backward into a chair. "Why does she want him? He's nothing. Trash."

"The question is not about her," Alexander said. "We do not choose who we love in this life. The question is about you. Do you love your daughter enough to forgive her and welcome her back into your home regardless of who she's married to or the mistake she made? It's up to you now. You must stand up for your daughter."

Mr. Masters's arrogant expression drained from his face and was replaced by one of bewilderment. His aggressive stance seemed to dissipate as his hands dropped to his sides. "What if…what if…" Masters couldn't bring herself to say it out loud.

But we all knew. What if she didn't make it?

"What will I do then?" Mr. Masters asked, his voice breaking. "She's all I have."

"Oh, for God's sake." My father's entire being trembled with rage. "What's it matter? You're rich. You can buy a new daughter if you want. What do I have?" He jabbed a red finger in my direction. "All I've got is this miserable excuse for a son. My own boy deserting his family. Can you imagine that, Masters? Would you boo-hoo about that?"

Alexander was on his feet by then. He grabbed my father by the shoulders and spoke to him quietly but firmly. "You, sir, are no longer welcome in my home. I'll arrange for tickets home. You will depart on the late-afternoon train."

"Leave it to me, Barnes," Masters said. "I'll send him back."

"Please, Masters, take pity on me." My father whined now, ridiculous and small. I was no longer afraid of him. He was a worm, not worthy of my love or fear. "The same arrangement we talked about can still work."

"But what do you give me?" Masters said. "What could you

possibly have that would entice me into rescuing you and your family?"

"You could feel like a good man," Father said. "A man who keeps his word. Unlike my poor excuse of a son."

I blinked away tears. How had I spent so much of my life trying to please this unfeeling man? No matter what I did, it would never be enough.

"Father, go now. No one wants you here, especially me."

"What do I tell your mother?" His lips parted in a snarl, revealing pink gums and his slightly crooked teeth.

"Tell her the truth." I was amazed at how calm I felt. Relieved, too. I was finally free of this web he'd woven to trap me. He'd been doing this all my life, and I'd allowed him to. No more. I was a grown man, one who could make whatever life I wanted. With Addie. "Tell her you were trying to trick me into marriage to save yourself. Admit that you love no one but yourself."

"You'll rot in hell," Father said, sputtering. "All of you will. Turning on a man like this."

"Jasper will help you with your bags," Alexander said. "Safe travels."

And that was that. My father, out of ideas of ways to get what he wanted, stalked out of the room and my life. I knew this would be the last time I ever saw him or spoke to him. I thought I would feel something other than relief, but that was not the case.

ALEXANDER and I sat with Masters and waited for Theo or Quinn to come with word of Lena. I sat quietly and prayed as hard as I'd ever prayed. I prayed for Lena's recovery and for her father's heart to soften and for the unborn baby and his or her father.

"How did you do it, Barnes?" Mr. Masters said, startling me

from my sudden piousness. "Raise all these daughters without losing your faculties?"

Alexander smiled. "It's not always been easy. They're all different and have had various troubles. We've just dealt with them as they come."

"What would you do?" Mr. Masters asked him. "If one of yours wanted to marry someone completely wrong for her?"

"I think our definition of who is right or wrong for our daughters is different," Alexander said. "I've never cared about their wealth or position but rather their potential."

"Potential? What do you mean, Barnes? Are we talking business sense?

"Not really, no. I judge them on what I believe is their aptitude for giving my daughter a joyful and love-filled life."

"That's just it. She marries this…this gardener—and her life will be miserable. How will they support her and a baby? She'll live in squalor like my mother did and grow old and bitter before she turns twenty-five. He'll end up leaving her, just like my father did, and then where will she be?"

"Offer him a position working for you," I said, blurting it out even though no one had asked for my opinion.

"Preposterous," Mr. Masters said. "He knows nothing about business and has no education. What would I have him do?"

"Start him out in an entry-level position," Alexander said. "Give him a chance to prove himself. Like you did."

"Like I did?" Mr. Masters scowled.

Alexander continued. "You worked hard and made clever decisions and now instead of living in squalor, as you put it, you're one of the richest men in America. Isn't that what you believe in? What you've done? It would be easy for you to give him a chance. Easier than losing your daughter, isn't it? And a grandchild? You've no idea the joy a child of your child will bring you."

"What would I tell people about him?" Masters asked. "That my daughter married a gardener?"

"Tell them he's an American," Alexander said. "And in America, we have the chance to better ourselves—to become more than our father was. A little help from you, Masters, and the boy might surprise you. I'm sure you've surprised people along the way."

"People underestimated me," Masters said. "That gave me more ambition, just to prove them wrong."

"My point exactly," Alexander said.

"He might be dumb as a block of wood for all I know." Masters rubbed his temples as if his head hurt. It probably did. Remarkably, the ache behind my eye had disappeared.

Masters sighed and looked down at his hands. "I've made a shambles of things, haven't I? To take her own life? Because of me. If she doesn't make it, I shall never forgive myself. It's only that I've wanted to give her everything this world can offer. The life my mother never got, or Lena's mother, either. They both died before I could give them what they deserved. But Lena? She's been my pride and joy. My everything."

"You can make this right," Alexander said. "God willing, you'll have a chance."

22

ADDIE

FROM UP ABOVE, DELPHIA AND I WATCHED AS JAMES'S FATHER GOT into the back seat of one of our cars. Jasper, who apparently would drive him to the station, put Mr. West's suitcases into the trunk.

"He's going?" Delphia whispered. "What's happened?"

"I don't know." We knew nothing, other than we'd seen Theo's arrival and heard hushed voices behind the closed door of the guest room where they were hopefully making Lena better.

Jasper got in the car and pulled out of the driveway, faster than usual, I noted, with some humor.

"What could have happened?" Delphia asked again, then answered her own question. "James told him. That has to be it. He finally told him he can't marry Lena."

She had to be right. Why else would Mr. West leave? He'd done it. "He's done it," I whispered out loud.

"He's done it," Delphia said. "Brave, brave James. Go downstairs and find him."

"But Mama said to stay here. I don't want to be in the way. And what about Mr. Masters? He'll be there, and I can't face him. It's all out in the open now. I think it must be, right?" I realized I was rambling, but the excitement and drama of the day had stolen my reticence.

"It must be." My sister reclined into the corner of the window seat and wrapped her arms around her knees. I did the same on the other end, our toes touching. How many times had she and I sat here together over the years?

There was a soft knock on the door, followed by Mama coming into the room. I held my breath, waiting to see what she had to say.

"Lena's going to be fine," Mama said. "Between the tea and Theo's medical skills, they got most of the poison out of her."

"Thank God," Delphia said.

"Mr. Masters is with her now," Mama said.

"Does he know?" I asked. "That James and Lena won't marry?"

"James told them everything," Mama said. "He told them about you, Addie. About his feelings for you."

"Oh," I breathed.

"What happened then?" Delphia asked.

"Mr. West didn't take it well. Your papa asked him to leave. Apparently, it was quite a scene. James belongs to us now."

To us? To me? Dare I hope?

"What about Mr. Masters?" Delphia asked. "Is he going to disown Lena? Will she have to live with us now?"

"He's come around," Mama said. "Your father gave him some good advice, and the man isn't too prideful to see that if he wants Lena in his life, he needs to accept her as she is. Including the baby and the man she's in love with."

"I can't believe it," Delphia said. "I didn't think he'd see reason."

"I have to say, I agree." Mama smiled. "Sometimes people astound me with their cruelty. Sometimes they surprise me with their capacity for forgiveness."

"A happy ending for Lena after all." Delphia spoke softly, without the sharpness that usually accompanied anything to do with Lena Masters. "Will she marry this man? The father of her baby?"

Mama nodded. "I'm assuming so, but that's for her to work out."

"Mama, what do I do now?" I asked. "About James, I mean?"

She came to sit between us on the window seat and patted my knee with her small white hand. "I know you didn't expect this and would never have asked James to do so, but he did the one thing he didn't think he could ever do. He chose his own happiness over saving his father. He chose you, dearest. It's a great responsibility—some might even say a burden."

"I don't know what you mean," I said. "James isn't a burden. I love him."

"I suppose I mean that he gave up something important to him so that he could have you. And it might feel like too much responsibility, as if you have to be perfect to make sure he doesn't ever regret his choice."

I laughed. "I never thought of that. I'll never feel that way. Standing up to his father had to be done, regardless of how he feels about me or even Lena. James could not be free until he did so."

Looking into my eyes, Mama ran her hands down my bare arms. "You're absolutely right. This was a rite of passage for James. One he had to do in order to be worthy of you. You've always been wise, my love. I'm so very proud of you."

"Darn right," Delphia said. "It's about time James did the right thing."

"Delphia, really?" Mama sighed, but I could tell by her smile that her earlier anger at Delphia had gone away.

"I'm sorry I interfered, Mama," Delphia said. "Addie forgives me. Can you?"

"Yes, of course, I can." She hugged my sister, holding her

close and kissing the top of her head. "The two of you have always been so different from each other, but the devotion and friendship between you has never suffered because of it. Wanting your sister to be happy can make a young woman do dangerous acts. You two will always have each other, and that's no small gift."

My sister and I grinned at each other.

"Do you think James will want to go back to New York?" I asked, sobering at the thought. "For his work?"

"I'm not sure. You'll have to decide between the two of you," Mama said. "What do you want?"

"I'd like to stay here. New York sounds dirty," I said. "But if James wants me to go with him, then I will."

"If you're married," Mama said, a note of caution in her voice. "I'll not have him dragging you across the country without a marriage license. If his mother and sister come to Emerson Pass, he may have even more incentive to stay."

"Where will we put them?" I asked.

"We'll decide all that later," Mama said.

"Addie in New York?" Delphia's eyes filled. "I never thought of that. Not once. I don't know what I will do without my big sister."

"You've got three others here." I spoke with more jocularity than I felt. The idea of leaving my family made my stomach churn. Would James want to take me away from everything I'd ever known? If he did, I would have to go. He was what I wanted more than anything.

"I told James I'd send you down," Mama said.

I rose to my feet and went to the mirror. My hair was all over the place. Mascara had smeared under my eyes. "I look a fright." I sat at the dressing table, torn between making myself presentable or going to James right away, regardless of my disheveled appearance.

"Don't worry. I'll get you fixed up quick." Delphia came to

stand behind me and started to take out the pins in my hair. "Please tell James she'll be down shortly."

Mama took my hand. "This is the last time I'll ask you. Addie, you're sure about James?"

"I'm sure." I spoke with truthful conviction. Whatever happened I could handle, as long as James was by my side.

"All right then," Mama said. "I'll see you both downstairs."

She turned to go, but I grabbed her hand. "Mama, thank you for always being here for us, no matter how difficult."

"That's a mother's job. You'll see for yourself someday." Mama gave us each a smile and then, in her graceful way, left us to our primping.

James wasn't in the sitting room when I went downstairs. In fact, no one was there at all. I went back into the hallway and heard voices coming from my father's study. James and my father? My stomach fluttered with nerves. Should I knock?

Before I could decide, the door opened and Papa greeted me. "I thought I heard footsteps. Come in, love. James and I were talking about the future."

My gaze skirted to my James. My James. Could it be? He smiled back at me from where he stood by the desk.

"I'll leave you two to talk," Papa said. "After all this, I need a nap before dinner."

"Thank you," James said, holding his hand out to shake Papa's.

"You're welcome, son." Papa winked at me before leaving us alone, shutting the door behind him.

James took my hand and led me over to the leather chairs where my parents so often sat together. When we were settled, he reached over to touch my cheek. "Lovely, lovely Addie. I'm sorry all of this has been so difficult."

"I'm sorry, too."

"Did your mother tell you everything?"

"Yes, I think so. We saw your father leave." I searched his face for clues. He seemed fine, even calm. It had been a huge ordeal for him, though. I knew that without him having to say a word. "Are you all right?"

"I'm good. Really good." James turned to face me. "How about you?"

"I'm fine. Unsure what happens next, though." I flushed, shy.

"What would you like to happen?"

I looked down at my hands, and warmth flooded my cheeks. "I think you know what I want. What do you want?"

"I want you, Adelaide Barnes. I want you to be my wife."

I lifted my gaze. He stared back at me with unflinching honesty and love. "I'd like that, too," I said. "Did you really cut ties with your father?"

"I did. I'm not sure if I'll hear from my mother or sister again. It's up to them, I suppose." He drew in a breath. "I've not felt this free in my entire life. I'm sad that it had to be this way, but sometimes a man has to put the woman he loves first. You're first, Addie. You'll always be first. From now on, every decision in my life will be to give you everything I possibly can. I just promised your father I would spend the rest of my life taking care of you and giving you everything you want."

"There have only been a few things I've wanted in my life," I said. "You're one of them."

"And your writing?"

"Yes." I looked up at the ceiling, gathering my thoughts. "When I was ill as a child, I never thought I'd live long enough to fall in love. I didn't think I'd have the normal aspects of a life that others took for granted. Then you came, and I thought I could see the rest of my days in your eyes. It seemed like a fanciful dream for a long time. But this summer, I knew I was right. We were meant to be together. I just didn't know how it would happen."

"You were right all along," James said.

"I'm grateful for all of it, James. My life. My health. My family. And now you."

"May I kiss you?"

I nodded, flushing.

James brought me to my feet and took me in his arms. He kissed me, taking his time. There was no urgency to it as there had been the first time. We were free to love each other. *Finally,* I thought, *my life is headed in the right direction. The direction of James.*

We returned to our chairs, our hands intertwined.

"Addie, will you marry me?"

"You know the answer to that."

"Next week?"

I laughed. "That's soon." Sobering at the idea of leaving my family, I asked him, "Will we go back to New York?"

He cupped my face with his hands. "You'd be willing to go with me?"

"I'll go wherever you are."

He leaned close, kissing me again. "Your father thinks we should stay here in Colorado."

"For my sake?" I asked.

"No, he thinks I would be happier here. We could work on your writing together—use my contacts in publishing when we have the manuscript ready."

"What would you do for work?"

"Your father had an idea. A good idea. One that sounded just right for me."

I waited. What could it be?

"He thinks I should be the next schoolteacher of Emerson Pass. The high school needs an English and history teacher."

"A teacher? Would you be happy doing that?"

"I think I would. We'd get to stay here with our family."

I grinned. "Our family? I like the sound of that."

"Your father offered us the cottage that Merry and Harley

used to live in. Apparently, your father gifted it to them years ago?"

"Yes, that's right. They lived there before they built the big house." The cottage had been empty for a few years now, but I remembered playing with Jack and Henry there when we were little. It was small but filled with light and had a nice yard. For children? Our children?

"Are you sure?" I asked. "Giving up your dream of being an editor to become a teacher seems like a big sacrifice."

He hesitated for a moment before answering. "For a long time, I've been scrapping and fighting to try to get out of the shadow of my past and my family. I'm tired. I shouldn't feel old and exhausted all the time. The only time I feel good is when I'm here. I've come here every summer when I could have gone home. What does that tell you?"

"It tells me this could be your home, too."

"This always felt more like home than anywhere else." Gazing downward, he rubbed one of his knuckles with his thumb. "I could try teaching and if I didn't like it, I could do something else. I don't know, Addie. All I know is that I'm ready for a change. My father and the Mr. Masterses of the world have weakened my capacity for ambition."

"I think the most important work is that of a teacher. Look at what my mother has done for this community. Do you know she taught adults to read when she first came here? She made a lot of difference to many people."

"She and your father have made all the difference for me. Mostly, because they made you." He kissed me again.

"When you first met Fiona, did you ever think your friendship would lead you here?" I asked when we parted.

"I certainly did not. I'm glad, you know, to be giving in to my destiny instead of fighting it."

"I'm your destiny?" My entire body buzzed and hummed with joy. He saw what I saw, wanted what I wanted. How good God was.

"Yes, and aren't I the lucky one who gets to have you? Marry me, Addie. Let's do it sooner rather than later and start our life together."

"Well, I *am* available for an end-of-summer wedding."

He grinned and surprised me by pulling me over to sit on his lap. I giggled, delighted and astounded at the same time as he lowered his mouth to mine.

23

JAMES

WE WERE ALL RELIEVED WHEN LENA MADE A FULL RECOVERY. THE day after her attempt on her life, I was able to see her. She was sitting up in bed eating a plate of peach slices when I knocked softly on the door of the guest room.

"May I come in?" I asked.

"James, yes, please do."

I was taken aback for a moment. She looked beautiful—different, with an inner glow that shone in her eyes. Her hair was unpinned and cascaded around her shoulders. She set aside the tray with her lunch and smoothed the covers over her lap.

"I wanted to see how you're feeling." I sat in the hardback chair near the bed.

"Very well, thank you. Other than I'm so embarrassed about everything. Quinn has been more than kind, but I can barely look her in the eye."

"You shouldn't be." I noticed an open book on the history of the gold rush on the nightstand that Masters had been reading yesterday. "Your father's been here?"

"He won't leave my side. I had to force him out of here today so I could have a little peace. He keeps staring at me as if I'm going to take more powder at any moment."

"You scared him."

"Yes, I'm sorry about that. And I'm sorry I scared you."

"You did frighten me. I thought we might lose you." I patted her hand before setting my own back on my lap. It was awkward for me to see her this way, especially after knowing what she'd done to herself. Or almost done to herself. She'd not succeeded. She was fine.

"I didn't think anyone would care," Lena said.

"You were wrong."

"My father knows everything now, and he's given me his blessing to marry Carl."

"Really? That's wonderful. I'm so pleased for you. Have you written to Carl yet?"

"Yes, Delphia took it to the post today. Father says if I'm feeling well enough, we're going to leave tomorrow."

"I hope you get everything you want." I squeezed her hand. "I truly do."

"I hope that for you, too," Lena said. "Tell me everything. What's happened with Addie?"

For the next few minutes, I told her what she'd missed, including our engagement. "I'm going to stay here, Lena. There's a teacher position Alexander wants me to take."

"Is that what you want? Because Father will make everything right with your job. He promised me."

"I'm sure. I haven't felt this alive since I was a kid. I want to be here, and who knows what can happen? This is where I'm supposed to be."

"With Addie," Lena said, nodding. "And the rest of them and the sky here, right?"

"That's right."

"I'm sorry about your family," Lena said. "Your father must have been really angry."

"Yes." I smiled, even though there was a sadness in me that would never leave. One didn't lose their father or even the idea of him without grief. "I did it, Lena. I did what I needed to do, and it felt good. It's a remarkable relief to have it behind me."

"I understand completely."

"The Barneses have offered to bring my mother and sister here. Did they tell you?"

"Quinn mentioned it. I hope it will be the right thing for you, James. I do worry."

"If they come," I said. "We'll take it as it comes."

"Perhaps your father will find another way out of his financial difficulties," Lena said.

"Perhaps."

We left it at that. What else was there to say? Only time would answer these questions. For now, I was content, knowing that my favorite person in the world waited for me downstairs.

A FEW DAYS LATER, Lena and her father departed for home. I stood on the platform waving as the train chugged away. Lena had promised to write when she was settled and had contacted Carl.

I'd brought them to the station alone, planning on stopping by to see Fiona and Li on the way home. A gardener watered pots of flowers as I drove up to the house. Li had built onto his original cottage to accommodate their large family. I let myself in through the gray picket fence and a garden teeming with flowers. I heard the young twins playing in the backyard. Given the time of day, Fiona would likely be there, too. I walked around the side of the house, taking in the sweet scent of lavender and roses.

Wisteria and vines woven through lattice and a stone walkway made a quaint scene. Fiona sat reading in a low-slung chair with a glass of iced tea on a small table next to her. From inside the house came the sounds of a violin. Li practicing. I'd know that beautiful tone anywhere. The small twins were on a set of swings hanging from a sturdy-looking wood contraption. They waved to me but went back to chatting together as I passed by them to stop at their mother's feet.

"James, how are you?" Fiona jumped up to give me a quick hug before gesturing to the empty chair beside her. "Sit. Tell me everything. We've only just returned from our trip to Chicago, but I know the whole sordid story already."

"Already?"

"Mama and Addie came by earlier. On their way to see Aunt Annabelle." She shot me a mischievous look. "But we'll talk about that in a moment. Have you just dropped Lena and her father at the train?"

"Yes, they're on their way. I can't say I'm sorry to see them go." I lowered myself into the chair, brushing aside a meandering ant before directing my attention toward my companion.

"They were on their way to have Addie measured for a wedding dress. You didn't waste any time." She jabbed my shoulder. "Good for you. And Addie, of course. I'm so relieved. When I left I thought she'd be heartbroken by the time I returned and you'd be trapped in a loveless marriage."

"There will be a wedding. Just not the one we anticipated."

Her hands flew to her mouth. "Oh, James, I'm so happy."

"I hope you're not angry with me."

"Why would I be?"

"It hasn't exactly been a proper courtship. Rather messy, in fact."

"What do they say about the path to true love? Li and I were messy too, and look how happy we are."

I reached over to brush my fingers against her wrist. "Has it been all right? Harder than you thought?"

"Not harder than we thought, but hard at times. People stare at us when we're away from here. It's what we expected. Fortunately for us, we're talented enough that people want to hire us anyway, even if our heritages don't match."

We sat for a moment in silence. The garden had a humming

sound to it this time of year, with insects and bees busy with their flower work.

"Mama told me about Delphia's part in all of this. Are you all still mad at her?"

I chuckled. "Who can be mad at her for long? She meant well. Delphia might be the most loyal person I've ever met."

"True enough. If she finds the right man, he'll be lucky."

"As it turned out, she did the right thing," I said. "It forced everything to come out in the open."

"I suppose so, but what a thing to do. Paying a boy to seduce her. Who thinks of these things?"

"Apparently, Delphia."

"That girl." She stretched her legs out long. "The sooner we get her married off the better."

Good luck with that, I thought. Delphia would decide for herself who and when she married. I hoped for her sake that her path to love was easier than mine and Addie's or Li and Fiona's.

The twins, who must have had enough playing on the swing for the afternoon, ran over to ask their mother if they could have a cookie.

"Go ask Gabriella," Fiona said. "But just one."

They ran off happily for their treat. What a gift it was to be unencumbered with adult worries and responsibilities and delighted by just the thought of a cookie.

Fiona and I chatted for a moment about the musical composition she and Li had just finished for the movie studio. "We're glad to be done with it, to be honest. I don't care for the city, as you know. I yearned to get home to my garden and piano. But they needed us in Chicago to record and that was that."

"Will you do more of this kind of work?"

"Yes, if we're asked to. The money's good. We were growing a little weary of giving all those music lessons. Li especially. It hurts his ears to hear some of the children." She brushed back a tendril of hair and directed her gaze at me. "Mama told me about the job at the school. Is this what you want, or are you doing it for Addie?"

"A little of both. Love, you know."

"Yes, love has a way of changing everything." She nodded but didn't say anything further. Fiona and I had met when we were both a lot younger. I'd been so full of ambition then, determined to become an editor. Now I could find that place inside me that had wanted all of it so badly. Love had replaced my ambition, at least for the time being.

"I should have figured it out about you and Addie," Fiona said. "Looking back, I can see the signs of how she felt about you. But she had to grow up first."

"Yes, I guess she did. We're anxious to start a life together. I've got to figure out how to make a home like this." I waved my hand toward the row of pots that contained purple and red flowers, none of which I knew the name of. "Maybe I'll learn to grow a garden."

"You'll make a wonderful nest for Addie. I've no doubt. In the meantime, we have a wedding to plan. What kind of music do you want?"

THAT NIGHT AFTER DINNER, Addie and I strolled through the rose garden at the big house. We talked about where we might like to decorate our little cottage and when I would start at the school and the latest edits on her manuscript. This would be my life, I thought. Sweet and uncomplicated, with Addie at my side.

"Do you want children?" Addie asked. "I've never asked you that."

"I'll be happy either way. As long as I have you." Now that we'd moved behind some large shrubbery, I pulled her against me to kiss her. She tasted of Lizzie's sweet lemonade.

With her arms around my neck, she spoke against my mouth. "Did you ever think you'd feel this happy?"

"No, never." I kissed her again with all those pink roses around us. My pink rose of a girl.

24

ADDIE

ON MY WEDDING DAY, I STOOD IN FRONT OF THE MIRROR IN MY bedroom. We'd just buttoned my dress, and I stared back at my reflection. Aunt Annabelle hadn't had time to make anything elaborate, but the simple white silk with its modest neckline suited me just fine. Tucked in at the waist, the bodice hugged my gentle curves.

My mother fastened the veil to my hair and stood back to look at me. "Lovely, darling," she said.

Fiona smoothed the short train of my dress and stood next to me in the mirror. "Perfectly perfect."

Cymbeline, powder brush in hand, gave me an up-and-down assessment. "Yes, you look beautiful."

Delphia, sitting on the window seat with Josephine, had been surprisingly subdued all day. She would not say it, but I knew this rite of passage pained her. For the first time in her life, she would go to sleep tonight without me in the same house.

After we'd moved all of my things to the cottage yesterday, I'd caught Delphia crying on the porch. She waved me away and refused to talk, but I knew it hurt to let me go. It had been the two of us for a long time now.

I turned to Delphia. "What do you think?"

"I think you'll do fine." Delphia gave me a weak smile. "And James better treat you like the queen you are."

Josephine wrapped her arm around Delphia. "Don't worry, sweetheart, you'll be next. Soon we'll be putting you into a wedding dress."

"I don't know," Delphia said. "Viktor hasn't brought any prospects to me."

Cym laughed. "Are you still waiting for that?"

"He promised me when I was a little girl that he would find my husband," Delphia said, jutting out her chin. "And none of you are allowed to make fun of me about it. He knows the kind of man I want."

"One like him," Cym said. "But you'll have your own man, uniquely made by God just for you."

Delphia looked skeptical but said nothing further, getting up to kiss my cheek. "Come on, sister of mine. It's time."

Suddenly, I was nervous. I looked around at the loving faces of my sisters and Mama. They were all smiling. Jo and Mama both had tears in their eyes. "All the people will be looking at me."

"Aren't they lucky to see such a pretty bride?" Cym said. "And I promise, it's over before you know it. I barely remember my ceremony."

"Same with me," Jo said. "And anyway, it's just the first day of saying 'I do.' Every single day of your marriage requires you to say yes all over again. Try to remember that during the hard times—love is always worth recommitting to. It's a choice every day to love each other and to make sure the other knows how much."

"Quite true," Mama said. "There will be times when you have to try a little harder to understand each other and come to compromises. Regardless, you'll find it the very best kind of work. Nothing will ever be as rewarding. Except your children, of course." Mama started crying. "Oh, my dears. How can it be that the years went so fast? I can see each of you as little girls by just closing my eyes. Now you're all grown. Even my babies."

Jo and Cym wrapped their arms around Mama, kissing her cheeks and reassuring her that they would always need her.

"Think of all your grandchildren," Fiona said.

"I'm very blessed," Mama said. "To have them all near me and to have the pleasure of watching them grow up without having to do any of the work."

"You're about to be blessed again," Fiona said. "It's confirmed. I'm having another."

"Fiona, you never said a word," Mama said.

"I didn't want to say anything until I knew for sure," Fiona said. "Anyway, we've been busy planning the wedding."

"I'm delighted for you," Jo said, beaming. "For me, too. I love being an auntie."

"I'm tired," Fiona said. "Worried, too. How will I take care of them all?"

"That's what you have all of us for," Cym said. "There's always someone to call in this family."

"You've all given me such a good life," Mama said, crying again. "I love being your mother."

"We love you, Mama," Fiona said. "More than you could ever know."

"All this fuss. I'm so sorry," Mama said. "I'm overcome suddenly and blubbering like a fool. I wish my mother could see you, Addie. She'd be very proud to see you in one of Annabelle's dresses."

"She's with me, Mama," I said, tapping my chest. "Always."

"Let us pray before going to the church," Mama said. "On this most joyous of days."

"Won't we be praying at church, too?" Delphia asked. "Why should we do it now?"

Josephine turned to address my little sister. "Delphia, please, try to be a good girl today. And don't give Mama any sass." She smiled, indulgently, and gestured for her to come and stand next to her.

Delphia stuck out her bottom lip. "I wasn't trying to cause trouble, I was just asking."

"Come here, goose." Cym wrapped her arm around Delphia's shoulders. "I know it's hard to be good."

"It really is. Especially when I never know what the rules are," Delphia said.

"Would you obey them if you knew?" Fiona asked, teasing.

"I might," Delphia mumbled.

We made a circle, holding hands. Mama's voice was soft and sweet in the warm room. A breeze rustled the curtains as we bowed our heads.

"Dear Lord, thank you for this day and for my beautiful girls. Thank you for blessing us with another happy union. Please be with my baby today as she marries James. Amen."

We echoed her amen and stood for a few seconds gazing at the floor for fear that we'd all burst into tears.

Regardless of the sentimentality of the moment, we broke apart. There were vows to exchange and a celebration to enjoy. A marriage to begin.

AFTER THE CEREMONY at the church, we all traipsed back to the big house, as we always did after one of us was married. Finally, it had been my turn to walk down the aisle on Papa's arm. I'd been strangely calm. My groom, however, had spent most of the short ceremony with misty eyes and a trembling voice as he answered the pastor's questions.

Now we were in the backyard. The sun had set already, and stars had appeared. Fiona and Li started in with a rousing jazz number, and most of us wandered out to the grass to dance. Instead of a formal meal inside, I'd asked if we could enjoy our wedding feast on the back porch. Lizzie had gladly arranged for it to be so, and she and Mrs. Wu had cooked all day yesterday and today to prepare cakes and treats as well as a roast pig. Not Daisy, mind you, who as far as I knew was behaving herself in the barn. The wedding cake, white with buttercream frosting, had been cut and consumed. Champagne continued to flow, and even the staff had been convinced to join us for dancing and drinks.

The air, scented with roses and lavender, had cooled and felt nice on my bare arms after the heat of the afternoon. James held me close despite the fast pace of the music. We had our own rhythm to begin this new season of our lives and eyes only for each other.

"Mrs. West, are you enjoying yourself?" James whispered in my ear. His breath smelled sweetly of champagne and cake. I shivered in his arms, nervous and excited about what would happen later when the party was finally over and everyone had gone to bed.

"It's been a lovely day."

"No regrets?"

"About what?"

"The wedding, I guess. Or me." He smiled down at me, his eyes catching the light cast from the porch.

"I'll never regret either."

"I meant what I said during the ceremony," he said. "Whatever you want, I will give you. If I can, of course."

"And I you."

"Are you worried about later?"

"A little. You?" I asked, knowing he referred to our wedding night. My sisters had gone out earlier and filled the kitchen of our newly cleaned and decorated cottage with food for our first days together. They'd also made up the bed in the room I would now share with my husband. Husband! I still couldn't quite believe it. James was mine and I was his.

We'd agreed to have our honeymoon next summer, for school would start in a few weeks and Mr. West, teacher of English and history, would be busy preparing. My mother had agreed to help him prepare, reassuring him that all would be well. James's mother had declined our invitation to move to Colorado, for now, at least. She'd written to tell him that his father was not well and that she could not leave him to die alone. In addition, his sister had eloped with her childhood sweetheart and hadn't been heard from since. I'd worried the news would send James into a mourning of some kind, but instead, he'd seemed resigned to whatever came. "I can no longer hold on to the belief that my actions can save any of them. It's a relief to finally accept that fact," he'd said to me a few days before the wedding.

"Was it strange for you?" I asked him now. "To marry without any of your family here?"

"Not really. I've spent all these years without them." He paused, obviously thinking through what he would say. "My sister's escaped as well, you know, and this makes me happy. My mother and father have made each other miserable all their married life, but at least she has a chance for a good life."

"I hope she will be as happy as we are," I said.

"I can wish for nothing better for her."

The song changed to a ballad, and he drew me closer and whispered in my ear. "When can we leave? I love your family, but I'm longing to be alone with you."

"Another hour? I don't really know, now that you ask. At my siblings' weddings, I can't remember ever wanting the party to end, but tonight it's a different story."

"It will be the longest hour in the history of man."

I laughed and rested my cheek against the lapel of his new suit, made in haste by our own Mr. Olofsson. "We have so much to look forward to." I gazed up at him, wondering what it would feel like to wake up in the morning and see his beautiful eyes staring back at me from across the pillow. "I still can't quite believe it's you."

He brushed his mouth against a spot just below my ear. "I can't believe you would pick me. Of all the men in the world?"

"You've always been the one. My one and only."

"It wasn't obvious to me at first, of course, but I am a man and therefore less intelligent than the woman who loves me."

"Oh, I *do* love you, James West." I wriggled my hand from his to touch the side of his smooth face. "You're mine for always, which makes me the happiest woman in the entire world."

He chuckled and brought my hand to his mouth and kissed the palm. "You smell very nice. If you were wondering about that."

I laughed. "Thank you. You smell nice, too." Over his shoulder, I saw my mother and father sitting together on the bottom steps of the porch. How many other exchanges had happened there over the years? Many, I suspected, given the largeness of our family.

Tonight, my parents sat side by side. My father had his arm around her shoulders, and her head was resting against him. Instead of looking at each other, they were watching us. A gentle smile on my mother's face told me of her delight in my happiness, but there was a bittersweet quality, too. I was one of her babies, after all, and this was the end of an era.

My father winked at me and then turned away to whisper something to my mother. She laughed and nodded, then took his hand and they joined us on the lawn to dance.

Along with Fiona and Delphia, my sisters and brothers were there too, all dancing with their spouses. Delphia was in the corner of the yard with the Depaul brothers playing some kind of game with marbles. I'm fairly sure money was exchanging hands. Given her self-satisfied grin, she must have been winning.

I nestled closer to James, knowing I would always remember this moment when my world was absolutely perfectly perfect. Whatever tomorrow brought, I would always have this rose-scented night and the sounds of Fiona's music in accompaniment to the joyous sounds of my family celebrating that once again love had conquered all. A match that had made no sense to anyone but me had finally come to fruition. I would not ever forget what a miracle it all was or the generosity of my parents. What a thing to be a Barnes, I thought. A glorious, lucky blessed thing.

Now, however, I was also a West. Mrs. James West. I could hardly wait to write it on an envelope, although I'd promised my new husband that I would use Barnes for my pen name. I might be Addie West at home, but the world would know me as Adelaide Barnes, author. Would his prediction come true? Only time would tell. Until then, I was content to be under the stars in the arms of the man I loved with my family all around me.

Nothing could be better than tonight, I thought. *This is the best day of my life.*

I was wrong, of course. There were many more joyous occasions in our future, ones that topped even this one. But they are stories for another day. Today was today, and I was young and in love. Whatever came, James would be with me. Knowing that, I could face it all without fear. His love gave me the courage I never thought I'd have.

"You've made me braver," I said.

"No, you've made me brave. It's all been you. From the beginning, it was you who was the courageous one, the one who opened my eyes to what my life could be. It'll always be you, my love—the woman who changed my life."

We danced for a while longer and then, as lovers do, sneaked away from the crowd and headed for our new home. If anyone noticed our departure, they didn't come after us. They'd been like us once, I thought as we got out of the car. Time may go on, but lovers will always be the same.

James carried me into our house, both of us giggling until the lights were turned off and my life as a wife began. And what a life it was.

ALSO BY TESS THOMPSON

CLIFFSIDE BAY

Traded: Brody and Kara

Deleted: Jackson and Maggie

Jaded: Zane and Honor

Marred: Kyle and Violet

Tainted: Lance and Mary

Cliffside Bay Christmas, The Season of Cats and Babies (Cliffside Bay Novella to be read after Tainted)

Missed: Rafael and Lisa

Cliffside Bay Christmas Wedding (Cliffside Bay Novella to be read after Missed)

Healed: Stone and Pepper

Chateau Wedding (Cliffside Bay Novella to be read after Healed)

Scarred: Trey and Autumn

Jilted: Nico and Sophie

Kissed (Cliffside Bay Novella to be read after Jilted)

Departed: David and Sara

Cliffside Bay Bundle, Books 1,2,3

BLUE MOUNTAIN SERIES

Blue Midnight

Blue Moon

Blue Ink

Blue String

Blue Mountain Bundle, Books 1,2,3

EMERSON PASS

The School Mistress of Emerson Pass, Book 1 (First historical installment).

The Sugar Queen of Emerson Pass, Book 2 (First contemporary installment).

The Spinster of Emerson Pass, Book 3 (Second historical installment).

RIVER VALLEY

Riversong

Riverbend

Riverstar

Riversnow

Riverstorm

Tommy's Wish

River Valley Bundle, Books 1-4

CASTAWAY CHRISTMAS

Come Tomorrow, Castaway Christmas, Book 1

LEGLEY BAY

Caramel and Magnolias

Tea and Primroses

STANDALONES

The Santa Trial

Duet for Three Hands

Miller's Secret

ABOUT THE AUTHOR

USA Today Bestselling author Tess Thompson writes small-town romances and historical romance. She started her writing career in fourth grade when she wrote a story about an orphan who opened a pizza restaurant. Oddly enough, her first novel, "Riversong" is about an adult orphan who opens a restaurant. Clearly, she's been obsessed with food and words for a long time now.

With a degree from the University of Southern California in theatre, she's spent her adult life studying story, word craft, and character. Since 2011, she's published over 20 novels and a five novellas. Most days she spends at her desk chasing her daily word count or rewriting a terrible first draft.

She currently lives in a suburb of Seattle, Washington with her husband, the hero of her own love story, and their Brady Bunch clan of two sons, two daughters and five cats. Yes, that's four kids and five cats.

Tess loves to hear from you. Drop her a line at tess@tthompsonwrites.com or visit her website at https://tesswrites.com/ or visit her on social media.

Made in the USA
Las Vegas, NV
21 March 2023